EAGLE SQUAD

Borgo Press Books by JAMES C. GLASS

Eagle Squad: A Novel of Suspense
Imaginings of a Dark Mind: Science Fiction Stories
Sedona Conspiracy: A Science Fiction Novel
Toth: A Science Fiction Novel
*Touches of Wonder and Terror: Tales of Dark Fantasy and
    Science Fiction*
Visions: A Science Fiction Western
Voyages in Mind and Space: Stories of Mystery and Fantasy

EAGLE SQUAD

A NOVEL OF SUSPENSE

JAMES C. GLASS

THE BORGO PRESS

MMXIII

EAGLE SQUAD

FIRST EDITION

Published by Wildside Press LLC

www.wildsidebooks.com

DEDICATION

This one is for Gail

ACKNOWLEDGMENT

Thanks go to Joy Oestreicher for her useful comments and suggestions regarding the first draft of this book.

CONTENTS

PROLOGUE

A snarling wharf rat, mouth flecked with foam, came out of the darkness. Jacob Bauer cowered in one corner of an empty room as the dog-sized animal lunged towards him. There was a fleeting instant of panic. Something was amiss; it was the wrong kind of rat. It should be small, white and cute, with little pink eyes. Bauer glared at the rat, and it fell over on its side. Bauer watched the death throes curiously, feeling detached yet somehow responsible, and then a telephone was ringing, but that wasn't right either because he didn't allow telephones in this part of the laboratory. He tried to find it, and it kept on ringing.

He awoke when a fumbling hand struck something sharp on the nightstand. Ester grumbled in her sleep and turned over beside him, pushing her buttocks against his back. He fumbled until he had the telephone in hand, and he was wide awake.

"Yes, this is Bauer," he whispered, then listened quietly for a long minute, frowning.

"Don't touch anything at all, and stay out of the room. I'll be over in a few minutes, Len, but are you okay? No cramps, or dizziness? I hardly recognize your voice." He listened again.

"Relax, and put some coffee on. See you."

He swung out of bed, shuffled to the bathroom and splashed water on his face. A balding, middle-aged man with sagging jowls and stomach watched him sleepily from the mirror as he performed his toilet rituals. He dressed in the dark, smiling when his wife began to snore. He tapped the bed sharply with his foot and the snoring stopped. I'll call her later from the lab, he thought. He went to the kitchen, found a day old bagel, some cream cheese, and made a snack. There was an uneasy feeling in the pit of his stomach.

The morning was clear and crisp, with an orange glow on the horizon as he peddled his bicycle through empty streets towards the nearby campus. The hill loomed ahead of him, bristling with silhouettes of buildings housing classrooms and laboratories that were his life for much of each day. A feeling of guilt returned. The university had been so good to him, but if he had his way he might soon bring it all down. Why couldn't he just do his work like the others? Because the others didn't care about consequences, he thought. They only wanted the power and prestige that came with heavily funded research programs, and they would do anything for that. He had wanted it too, and had played the game well, but now he wanted out as soon as the project was finished. The way things were going that might be never. The string of failed experiments was both discouraging and mysterious, and his masters were not pleased.

Bauer leaned over the handlebars, pumped hard up the winding narrow road towards the hilltop campus. He raced past the darkened library and administration building, circled a wide grassy quadrangle in the center of campus and sweated a staggering path up a dark walkway towards the glowing beacon of the Robert F. Gordon Science Center at the very top of the hill. The white marble building, a windowless four story rectangular box, glowed softly in yellow light from dozens of powerful lamps pointing upwards from the flower gardens at its base. He parked his bicycle with three others in a rack near the front entrance. One he recognized as Len's, the others he hadn't seen before. At a wide door of thick glass he inserted a plastic card in a slot below a speaker and television screen. The PROCEED appeared on the screen.

"Jacob Bauer, analytical chemistry," he said slowly.

Somewhere in the bowels of the security system, a voice-print identity comparison was made. CLEAR appeared on the screen. Bauer pushed on the door and entered the building, crossed the dimly lit empty lobby to the elevators and pressed a button, looking up at the floor indicators to see that both elevators were at the third floor where his laboratory was located. He waited impatiently while one descended, and then rode it up to his floor. He stepped out into a brightly lit corridor stretching far in both directions. A uniformed guard sat at a desk near the elevator, watching several television monitors and eating a sandwich. He grinned as Bauer approached him. The man had dark circles under his eyes, his face a ruin of old acne scars.

"Getting an early start today?"

"Not really. Len called, and I've got some troubleshooting to do." Bauer signed his name in the security record book. Len had signed in at dinnertime the previous evening, had not yet signed out.

The guard chewed thoughtfully. "Haven't seen Len all night. Haven't seen anybody all night," he said.

"He called from the lab, and his bike is downstairs. I won't be long." Try staying awake, he felt like saying, but didn't.

The man wrote something on a pad in front of him and yawned. "Have a good day, Doctor Bauer," he said cheerfully.

"Sure," said Bauer, and he started down the corridor to his right. Behind him the guard returned to watching the television monitors, but his eyelids fluttered and he was soon dozing as he did for much of his shift each night.

The laboratory was at the far end of the corridor, and Bauer found the door unlocked. Don't students ever use their keys? Irritated, he pushed the door inwards and stared into a dark room. He flicked the light switch on and off, but darkness remained. Across the room, light shimmered beneath a closed door. The synthesis lab. He left the hall door open and felt his way across the room past benches covered with animal cages. The animals were excited by his presence; he could hear the scratching of their tiny feet as they scuttled back and forth in their prisons.

"Hey, Len," he called loudly, "give me some light out here

before I knock something over."

There was a sound of metal sliding on metal in the room beyond the door. It sounded like Len was working in the fume hood, but couldn't he at least answer?

"What happened to the lights in here?" he shouted, and reached for the door. Behind him, the door to the hallway slowly closed as if pushed from the inside. He heard a click in the other room as the light there suddenly disappeared, and he was in total darkness. His breathing quickened. He pushed the door open wide, saw a single red light glowing dimly ahead of him and shuffled towards it, keeping his arms out to avoid collisions with the benches he knew were there.

"Len, are you all right?" His voice was trembling, and he wondered if the red light was on the timer. His foot struck something soft, he stumbled and looked down.

Len was on the floor, face contorted in agony, staring at the ceiling.

Bauer's first instinct was to turn towards the fume hood, sniffing the air for escaped gases or fumes that could kill him in seconds, and then his hands found the open hood and began to close it.

He heard a single step before gloved hands seized him by the arms and neck, slammed him hard into the fume hood until he was sprawled in it from the waist up. The grip on his neck was so strong his voice was paralyzed, and bright colors flashed before his eyes. The sliding door to the fume hood came down painfully across his shoulder blades simultaneously with the sound of a glass ampoule shattering, and he took one musty breath. Gasping, then vomiting, his brain was dead before the convulsions began and his feet drummed a random tattoo on the floor. The following silence was broken by the gurgle of a freshly dead man evacuating his bowels.

Strong hands lowered him gently to the floor as the light in the fume hood suddenly came on, revealing two hooded figures clothed in black. One turned on the blower in the hood for a moment, then rearranged the positions of beakers and a broken ampoule while the other changed a bulb in the red light on one wall. The fume hood door was lowered halfway. The two people looked around the room silently, nodded to each other, then left, turning the room light on before closing the door. They walked quickly to the hall door and locked it behind them before moving along one wall down the hallway. The guard slept lightly, head nodding as one black figure, an aerosol can in one hand, stepped up lightly behind him and sprayed his head with a fine mist. The guard's chin flopped against his chest, and he moaned softly. Both people moved to a waiting elevator and entered, pulling off their hoods with difficulty over the gas masks they wore beneath them. A moment later two students, wearing jeans and sweaters, left the building, loaded book packs on their backs. They mounted bicycles and coasted out of sight down the hill towards the awakening town as Ester Bauer arose to make morning coffee before the expected return of her husband.

CHAPTER ONE

Jack Nelson lined up on the split-receiver, a black kid with wide, frightened eyes, and watched the big Bemidji quarterback. Look right, throw left, look left, throw over the middle. That was the pattern, at least over the last four possessions, and now the guy was backed up against his goal line. The crowd screamed as the ball was snapped. Nelson gave the black kid a hard shiver, knocked him to one knee and drifted back four steps. He broke to his left, saw the receiver coming across the middle with one step on a linebacker. The ball was there, and then Jack Nelson had it, cutting against the grain and crossing the goal line before even the surprised quarterback had a chance to react. The home crowd sat in stunned silence while six busloads of students from Simenson University screamed their lungs out from the far end of the field. Jack trotted back to the sidelines to accept the congratulations of his team mates. Ten minutes later the Cougars from the new school near the Canadian border had won the first game in their second season together as a team, extending their winning streak to seven.

The droning bus ride north was quiet, each young man nursing private aches and bruises. Occasional whiffs of pine scent floated past dozing faces while outside a full moon was rising over the dark silhouettes of fir trees in the north woods. Arnie Kant dozed next to Jack. At six feet-eight and two hundred and seventy nine pounds the good-natured defensive end was called Boulder by his teammates. He found this amusing, but football he took most seriously. That day he had sacked the quarterback twice, and made seven unassisted tackles. The price was pain, which he now nursed quietly. He had closed his eyes, toughing it out like a wounded Tiger when Jack turned to whisper to him.

"Arnie, you awake?"

"Yeah."

"You were great tonight, man. All over the field. Graham was running for his life most of the time."

"He's a good quarterback, Jack."

"Sure he is, when he has time to throw. Not tonight."

Arnie chuckled. "And when he did throw, it kept going to you."

"Ya, sure," said Jack. Both men laughed, and then Arnie was serious again.

"Coach Patterson said the Vikes and Packers had scouts there tonight."

"Oh, ho, that's why you were so up."

"Hey, I play to win. You know I've got to play pro ball. Either that, or be a bum."

"Come off it, Arnie."

"Those scouts were watching you, too, but if they offered you a job you wouldn't take it, right?"

"Of course not; I want to finish school."

"I mean after graduation."

"Well, I'll get my commission, and then I've got my active duty to serve. After that I guess I'll be an engineer for someone or maybe stay in the service."

"See, all planned out. For me it's play pro ball or teach little kids and collect food stamps."

"Bullshit. I've seen you work with kids, and they love you. You're weird, Arnie."

The big man looked at the seat ahead of him and grinned. "You're right. I could be happy living on food stamps if I had enough of them. Karen wouldn't be a problem; I'd keep her happy even if we were poor."

"In your dreams. I don't know how she could handle both of us, Arnie. You know, one of these days I'm going to learn when to take you seriously."

"I really was great tonight, wasn't I?"

"Shut up, Arnie." Jack turned his head towards the window and feigned sleep. Arnie smiled at the man's muscular back for a moment, unable to remember having a closer friend or roommate than Jack Nelson. He closed his eyes and quickly drifted off into a light sleep filled with crowd noises, the impact of hurtling bodies, and pain.

* * * * * * *

The bus station was a study in chaos. Four busloads of students had already arrived, a pep band was playing loudly in the lobby while the mob of young people, having emptied all the candy machines, milled around looking for something else to eat. Two more buses pulled in and two more students carried off one where an elegantly stocked bar had been carefully hidden. Cans of beer were being passed around overhead and bathroom doors off the lobby were open more than closed as people relieved themselves after the long trip.

Karen Butler leaned against a ticket counter, watching the happy throng with a mixture of amusement and disdain. A bit juvenile, she thought, but somehow she shared their excitement. Her undergraduate days were past. Graduate school required focus and discipline, two traits she shared with Jack, but it was his warmth and affection that brought her to a bus station in the wee hours of the morning. She adjusted the band on her blond ponytail, and was conscious of the stares by several young men nearby when she did it. But then a tiny pompom girl wriggled up to her, smiling in a way calculated to melt even the hardest soul, and force a smile in return. Karen did not smile.

"I saw you waiting," she gushed. "Do you want a beer or a coke, or something? Oh, he is such a hunk! You should have seen him tonight; it's like he can read minds, you know."

Please spare me from this, thought Karen.

"It must be great having a guy like that. I mean, Jack is so good at everything."

Karen arched an eyebrow. "Everything?" she asked suspiciously, pleased with herself when the girl blushed.

"Oh, well, I don't mean his private life. I mean...."

Thank you for sharing, now please go away, Karen wanted to say, but the team bus had just pulled in and the crowd was spilling outside to greet it. "They're here," she said, and pointed.

"Oh, yes!" yelped the girl, and then she juggled towards the bus, shaking her pompoms overhead while Karen leaned back with relief against the ticket counter.

There was a delay while coaches made announcements on the bus, and then the door opened and weary players came down the steps, smiling shyly at all the happy faces and wincing at the loud, brassy music of the band. She saw Arnie first, then Jack right behind him, elbowing their way through the crowd to where they knew she would be. Arnie came up to her with arms outstretched.

"Karen, baby, I couldn't hold back. I had to tell Jack about our secret relationship." He smothered her in a bear hug that made her grunt, then released her as Jack stopped and put down his duffle.

"How do you feel about that, Jack?" she asked.

"I think group sex is perverted," he said, and pulled her to him as her arms went around his neck. Over his shoulder, she could see the tiny pompom girl watching them. Unable to resist the sudden impulse, she took his face in her hands and gave him a long open-mouthed kiss. Eat your heart out, she thought.

"Hey, cut that out! You're making me horny," said Arnie.

"You're always horny, Arnie," said Jack, and looked closely at Karen. "How's my girl?" he whispered.

"She's fine, now, thank you. I hear you guys were superstars tonight."

"How'd you hear that? The game wasn't even on radio."

"Oh yes it was," said Karen. "Kent Conrad went down there and did a play by play on his phone. He brought it back in his Camaro and had it all on the net at eleven."

"There's a crazy man for you," said Arnie. "He must have averaged ninety coming back."

"At least people are interested," said Jack. "Come on, let's get out of here. I've got studying to do in the morning." He picked up his duffle and looked at Karen.

"I'm in the lot across the street," she said.

The three of them left the station, crossed a quiet street to a parking lot crammed with compact cars and motorcycles. They stopped at a red Honda Civic, waited while Karen fumbled with a ring of keys.

"I just bet I get to sit in the back again," grumbled Arnie.

"It's either that or banging your knees on the dash," said Jack. "These cars are built for normal humans, Arnie."

Karen got the door open and Arnie squeezed in the back along with a duffle. Two more pieces of luggage went in the trunk and Jack sat in front with another smaller bag between his legs. Karen started the car, shifted gears and found her hand on Jack's leg. She looked at him mischievously.

"It's going to be painful when I go into second or fourth," she said.

Jack rolled his eyes and gave her a lecherous grin. "But I do love you," he said, and then moved his leg away from the gear shift.

They pulled out of the lot as people began leaving the bus station in pairs and groups, then drove down the empty main street of Simonsen Park towards the university campus dormitories just outside of town. A few homes for the four thousand-plus permanent residents of the university town were scattered along side streets. All were new, sprawling ranch-style homes with large lots surrounded by pine trees and short walls of yellow brick. The stores were new as well, since the entire town had been born with the university only a decade before: gas stations, two grocery stores, a couple of fast food chains and a single theatre currently featuring two old films titled *Porky's Place* and *Porky's Revenge*. They passed the only bar in town, The Plumbing Shop, quiet now, but soon to be noisy again when the bus station parking lot was emptied out. There was no off-sale liquor store in town, except at The Plumbing Shop. At the other edge of town, nestled in pines, was The Heidelberg, an A-frame chalet serving European foods with some class, but at prices even students could occasionally afford. With seven thousand students, a faculty of over three hundred at the university, and no other real restaurant within forty miles, business at The Heidelberg was brisk.

At the edge of town the road began to climb. Jack rolled down a window, and pine scent flooded the stuffy car. Ahead of them rose the dark silhouettes of brick dormitories, only a few windows showing lights, and then they were at the border of campus, a sprawling array of white granite buildings arranged in spokes radiating outwards from a seven story tower which was the administration building. Unseen were the underground tunnels connecting all buildings, with shops, cafeteria, book store, even a cabaret for the long winter nights. Nearby rose the dome of the nuclear power plant which provided energy for both the university and the town. It was a technological community, proud of itself and totally self-contained.

They stopped in front of a dormitory. Jack unloaded luggage while Arnie struggled to get out of the tiny car. "My legs are all weird," he quipped. "Thanks a lot, Karen."

"Good night, Arnie," she said, smiling. The two men carried luggage into the building while Karen sat in the car, engine running. Jack returned in a moment, sliding into the front seat and leaning over to kiss her cheek.

"Alone at last," he said huskily.

"You let Arnie take the luggage up by himself?"

"He insisted. Practically threw me out of the elevator, and told me to get back to you."

Karen laughed, put the car in gear and pulled away from the building. "I wish we could find him a nice girlfriend, Jack. He's a sweet guy."

"What we need is someone who's big, beautiful, horny, a great cook, and has an encyclopedic knowledge of football.

Know anyone like that?"

"Could be a Swedish girl. I'll keep my eyes open. You had a good game tonight."

"Yeah, not bad for the opener. Arnie was awesome. He tries so hard when he knows scouts are watching him. I don't know what he'll do if he can't play pro ball. He makes jokes about not playing, but the game is everything to him."

"Well, it's important to you, too."

"Sure, but not like Arnie. I mean, it's just a game to me, and without the scholarship I couldn't afford this school. God, a full-time job wouldn't even pay the tuition. I like the exercise, the discipline, being a part of the team. I like being a part of something unified, with a single purpose."

"Like the military," said Karen, looking at him seriously.

"Yeah, like that. Sports and military overlap a lot: being the best, team spirit, discipline."

"Always the discipline. You talk about that a lot, Jack."

"Does that bother you?" he asked.

Karen kept her eyes on the road. They were coming up to the president's house. The lights inside were all on, and a county sheriff's car was sitting in the curved driveway in front of the two story, brick structure. "Not really," she said thoughtfully. "It's just that sometimes I think I've fallen in love with an ancient warrior who's out to right all the wrongs in the world. Dedication, perseverance, *et cetera, et cetera*."

"Hey, even chemists have concern for the human condition. You guys must care about people too. Better living through chemistry, and all that."

"Or dying," Karen said softly.

"What?"

"Nothing," she said, smiling and shaking her head at him. "Let's change the subject."

"Okay. Right now I'm wondering what a police car is doing in front of the president's house this time of night?"

"Probably the trouble on the hill this morning. The rumors have been flying all day. Do you know Doctor Bauer?"

"I had physical chemistry from him. Decent guy, but his lectures would put a hungry shark to sleep. Catatonic."

"A guard found him dead in his hush-hush lab this morning, and one of his graduate students is missing. The more imaginative rumor is that the student killed him."

Jack looked at her incredulously. "I can't see anyone doing in old Bauer. He wouldn't hurt a bug."

"Maybe so," said Karen, "but from what I've heard, he's done some really terrible things to rats."

CHAPTER TWO

When Curtis Lundeman stepped out upon the front porch of his home he was in an expansive mood, and the world was good. For a moment, the president of Simenson University was totally at peace with himself; the fight with his wife the previous night was forgotten, along with the previous day's stress of a faculty senate meeting and other nonsense. He breathed in cool air and surveyed his command in the orange light of an early morning sun filtering through trees and awakening the birds. Below him, in a green hollow watched over by the vast research complex he had personally negotiated funding for, the polished marble campus glowed like an ancient seat of learning reborn.

Lundeman was proud of what he had accomplished here, even though he had been necessarily harsh at times, so much so that certain faculty members still walked softly around him. Only the goal was important, the goal of creating an educational institution of high quality that would have a positive impact on a shaky world. The thought of it made him tremble, giving him true meaning and sense of purpose in what he otherwise considered to be a drab life. There it was before him, growing, and glowing in the morning sun.

He looked forward to the day: a little work in the office, lunch with two representatives from the National Science Foundation who were looking at his plans for an institutional grant, and then the trip south for the football game and what he hoped would be another big victory for the Cougars. Why was it, he wondered, that universities were so often measured by the greatness of their football teams? A sad fact, but one he accepted and made use of in his talks to business groups. Football made money.

The campus was quiet, the sound of his footsteps coming back to him from granite walls. At a distance, he saw someone mount a bicycle in front of the physics building and ride away. Lights were on in the chemistry complex; it seemed the chemists were always there, cooking a new brew. Lundeman was happy with them. Chemistry made money, lots of it.

He walked past beds of flowers surrounding the cylindrical hub of campus which was his office building, known among various faculty factions as the galactic core, the seat of power, the phallus of academe, or simply the palace. His office was on the first floor, and he used a key to let himself in, made a pot of coffee in the little kitchen that had once been a closet, and settled himself at his desk. He inserted a disk of Mozart's Requiem in a player, turned the volume down low and began to work as the aroma of brewing coffee filled the office air. The work flowed smoothly, the coffee was hot and tasty, and the music lulled him into a state of peaceful detachment. Such a fragile state, so easily shattered by the sound of a ringing telephone.

The telephone rang three times before he answered it. He listened for a moment, then leaned back in his chair, putting one hand to his forehead to dab at beads of sweat that had suddenly formed there.

"When did you find him?" he asked, then listened.

"Didn't the guard know anything at all?"

Pause to listen.

"Keep him under wraps, Max. I don't want him talking to anyone until I've cleared it, do you understand? Good. No, you did well, Max. I'll remember that. Hold tight, and I'll be over with someone. No, not the police. We can't allow them in a restricted area. Don't let anyone in until I get there. Tell them there's contamination. Right. You've got it, Max. I knew I could count on you."

Lundeman hung up the phone quickly and stared at a wood-paneled wall, drumming the fingers of his left hand on a polished desk. He picked up the phone, punched four numbers, continued drumming until there was an answer. His voice was low, sharp and accusing.

"So you're in already," he said quickly. "Let's see if this is news to you; I just got a call from the hill. They found Jacob Bauer dead in lab four an hour ago. I don't suppose you'd know anything about that? You know exactly what I mean; don't give me that shit. You answer to me, don't forget it. If I find out you're bypassing me I'll have your ass. Understand? All right. All right! Is your car here? Go home right now. I don't want you seen around here. I'll see you Monday, but I've got to call the Langley people now and get a crew out here. Yes. Goodbye."

He hung up the phone gently this time, breathing deeply as self-control returned, then from memory punched a long sequence of numbers and waited again before speaking carefully and succinctly.

"Curtis Lundeman for room five-two-four. Curtis Lundeman. That's C-U-R-T-I-S."

There was a moment of waiting for voiceprint identification before he spoke again.

"We have a red contamination problem in four. I need a crew out here stat. Medical treatment is not necessary."

When he put down the phone, his forehead was dry again. Moving slowly, he returned two files to a cabinet, locked his desk, rinsed out a cup and unplugged the coffee-maker before leaving his office. He tried the front door of the building after locking it, walked casually across campus and up the hill to the entrance of Gordon Science Center. The walk took only five minutes, but a white Dodge van with U.S. GOVERNMENT stenciled in blue on the front doors was waiting for him when he arrived. No football game for me tonight, he thought.

The revolving glass doors at the entrance yielded to his touch. Three men, one of whom he recognized, looked at him from the reception desk. Max Schuler, head of security, was obviously relieved to see him, smiling as his reinforcements arrived. Unlike Max, who was in slacks and a flannel shirt, the other two men were gloved, dressed in white, each carrying a transparent helmet under one arm. The men, both blond and in their late twenties or early thirties, turned to examine Lundeman with exceptionally blue eyes. One extended a gloved hand, and the university president held it lightly in his for only an instant.

"I'm Sanderson, and this is Harris," said the man, nodding towards the other who stood beside him silently and without expression. "You called in a problem?"

"We'll take the elevator up," said Lundeman. "Max, you wait here, and keep everyone out. Tell them we've had a bad chemical spill."

"Yes, sir," said Max, looking relieved.

When the elevator doors closed behind them, Sanderson and Harris began stripping off their white decontamination clothing.

"No use sweating any more than we have to," said Sanderson, smiling. Beneath the clumsy suit he wore grey slacks and a white body shirt stretched tightly over a heavily muscled frame. Harris was dressed the same, but he was a slender man who moved slowly with the fluid-like grace of a dancer. His eyes were those of a shark: cold, without expression.

"I want a quick word with the guard," said Harris. "You go on to the lab, but I want to see it before you disturb anything."

When the doors opened, the guard, face red and puffy, rose from his desk to meet them. He looked first at Lundeman, and said nothing. Harris took him firmly by one arm and led him back to his desk as Sanderson followed Lundeman down the hall. The lab was cold when they entered, and the animals were quiet in their cages. There was an open door on the far side of the room, and the body of a man was sprawled there on his back, eyes staring upwards, mouth open.

"He looks surprised," said Sanderson.

"Poor old Bauer," said Lundeman. "He wasn't much of a teacher, but he did some good research, and the students liked him."

Sanderson looked into the fume hood. "He was working in here. Broken glass all over the place, but otherwise nothing.

Does this mean anything to you, Doctor Lundeman?"

"No. Maybe he broke something poisonous. I'll have to look up his contract to recall what he was working on."

"He was working with SB4," said Harris, who had entered the lab with stealth and was padding around the room behind them. He leaned over to look at the body, pulled down the dead man's collar, peered closely at something and straightened up. "For your information, Doctor Lundeman, that's a nerve gas."

"Ah yes, now I recall it," said Lundeman.

"The gas is stored in ampoules, like the one broken in this fume hood. There's no other equipment or chemicals in there, no animal cages, nothing. Just a broken ampoule. Now, if the exhaust fan were on and the fume hood window pulled down even two-thirds closed, the gas from that broken ampoule should not have reached the room, yet it appears it did."

"Bauer was killed by SB4, then. An accident due to poor technique." A simple explanation would be best and most easily accepted by grant officers, hoped Lundeman.

"I don't think so," said Harris quickly, "and I don't think it could be suicide either. There are bruises on the back of his neck, and pieces of glass on the floor by his head. He was forced into the hood, and the ampoule broken by his face. See the cuts near his right eye?"

Lundeman forced himself to look closely at Bauer's staring face. The cuts were there, a tiny piece of glass glistening in one of them. "Are you suggesting murder?"

"I am," said Harris, "and a sloppy job of it. Do you know of any reason someone might have to kill this man?"

"None at all. He was a quiet person who did his job and got along well with the students. He had a graduate student working with him, by the way. Where is he?"

"Len Dieter," said Harris, looking at a small notebook he had scribbled in. "The guard remembers Bauer saying the student had called him from the lab, asking him to come in, but the guard hadn't seen him all night. We'll check this all out with the student later. It seems he wasn't here when Bauer arrived, and the guard didn't see anyone leave."

"This Len Dieter still hasn't arrived, even though he called Bauer to come in. I find that strange," said Lundeman.

"Perhaps," said Harris, "but we'll check it out. Central office is sending someone, and he'll be here by this evening. Maybe the student will turn up by that time. My people will look for him right away. In the meantime I'm ordering an autopsy, and the official cause of death will be heart failure. There's no need to complicate things any further right now."

"Certainly," said Lundeman, "and I don't want any stories about nerve gas accidents here, either."

"Publicity will be kept to a minimum," Harris assured him. "I'll control that locally. We'll need to talk with you again later. We have to move fast, particularly if there's a security problem involved. For now, let's get his body out of here. Sanderson, get the stretcher and bring a body bag."

"Right," said the big man, and he quickly left the room, elbowing his way past the guard who stood at the doorway, gazing at the body of Jacob Bauer. Harris seemed startled.

"How long have you been standing there?"

"Just for a minute. Can I go now? It's two hours past the end of my shift, and my replacement is here."

"Go ahead, but be quiet about all of this," snapped Harris.

"Yes, sir," said the man. He turned and shuffled out of the room. Harris looked at Lundeman, a question in his eyes.

"He'll be okay," said Lundeman. "He's been with us a long time."

The guard left the building and went home for breakfast, where he told his excited wife everything he had seen and heard that morning.

* * * * * * *

Irene Lundeman relaxed the morning away under the gentle, capable hands of Allen, her hairdresser. The salon was empty except for Allen, herself, and Allen's partner Eric, who struck a bored, effeminate pose in a barber chair near the window. Allen played the affected hairdresser well, clucking over her like a mother hen, but as he washed her hair his hands strayed to her neck, shoulders and back, rubbing with just the right pressure and rhythm to give her a minute tingling and throbbing sensation between her legs.

"Something swept up, I think: symmetric and softly curling at the top to accentuate your height, and those gorgeous cheekbones. Curtis will not leave you alone today," he promised.

"Curtis won't even notice, Allen. He never does. You know I come here for myself."

"I am your devoted servant, madam."

"You're so sweet to me, such a blessing in this dismal little town."

Allen leaned her back in the chair, folded a towel around her head and kneaded softly. She tilted her chin up as his fingers worked, occasionally caressing her throat, and he felt rather than heard her breath quicken.

"Oh, you have such marvelous hands," she moaned.

"Pooh," he said teasing, then smiled as she whispered to him and reached up to touch his face.

"Don't play the gay with me, Allen. We both know better." She leaned back against him.

"Do you want us to be alone, dear?" he whispered.

"Yes," she breathed. "Tell Eric to take a walk."

Allen chuckled. "Eric, my lad," he said brightly, "it's a lovely morning, and business is slow. Why don't you take a stroll in the park?"

Eric looked at them angrily, rolling his eyes. "Again? Why don't we just buy a cot for the storage room, or put up a curtain so you can consult in private? Really, Allen, this is disgusting. I will be back in exactly twenty minutes, so make it quick."

Eric stormed furiously out of the shop and walked to the park, where he found a friend and spent some lovely, intimate moments of his own that eased his jealousy of Irene Lundeman.

* * * * * * *

At seven o'clock the blue Lincoln Town Car pulled majestically into the circular drive before the president's residence and stopped by the front door. Curtis Lundeman got out of the driver's side and walked slowly around to where his wife waited for him to open her door. She swung her long legs out of the car and used his extended hand for support in making a graceful exit.

Inside the house they pulled off the full-length leather coats they had worn to dinner. Irene sat down on a white sofa to take off her boots, and sighed contentedly.

"I had a lovely time tonight," she said happily.

"I'm glad," said her husband. "I was afraid you'd be bored at the game, and business prevented us from going anyway."

"Oh no," she said. "It was so nice with just the two of us for a change. I do enjoy entertaining your important guests, of course. Do you think I make them feel comfortable?"

"Of course, dear. I've never doubted your abilities to charm people." Lundeman smiled when she looked at him sharply, but then her expression softened again. "You are always the perfect hostess," he said seriously, "very relaxed, and obviously satisfied with yourself."

"I do want to help you, Curtis, if you'll let me. You were so quiet today, I wondered if you were still angry about last night."

"Not at all; it's forgotten."

"You have a right to be angry. I really was a brat. It's just that most of the time I feel so useless around here, and this town drives me crazy with boredom."

"We must find you some sort of hobby to pursue, something creative," he suggested.

"I don't want you to worry about this, darling. I'll find something to do while you build your little university and then we can move east to one of the real centers of learning and culture."

"That's the plan," he said, smiling, "and I'm not angry with you. There are other things on my mind. Do you want a drink?"

"Yes, if you're having one, a little scotch over ice."

He went to the kitchen and returned with the drinks a moment later. Irene patted the sofa, motioning him to sit beside her. He sat down and they touched glasses. "To next summer, and sailing off Nantucket, and a salty breeze in your hair," he said, then drained his glass in a single gulp.

Irene took a tiny sip of whisky, looking concerned. "You're worried about something, aren't you?"

Curtis looked at his empty glass. "It's probably nothing special, but a faculty member was found dead in his lab this morning."

"Dear God, how?"

"Likely a heart attack, but it happened in a secure area so there'll be an investigation. I'm being interviewed again tonight."

"You have to leave?"

"No, someone is coming over here at eight o'clock. Do you mind?"

"Of course not. Here, I'll get you another drink and fix us a little desert before your visitor arrives." She took his glass, planting a warm moist kiss on his forehead before disappearing into the kitchen, leaving him on the sofa marveling at his good judgment in choosing such a woman to be his wife.

At exactly eight o'clock, a county sheriff's car pulled into their driveway as Curtis watched from a window. A lone civilian, grey hair, slightly hunched over in a grey overcoat, got out of the car and walked casually to the house. Curtis opened the door as the man stepped up on the porch, looking startled.

"Doctor Lundeman?" Curtis nodded as the man fumbled in his coat pocket, then held up an identification card with his picture on it. "I'm Charles Ebensack, NSA Arlington. Could you spare me a few minutes, Doctor?"

"Yes, come in. I was expecting someone from Central Intelligence."

Ebensack smiled, took off the heavy overcoat and adjusted his tie while taking in the plush furnishings of a university president's house. Curtis hung the coat in a closet and motioned

Ebensack to the couch as Irene made her entrance into the room. She walked straight to Ebensack with a dazzling smile and hand extended as Curtis announced, "This is my wife, Irene." He had seen men quiver in her presence when she looked this way, some perhaps intimidated by her height, but Ebensack regarded her calmly with a little smile, took her hand gently in his and made a little bow. Curtis had seen the style in Eastern Europe, and he suspected that had Irene thought to raise her hand a little more, Ebensack would have kissed it while looking into her eyes.

"Can I get you something: a coffee, perhaps, or something sweet?"

"Nothing, thank you. I'll only be here a few minutes."

"Then I'll leave you to your business. Curtis, dear, if you need anything I'll be in our room, reading." She turned to her guest. "Nice to meet you, Mister Ebensack."

The man smiled warmly at her, said nothing, and Curtis detected both pleasure and amusement in his eyes as Irene turned and made her dignified exit from the room.

"An exceptional woman," said Ebensack.

"Thank you," said Curtis. "What can I do for you?" They sat down to relax in soft waves of white fabric.

"Just a few questions about the unfortunate incident in laboratory four this morning. An autopsy has been performed, and the official cause of death will be listed as heart failure. Doctor Bauer's family has some history of heart problems, and his wife can accept this without question. They have no children. Most unfortunate."

"Then there's no question of suicide or murder?"

"Ah, there's the rub," said Ebensack gravely. "There's no evidence of heart or arterial disease, or any other condition that might cause a massive coronary. There is no sign whatsoever of myocardial infarction. It would appear that his heart simply stopped, and this is an unusual physiological phenomenon. The broken ampoule could be related to his death. SB4 inhalation blocks every nerve in the body almost instantly. Do you think this could have happened accidentally, Doctor Lundeman?"

"It's possible. Look, I'm not a chemist, but I'm familiar with the original research proposal. Bauer's work was on finding an agent to block the effects of SB4. Maybe he was careless. There was nothing except the broken gas ampoule in the fume hood, and that material is supposed to be handled in a sealed glovebox, where there's no danger of exposure."

"That seems reasonable," said Ebensack reflectively, "but of course there's the question of suicide."

"Unlikely," said Curtis, warming to his understanding and explanation of the problem. "As far as I know, Doctor Bauer had no reasons for suicide. He seemed healthy, was enthusiastic about his work, and I've heard nothing about any personal problems he might have had. He was a rather outspoken man, and not what I would call private. He was well respected for the quality of his research here."

Ebensack wrote something down in his notebook and frowned. "So there's no obvious motive for suicide, even though one never really knows what goes on in the bedroom, and we also have the bruises to explain."

"Bruises?"

"Yes, across the back, one cheek, and two small but prominent bruises on the back of his neck, as if he had been grabbed by a very strong hand. Put this together with the fact there were many tiny pieces of glass in his face, and you might think he was beaten, then forced into the fume hood where someone broke an SB4 ampoule by his face. That's not suicide, Doctor Lundeman, that's murder."

Curtis felt the coolness of tiny beads of perspiration evaporating at his hairline. He willed himself to remain calm by remembering a cliché for stage comedians and university presidents. Never let them see you sweat. When he spoke, his voice was firm and reassuring.

"What you say makes sense, but I can't imagine anyone wanting to kill Jacob Bauer. Like I said, he was well respected here."

"He had no enemies? No rivals for a particular position, or a facility?"

"None that I'm aware of. He was not what I'd call an ambitious man."

Ebensack wrote a few words in his notebook. "Did you personally like him, Doctor?"

"I hardly knew him. We met at receptions and senate meetings, and he came over to my office once or twice for a chat. My door is always open for the faculty, and I encourage them to come in for visits."

"Did you ever have any conflicts with him?"

"Not really. I mentioned he was a very outspoken man, and we argued in the senate about our policies regarding classified research on this campus. He was basically opposed to allowing overly classified research here, and was quite vocal about it. The issue has been sent to the faculty senate research committee, and they're working on a policy statement now. The main issue seems to be easing restrictions on graduate thesis publication. Federal input has been very helpful in this matter, by the way, and I appreciate that. We should have the problem resolved in the next few weeks."

"Can you think of any faculty members who would be threatened by Bauer's opposition to classified research?"

"Absolutely not. The majority of our outside funding here comes from some kind of classified research, and the faculty certainly isn't going to do away with it. Bauer knew that when he argued in the senate, but he was not afraid to express an unpopular opinion, and did so. I respect that."

"It's hard to tell how some people will react to a situation, Doctor, and what one person regards as nothing may be seen as a life-threat to another. I'll be checking into this further, and I'd like to have your cooperation."

"I'll help you in any way I can. All I ask is that you be discrete about your inquiries, and please remember this is a university. People don't get killed for expressing ideas here."

"Perhaps, but unfortunately human history is filled with people who killed others because of their ideas. If a man is threatened by an idea, he will react to counter that threat with some permanence. This is a human trait, and universities are composed of human beings. It seems likely to me that Jacob Bauer was a threat to one or more people on this campus, and I will begin by finding out who they are."

"But please keep in touch with my office," said Lundeman quickly. "Some faculty members will be very sensitive to an investigation, and you should know who they are before you make any contacts."

"I understand, and I'll certainly let you know what I'm up to. My office will insist on that. This might take a few days or weeks, Doctor Lundeman. I'll be staying with Harold Cox, so just call his office if you have any messages for me."

"The county sheriff?"

"Yes. We went to school together, a long time ago. Such a small world we live in, don't you think? I can do my work, and have a nice visit with an old friend at the same time."

"That's nice," said Lundeman, standing up. "Is there anything else I can do for you now?"

Ebensack got up slowly, thinking. "I can't see anything more at the moment, but I'm sure something will come to mind later. You've been helpful, Doctor."

Lundeman helped the man with his heavy coat, and opened the front door for him. The evening air felt cold on his face and head, and he suddenly realized his arm pits were damp as well. The men shook hands, and then Ebensack held on as he suddenly thought of something new to say. "Tell me, Doctor, do you honestly think anyone could have regarded Jacob Bauer as a dangerous troublemaker?"

"No, not Bauer. He was just opinionated; everyone understood that." Their hands clasped together, Lundeman wondered if Ebensack felt the tremor that passed through his body.

"Yes, well, good night, doctor Lundeman, and thank you. I'll be in touch again." He let go of Lundeman's hand, walked slowly to the sheriff's car, deep in thought, and got in while Lundeman shivered in the evening air.

As the car pulled slowly out of the winding driveway, the university president stepped back into his house and closed the door. When he turned around, Irene was standing in the kitchen doorway, a strong looking drink in one hand and a facial expression usually reserved for those times when she had a particularly damaging piece of gossip to report.

"Well, dear," she said nastily, "you didn't bother to tell me it was murder."

CHAPTER THREE

The appointment was at three o'clock, but butterflies had been in Jack Nelson's stomach since noon. It was game time again, and adrenaline was pumping. At times like this he tried to go inside himself, but Karen was with him, feeding him cokes in a dark corner of the student union beer bar and making him talk it out.

"I don't know what you're so uptight about. You have everything they want: high grade-point average, athletic ability and leadership experience on the team. It's just a formality, Jack."

"A lot of it is politics, Karen: how you play the game, how many people like you. There are maybe a dozen slots open in Eagle Squad this year, and fifty guys who want in. Everybody's competing with everybody, and there are no close friends over there. Sometimes I wonder why I even want to go into the military."

"So why do you?" she asked.

"You know it's important to me."

"I know, but don't let your whole life hang on it. If you don't get in, it's their loss. You can still be an engineer, and the pay's better."

"I don't want to spend the rest of my life just making money, and you don't want it either."

"I want you be be happy with what you do," she said. "What you do and how much you earn makes no difference to me."

"But you're not a big fan of the military."

"No, I'm not, but I know it's necessary to have it, and if

you want me to be a military wife I'll be that." Her face was suddenly flushed, and Jack took her hands in his at the center of their little table in the dark corner.

"You never let me get away with bullshit, do you?" he said softly.

"Never," she snapped back.

Jack looked at her steadily for a moment, then sighed. "I'd better get over there. Meet me in the library at six?"

"Yes. Good luck, Jack. Just be yourself."

"Right," he said, made a funny face at her, and she rolled her eyes in mock disgust.

He left her alone to read, and walked in sunshine to the windowless, one story concrete building that housed the Department of Military Science. A maze of hallways led to classrooms, projection rooms and a small library. At each end of the building, narrow staircases led downwards to a full basement containing a rifle and pistol range with ten positions, storage and equipment issue rooms and a large open area which doubled as gymnasium and drill field. It was a modern facility, a campus pride, and it was widely known that the United States Army took a special interest in it, sending only their best people as teachers. Jack walked past a reception area where two secretaries sat pecking away at word processors without looking up. He walked to a closed door marked COMMANDANT, took a deep breath and knocked three times on the door jam.

"Come!" someone shouted from inside. Jack opened the door, pulled himself up to full height and centered himself in the doorway.

"Jack Nelson, sir. We have an appointment at fifteen hundred, sir."

As Jack stood rigidly in the doorway, Colonel William Holleque rose from behind his desk and walked towards him, hand extended.

"Jack, come in. Good to see you." He took Jack's hand in a quick, iron grip, then released it. There was an aura of strength surrounding the man: hard, angular body with a face chiseled from brown marble, skin like leather, short-cropped blond hair turning white at the temples, and light blue eyes that could look into a soul. His movements were quick and deliberately orchestrated. He projected a constant image of complete control, and one could not lie to the man or try to deceive him. His eyes wouldn't allow it. Even so there was something fatherly about him, something caring, and everything one said seemed to be important. He was probably in his late forties or early fifties. Nobody knew. He looked like a thirty-year-old, and among the four hundred cadets, he was simply known as The Man.

They went back to the desk, Jack seating himself in a straight-back chair in front of it. The colonel sat down, and punched an intercom button. "No calls, Margaret," he said sharply, and the intercom clicked twice. An open file was on the desk, and Holleque studied it for a brief moment, then smiled at Jack.

"What can I say, Nelson? Your record is excellent. Everything we like to see in a candidate for Eagle Squad, provided you have the proper motivation." He turned a page in the file.

"Motivation, sir?"

"Why do you want to be in Eagle Squad?"

"Because it's the best, sir. I want to be part of the best, and I feel I'm qualified for it."

"Every man in that unit intends to be career military."

"I know, sir. That's also my intention."

"Four years active duty minimum, and the scholarship won't even pay your tuition."

"I have a football scholarship, sir, but the extra money will help, and I want to get the best possible training. That means Eagle Squad."

"The field exercises are demanding and dangerous. Two cadets have been killed in the last three years. Your whole life can end before you even graduate. What would your parents think of that?"

"My folks have encouraged me to go for it, sir. Dad goes back a long way with a presidential task force and the national committee. I was raised ultra-conservative, sir. My folks are very pleased about my wanting to go into the military. That's why I'm here, in the best military science program in the country. My folks know the risks, and so do I."

"You're willing to die for your country?"

"I don't intend to die in combat, sir. The guy I'm fighting will have to do the dying."

The cold blue eyes searched his soul. Was there a trace of a smile on that chiseled face? Holleque turned a page in the file and then another while Jack waited quietly, ramrod straight in the chair. Time moved like molasses through cheesecloth. Finally the colonel closed the file and leaned back in his chair. His voice was crisp.

"Very well, Nelson, you have my positive recommendation at the board meeting on Friday. I promise nothing, but the board has never gone against a recommendation of mine. With their approval, you should receive a notice within a week, giving you the drill schedules and forms for your professors to fill out when you have to be excused from classes to attend field exercises. This is in addition to your regular military science classes, of course. You'll receive no extra credit for the field work, but it's a central part of your training."

"I understand, sir." Jack fought for control, wanting to grin, shout, jump up and down, anything to vent his feeling of victory in achieving a goal he had dreamed about for over two years. To the colonel he only showed a muscular, blond athlete, sitting at attention without expression and exuding an aura of total confidence and dedication.

They stood up together and shook hands again. Holleque seemed at ease as they walked to the door. His voice softened. "I handle Eagle Squad myself, Jack. I think you'll find I'm demanding but fair, and my people are handpicked. I expect nothing but the best from them, and so far that's what they've given me."

"I'll give you my best, sir."

"I'm sure of that," said Holleque, "but now I have another appointment."

Jack squared away at the door, suppressed an urge to salute, for he was not in uniform. "Thank you for your time, sir."

"Have a good day," said the Colonel. Jack stepped backwards out of the room, executed a left face and walked briskly away.

Holleque closed the door and walked back to his desk thinking, Holleque, my man, you have found yourself another right-wing gem. As he settled in his chair the intercom buzzed again.

"Yes, Margaret?"

"You had a call from President Lundeman, and he wants you to call back. A Mister Ebensack from NSA Arlington called and set up an appointment for Thursday morning at ten. He said it would only take a few minutes."

"What's that about?"

"He didn't say, sir."

"All right, I've got it down. Thanks, Margaret." Holleque punched the intercom, tapped his pencil on the polished desk a few beats, frowning, then picked up the telephone and dialed the president's office.

* * * * * * *

Karen was still thinking about Jack's interview when she entered the lab. The door was unlocked, so it was likely Doctor Reimer had already arrived. The animal room was dark, but there was light beneath the closed door to the adjacent lab. The animals chattered and squealed in their cages, smelling her perfume and anticipating a meal. Among her menial tasks as a graduate student it was her duty to feed them. Karen turned on the lights, retrieved food dishes from the cages and filled them with pellets.

There were muted sounds from the adjacent laboratory. At first Karen couldn't identify them. She listened carefully in the silence of her room as the animals fed. Sobbing. Someone was crying behind the closed door. She walked to it, knocked softly.

"Hello?" Is something wrong? It's Karen. The animals are

fed. I need to check on how my assemblers are doing."

The sobbing stopped, and there was a long pause. The doorknob rattled and Karen stepped back as the door opened. Judith Reimer, her thesis advisor, held the door open and smiled wanly at her. Reimer's eyes were red, and she wiped at them with one hand.

"Sorry. I'm having a bad morning. Come on in."

"What's wrong?" asked Karen, and then remembered. "Is it about Doctor Bauer? I was so sorry to hear about him. So tragic."

Reimer closed the door behind them. "More tragic than you might think, but don't mind me. I'm just being dramatic."

She wiped her eyes again and ran her hands over short-cropped grey hair that made some people think she was on the physical education faculty or even a coach. Karen had quickly learned that behind that hard face with thin lips was a genius who could model molecules hooking together in her sleep.

"There are rumors flying about how he died, and his research assistant is missing. Could he be responsible?"

"So much for military intelligence. That would be an easy answer," said Reimer. "They're interviewing all of us who have classified projects. Months to get us our security clearances, and now we're murder suspects. Brilliant. I don't even know what Bauer was working on."

"I didn't know you had a classified project," said Karen.

"Well now you know. It doesn't involve your thesis research, so don't worry about that. Nobody will be telling us you can't publish your work. That has been a problem on this campus, a problem doctor Bauer championed in the faculty senate."

Reimer paused, pressed her lips together angrily. "Maybe he was too loud about it, and pissed off the wrong people." Her eyes darted around, and she put a fist to her mouth.

"Sorry. I'm talking silly. This has nothing to do with you. A friend has died, and I'm a little scared about being interviewed by the feds. I don't trust those people to get anything right. Back to work, now. How are the assemblers doing?"

"The chain lengths were up to ninety when I checked last night."

"Not so hot. Should have been a lot longer by then. Change the temperature, the PH, or try another polymer with fewer side chains. The mites have to work much faster than what you're getting, and we're not going to spend time playing with their structure right now. We want to get your thesis finished and you graduated to do great things in the world."

Reimer put a hand on Karen's shoulder and squeezed. She was her old self again, quick and decisive. "I'll be in my office all morning," she said.

Karen spent the morning and early afternoon running one electrophoresis test after another and the results were all the same. Her chain links had only gone to two-hundred-thirty units overnight, a fifth of what she had hoped for. She set up six new experiments with varying PH and temperature and was ready to leave for the day to meet Jack. The door to Reimer's office was ajar when Karen went to see if there was anything else she should do.

Reimer was talking to someone on the telephone, and she was crying again. Karen listened briefly, and quickly left the laboratory before Reimer could know when she'd gone. And the last words she'd heard troubled her the rest of the day.

"I'm scared, baby," said Reimer to someone. "I could be next, and I don't know who to be afraid of. Please come over tonight. I need a lot more than a hug from you."

* * * * * * *

"Hey, spacewoman!" Jack said loudly, and other people in the library looked up from their books. "I've just had a major career breakthrough, and you don't seem to be interested in it."

Karen blinked her eyes and looked surprised, then hurt. "I have been listening to you, Jack. What do you want me to say? I knew you'd get it, so it isn't big news to me. I'm happy for you. It's what you wanted."

"You seem kind of down."

"No, I'm thinking about something else. After you left the union I went back to the lab to feed my animals and do some work. Doctor Reimer was there crying."

"Who's Doctor Reimer?"

"My thesis advisor; you've heard me mention Judith Reimer. She's a physical chemist: polymer chemistry, nano-tech, that sort of thing. Anyway, she was crying, and I was so embarrassed for her.

Karen quickly told Jack what had happened in the laboratory.

"Hey, hey," said Jack. "Sounds like she has a boyfriend."

"Listen to me. She believes it was murder, and said so. I can't forget that crazy, frightened look in her eyes when she first started talking to me. Then the wall went up, and we only talked about my work after that. She feels threatened by something. I'm sure of it.

"It's none of your business. You can't help her unless she asks for it."

"I've never seen her vulnerable like that."

"We're all vulnerable."

"Even you?"

"Vulnerable to your charms. Let's get out of here, and go for a walk."

They walked outside, where a cold wind came down from the hills. The campus was brightly lit; they walked arm in arm past silent, granite buildings and around the quad to a winding path lined with brick leading up into the hills. Every fifty yards a small wooden bench was placed looking down on campus, and after a winding climb of four hundred feet there was a covered overlook with tables and cooking grates. They leaned on the four-foot stone wall encircling the overlook, watched the lights from the campus town and a fire tower on a neighboring hill in the north woods. It seemed even the birds were asleep, and then Jack turned Karen to face him, taking her in his arms, and they kissed softly, without haste or force. He leaned her back slightly over the wall, pressing against her until she felt his hardness, and reaching with her hand she pushed down gently, but firmly.

"Ouch," he said.

"Ouch is right. I can think of better positions."

"Just a healthy, American boy," he quipped, but his breathing was deep and he held her hand where it had pressed him.

"I do love you, Jack," she murmured.

"You're my woman," he growled theatrically.

"No, tell me you love me, macho man."

"I love you," he whispered.

"That's more like it. You'll say it easier with practice."

At that instant, there was a footstep on the dark path behind them, a tiny stone grinding under a shoe.

"Shit," said Jack.

They held each other closely, waiting in silence for someone to appear, feeling uneasy until there was a scuffling sound further down the trail.

"Someone watching us?" asked Karen.

"Sounds like whoever it was is headed down now."

"Kinky."

"People come up here all the time. If I saw us, I'd know we wanted to be alone."

"I didn't hear anyone coming up the trail, Jack. Please, let's take the dirt trail back. It's spooky here."

He wouldn't tell her about how uneasy he felt. For just an instant he had felt danger, either real or imagined, and his body was ready for a fight.

"Sure, it's light enough, and we'll get back quicker," he said. "The dance started at nine, didn't it?"

"Yes."

"It's a quarter-past. Let's go boogie."

They picked their way down the steep narrow trail, dropping on a line through thick woods and sharp underbrush. The trail came out of the woods by the brightly lit house of the president, and they crossed the grassy quadrangle towards the student union. Near them, two figures dressed in khaki, black jump boots and red berets suddenly appeared, walking briskly towards the military science armory. As they approached the building, both men turned to look at Jack and Karen for what seemed like a long time, then disappeared inside. Karen, eager to dance, walked jauntily ahead, noticing nothing, but when Jack saw the two men watching him, uneasiness returned.

Red berets were the badges of Eagle Squad.

CHAPTER FOUR

Black boots pounded the floor beneath the high beamed ceiling of the big room. A single platoon was drilling in civilian dress on the polished wooden floor as five foot-nine inch Master Sergeant Jesus Rodríguez barked commands through the high-gain amplifier of a megaphone. He stood rigidly on a high platform at the side of the armory gymnasium, steadily increasing the frequency of his commands: "Column left, march! By the right flank, march! To the rear, march, rear, march, left flank, march...." The platoon was soon hopelessly confused, a few stalwarts still in step, the rest wandering aimlessly.

"Platoon, halt!" screamed Rodríguez.

There were sounds of shuffling feet, and murmuring echoed back and forth in the room.

"Fall in!"

Silence. Rodríguez glared down at his young troops, preparing to pronounce sentence.

"You young people are pathetic," he said softly. "You think you're a drill team. You have deluded yourselves into thinking you are ready to represent this battalion and this university with some kind of honor. At this moment, you will bring us only disgrace. Three days, people. Three days. One last review, and if you cannot represent military precision I promise there will be new faces where you are now standing."

Silence again, a pause for effect. Rodríguez turned to gaze at the young man standing three steps in front of the platoon. "Next Friday, Wilson, at fifteen hundred, I will see a flawless performance here. I hold you personally responsible for that."

"Yes, Sergeant!"

Rodríguez turned around sharply, stepped back onto the balcony that circled the room. As he walked away, a young voice boomed in the stillness.

"You people have embarrassed me today. More importantly, you have embarrassed yourselves. Do you enjoy that? I thought you were handpicked. Do any of you have physical or mental problems I should know about? No? Then let's do it right this time. Platoon—attention!"

Rodríguez smiled. Wilson was showing the first signs of leadership. He was learning to pull their strings, their macho strings. Rodríguez knew all about macho. He had been raised with it.

The Man was waiting for him at the end of the room, leaning over the balcony on folded arms and watching the action on the floor below. He remained in that position when Rodríguez approached and stood casually next to him, hands on hips.

"What do you think, Sergeant?"

"Another week. It's not automatic yet, but when they do it right it's as good as I've ever seen it. Wilson has come along, too. He's finally asserting himself out there."

"Another red beret?"

"No, sir. When it comes to dangerous situations, he'll always be a dedicated wimp. Too much mother in him."

"Too bad," sighed The Man. "Good eye for drill. Let's keep him where he is."

They went to a small lounge facing out on the balcony. Rodríguez filled two cups with coffee from a metal urn, and dropped some coins in a dish. The room was furnished with a hardwood conference table and chairs, and a cork board covered with announcements filled one wall. The coffee urn was next to a small, metal sink, and at the back of the room someone had placed an old couch and a plain coffee table that was covered with magazines. The two men sat on opposite sides of the table and sipped their strong hot coffee black.

"You're coming up for rotation, aren't you?" asked Holleque.

"Yes, sir. In another year."

"What're you going to do with it?"

"Overseas, I hope. I've applied for Wiesbaden."

"Then what?" Holleque studied the table top.

"Wish I knew, sir. That'll be my twenty years, and I'm not going any further if I stay in, but in civvy life I won't find many jobs for a small arms instructor."

"Demolitions, too," said Holleque thoughtfully.

"Yeah, demolitions. Maybe I could work for mining, or forestry, or—"

"Urban renewal," said the colonel, and both men laughed.

"What about you, sir? Gonna go for General before you get out?"

Holleque smiled the enigmatic smile reserved for times when people asked him personal questions. "It would take a good war for that to happen, Sergeant. No, I think full bird is going to be it for me, and that's okay. I've had a good career, and ending it here in two years sounds fine to me. Not retirement, you understand, but something different, something a little more lively that teaching kids to recognize their left feet, you know what I mean?"

Rodríguez nodded, and sipped coffee.

"I like working with you, Sergeant. You understand the male ego, and how to make it do things it thinks it can't do."

"Thank you, sir."

"Not at all. You know how to motivate young people better'n most Sergeants I've known. I've been kicking around a couple of ideas you might have some interest in. When we have some free time, let's talk about it."

"Anytime, sir," said Rodríguez, suddenly realizing how beautifully his own ego had been stroked. "I'm open to anything."

"Later," said Holleque, rinsing out his cup in the sink, then wiping his hands on a paper towel. "Right now I have one more meeting to get through."

Rodríguez shook his head sympathetically.

Holleque left the room, walked the labyrinth of narrow corridors back to his office, entered through a back door and settled himself comfortably at his desk before punching an intercom button. "Any calls, Margaret?"

"No, sir, but a Mister Ebensack is here to see you."

"Of course, send him right in."

The door opened, and it was a middle-aged man who stood there looking dapper in a black wool suit with vest, red-striped tie and highly polished shoes. His grey hair was neatly trimmed, and the way he held himself suggested a military background. The way he dressed made him look like a lawyer. The man extended a hand as he entered the room.

"Colonel Holleque, so nice of you to make time for me." He flashed an identity card which Holleque barely glanced at. They shook hands as they studied each other for an instant, then the Colonel motioned Ebensack to a chair and sat down again behind his desk.

"What brings the NSA out here? I haven't seen one of you spooks in years." Holleque gave him a friendly smile.

"Oh, I assure you we're around, sir, looking after our interests, and we do have a lot of interests on this campus. There are research grants, you know, in chemistry, physics and psychology."

"All classified, I suppose. There has been some hoopla about that."

"Yes, all classified, all work done in controlled areas, so we're naturally concerned about security, particularly on research hill. That's why I'm here now, in fact. There seems to have been some kind of breech in security."

"What's the problem?" asked Holleque, and raised an eyebrow.

"To the point, Colonel, a faculty member and chemist, Jacob Bauer, was murdered in his lab on the hill last weekend. A student of his is a suspect, but we haven't found the young man yet."

Holleque's eyes widened. "The newspaper said he had a heart

attack, and a history of heart problems."

"True as far as it goes," said Ebensack, "but the heart attack in this case was induced by a good whiff of SB4, a recent nerve gas development. There were one or more people involved. They forced him inside a fume hood and gassed him there. Sloppy job, definitely not professional. I do hope you will keep this all in the strictest confidence, sir."

"Of course."

"Particularly for the sake of Bauer's wife, left alone. How awful it would be if she knew someone murdered her husband."

"I understand, but why tell me it was murder? Do you need my help in some way?" Holleque's eyes were again soul-searching. He looked at Ebensack, and saw years of intelligence experience looking back at him calmly, studying him, watching for reactions.

"Not directly," said Ebensack, "but perhaps you can provide me with some observations, or opinions. There has been a pene-tration of security here very early on a Saturday morning, or late in the evening last Friday. Any information on the move-ments of people on campus during that time would be very useful to me. You operate a group of cadets, I understand, who keep an eye on campus, a sort of patrol. I've seen a few of them myself; they wear red berets with regular army uniforms, and jump boots."

Holleque chuckled at the misunderstanding, dismissing it with a wave of his hand. "You're talking about Eagle Squad. Those people are the handpicked physical and intellectual elite of the battalion, and I'm proud to work with them. They do not spend assigned time patrolling the campus, and whoever told you that is way off base. On their own initiative they proposed a coed escort service some months ago. It has been used by students and even some faculty members. There have been no sexual assaults on campus since the service began, and there had been some problems before, enough so that women were afraid to walk even in pairs from the library or union back to their dorms at night."

"So nobody will mess with a red beret." Ebensack smiled.

"Two red berets. They always work in pairs."

"Are they armed?"

"Certainly not," said Holleque, his voice rising. "This is an escort service, Mister Ebensack, not a police action. These people are students."

Ebensack smiled again, and wrote something down in a little notebook. "Nonetheless, there's a chance that in the course of their rounds last Friday or early Saturday they might have seen something that would help me. If possible, I'd like to speak to them."

"I'd rather you didn't," said Holleque quickly. "These are kids, not professional soldiers. If someone from NSA starts questioning them it's going to be upsetting, and will accomplish nothing I can't get by asking them to file a report on what they saw up to eleven P.M. Friday, when the escort service ended. If you like, I'll ask for their individual observations after that time. Coming from me, such questions won't be threatening or accusative, as they might be with a federal investigator. These kids have grown up in rural communities where people know and trust each other, and honesty is taken for granted. I try to maintain that atmosphere here."

"Okay," said Ebensack, "you have them file their reports, but eventually it might still be necessary for me to talk to them. Please understand, Colonel, I have to examine every possibility. A security penetration has been made, and with some skill. There has been a murder, quick, silent and brutal, and a sloppy attempt to cover it up. I see a group of athletic young people with special military training, patrolling the campus at night, and I think I've found a group of people who would have both the ability and opportunity to strike a secure area and get away unseen."

Holleque looked as if he thought Ebensack was a madman. "My God, you suspect a red beret. I just told you Eagle Squad is handpicked; those kids are some of the finest, most respected students on campus, and you suspect them of murder."

"Try to understand, sir. Everyone on this campus and in town is a suspect. I can't leave anyone out. If I have to question one of your students we could do it in this office, and in your presence. Would that be acceptable to you?"

Holleque thought for a moment, eyes moving back and forth between his desk and Ebensack. "Yes, if we must have questions, then I suppose it's best if I be there. A familiar face might help. You understand I'm only trying to protect a group of kids I think highly of."

"Of course," said Ebensack gently. "I'll be as discreet as possible, and questions may not even be necessary. I gather you work very closely with these students."

"I handle them personally."

"Do they get extra training the other students don't receive?" Ebensack was writing in his notebook again.

"Yes. There's an extra session with small arms each week, a night reconnaissance drill in the hills once a month, three weekends of field exercises a year, and then in the summer they attend a two week jump school at Fort Benning."

"You do all this by yourself?"

"I have a staff of six to handle the teaching duties. My primary aid is Sergeant Rodríguez; he oversees the weapons training and assists me in the field drills."

Ebensack was scribbling furiously. "Is he in the building, now?"

"I had coffee with him a few minutes ago."

"Could I meet him for a moment? I don't have time for another interview."

Without replying, Holleque picked up his telephone and punched some numbers.

"Ah, good, you're still there. I have someone in my office you should meet right away. Could you come down now? Good. See you." He put down the telephone, looked at his watch and sighed.

"This will just take a minute," said Ebensack apologetically.

"I'm afraid my mind is wandering a bit," said Holleque. "I

have another class to prepare for." He looked at his watch again as Ebensack opened his notebook and began doodling in it.

"Go ahead," said the NSA investigator. "I have some notes of my own to write here."

Colonel Holleque's face flushed, but Ebensack wasn't looking at him. Silently, the Colonel opened a file and began to read, but a moment later there were three sharp raps on his office door.

"Come!" snapped Holleque, startling his guest. Rodríguez entered, brown eyes darting back and forth between both men, feeling for a pulse. Ebensack stood up and introduced himself, quickly went over Bauer's death and why he was investigating it, and that he would have some questions for Rodríguez in the future. The Sergeant listened carefully, and when Ebensack was finished, said, "I understand, sir. The department secretary will give you my schedule."

"And now we really have other work to do," said Holleque.

"Of course," said Ebensack, closing his little notebook and stowing it in a coat pocket. He started towards the door, then turned around and walked to Holleque's desk, extending his hand. Holleque arose, taking his hand in a firm, dry grip. Ebensack smiled.

"Thanks so very much for your time. I'll check back in a week or so to see what your students had to say in their reports, and you can leave any messages for me at the president's office."

Holleque escorted him to the door, where he turned back once more before leaving.

"Nice to meet you, Sergeant."

"Yes, sir," said Rodríguez.

Holleque closed the door gently, strolled back to his desk and sat down, ignoring Rodríguez. He sat there for a moment, chewing a fingernail, and there was a look on his face that Rodríguez had seen before, in a distant desert. It was the look of a man about to go out on night patrol, knowing that before the sun rose again he would likely kill or be killed and the world would not care. It was a dangerous look, and then he heard the Colonel growl something so quietly it was as if he were thinking out loud.

"That motherfucker," said Holleque, "is going to be a problem."

* * * * * * *

Karen went directly to the lab after supper. She hadn't seen Jack since coffee that morning, and already she missed him. The Eagle Squad drills overshadowed football in Jack's excitement, and all he ever talked about was the other red berets, weapons, and The Man. They had less time together now, but it was good time, and they were happy with themselves as well as each other. When she looked at her watch it was nearly six. She had promised to meet Jack in the library at seven, and had a thousand things to do before then. She put on a white lab coat and buried herself in a pile of little tasks.

Later, she had locked the lab door and was timing the run of a rat named Morris when the door suddenly rattled with the sound of a key clumsily inserted in the lock. The door knob turned, but the door wouldn't open. After a moment, there was more rattling, then a soft curse. Karen looked at her stopwatch as Morris neared the end of the labyrinth. "Hold on a second. I'm coming."

More rattling, more curses, then a pounding on the door. Morris reached the end of his run and gave thought as to which of three levers he could push without getting an electrical shock. His drugged brain didn't care, so he pushed one at random and nothing happened. Karen clicked off her stopwatch and raced to the door, fumbling it open and stepping back in surprise as Doctor Judith Reimer lurched into the room, quite drunk, and spilled the entire contents of her handbag on the polished laboratory floor.

"Oh, shit," she muttered, and got down on her hands and knees to clean up the pile of debris. Her heavy overcoat was open, and tears in her pantyhose radiated upwards from her shoes. An unlit cigarette dangled from her lips, flopping up and down as she mumbled to herself. Wind-blown hair hung down over her eyes.

"First the car, then I can't find my keys, then the door and now this. I think I'll go back to the bar." Judith Reimer, Sloan distinguished Professor of Chemistry, groveled around on the floor, picking up cigarettes, lipstick, coins, antacid tablets, bits and pieces of gum and candy wrappers and crumpled Kleenex. She threw everything back into her purse, then paused for a moment on all fours, like some giant frog, breathing deeply. "I think I'm having a panic attack," she said. "Help me up, please."

Wordlessly, Karen got her hands under the woman's arms and hauled her up on shaky feet, depositing her in a chair by the table-top rat labyrinth. Reimer looked at her with rheumy eyes.

"You are a strong kid. Do a lot of wrestling with that jock boyfriend of yours?"

Karen's eyes narrowed. "Can I get you a glass of water?"

"Sure. And put some bourbon in it."

Karen filled a glass of water at a sink. Her research advisor teetered a little in her chair, then turned to look at the maze. "Hey, Morris. Look at that little sucker get off on electricity. Go for it, guy."

"Oh, God, I forgot him," said Karen. She pushed the water glass at Reimer, then pulled the plug on the labyrinth where Morris, having discovered the electrified lever, was repeatedly shocking himself. She picked up the twitching rat in her hands and deposited him in a small cage while Reimer drank most of the water and splashed the rest of it in her face.

"Oooh, I've had just a tad too much tonight. The room is goin' round and round." She put a hand to her forehead.

Karen watched Morris staggering around in his little cage, bumping against the wall, body twitching, eyes rolling. "This stuff is bad," she said. "He's totally out of it."

"What'd you give him?"

"The vial marked L5."

"Well you gave him some good stuff. Right now, if you tell him you want to cut off his paw he'll hold it out for you. He doesn't care about anything anymore. Imagine what it would be like if you sprayed an army with that stuff. Hey, I ought to take a shot of it myself." She laughed, then stared at Karen morosely.

"I guess I don't feel too good about myself tonight. The booze doesn't seem to work very well anymore."

Karen remained silent. Her face felt hot, and her fingers played nervously with a button on her lab coat. Reimer took off her glasses, rubbing both eyes with the heel of her hand.

"Don't look so stunned, Karen. The old prof drinks too much, that's all. It's nothing you've said or done. I'm just sick of my work, and this place, and the people who run it, and.... You know, I got to thinking about Jacob again tonight, and he never hurt anyone in his life, and he's dead, and I'm alive. He has a wife, and I have nobody, and he's the one who gets killed. No warning. All his yelling in the senate, and for what? Nothing will happen, and if it did the university would fall down, and we'd all be out of a job."

"I don't understand any of this, Doctor Reimer."

"Of course you don't, and I don't want you to understand it. Take my advice and find a good job in industry where they don't change the rules every other week and allow you to follow a code of ethics. Everything here is money, money, money, and education be damned."

"Then why don't you quit, and go somewhere else?"

Reimer chuckled. "I was wrong. You should go into academe, and become an administrator."

"Really, Doctor Reimer, why stay here if it makes you so unhappy?"

The professor let out a long sigh. "Do you know how many job openings there are for an old gal like me? Industry thinks I'm too theoretical, and academe thinks I should be a department chairperson. I refuse to do that. Pushing paper and wiping faculty noses is not my way of life. If I abandon research I'm stuck here, unless I push paper. That's the trick they pull if you make money for them. They give you good raises, promote you fast, and before you know it you're too expensive to go anywhere else. Clever, these administrators."

"I'm sorry," said Karen.

"Ah, youth," said Reimer dramatically. "The world is a giant oyster, and you're going for the pearl. Trouble is, you get to the pearl and find out it's a black one, covered with blood, and all the great ideas you had about helping humanity have been twisted and perverted by the ones who control the money, so you spend your time developing and testing chemicals that blow minds in new and interesting ways, like Morris here." She pointed at the rat in his little cage. He sat quietly, now, staring at both of them, an occasional shudder running through his body as if he had hiccups. Reimer leaned over and snapped her fingers sharply in front of his face. No response, not even the blinking of an eye.

"Gone, gone, gone," said Reimer tearfully. She fumbled in her purse for a tissue and blew her nose loudly. "Oh, God, I'm a mess. I should go home and sleep, but I'm afraid to." Another blow, daintily this time.

Karen pulled herself up to her full five feet-ten. "What are you afraid of?" she asked indignantly. "Has somebody threatened you?"

"Me and my mouth again. Not your concern, Karen. Just do your experiments, write your thesis, and stay out of campus politics. Your time will come soon enough." She chuckled, and seemed to suddenly calm down. "What I need is a cigarette, and a good night's sleep, and maybe a roll in the hay to make it all worthwhile again." She wiggled one eyebrow seductively, but Karen stared at her coolly, arms crossed in front, unmoved by the sudden bravado.

"You're in trouble, and you won't tell me about it because I'll be in danger if you do. That's what I think, Doctor Reimer."

Reimer looked up at the statuesque girl with the sharp cheekbones and piercing auburn eyes and thought to herself, Oh, honey, I can see what he sees in you, and you are a darlin', and right now I'd like to run my hands all over you, but I don't dare because you are as straight as an arrow.

What she said was, "I have some personal things to work out,

Karen, and the less you know about that the better off you'll be, but if the time comes when I really need your help I'll scream loud and long. Okay?"

Karen looked so serious, arms folded, back straight and tensed. Oh, you are gorgeous, thought Reimer.

"I don't suppose I have any choice," said Karen.

"No, you don't."

"If something happened, and I thought I could have helped, I—"

"Don't worry about it. I've been around the horn a lot of times, and I know what to do. Well, most of the time I do. Why get people involved if they're not involved, know what I mean?"

"But I am involved. I work in this lab, and I work with you, and look what I just did to Morris. Is that what this is all about? Some sort of secret projects you're working on? You told me to make these tests, and you didn't seem surprised by what happened to the animal."

"Partly true. There was a vial marked neuter. He was supposed to get that before the L5, and then the timed run. I assumed you—"

"Yes. I followed your instructions exactly, with the shots five minutes apart, and ten minutes before the run. There were no negative symptoms until he got near the end of it."

"Shit," mumbled Reimer softly. "The block is still breaking down too fast; I thought we'd used enough chelator this time, but stuff is still precipitating out."

"Who's we? Doctor Bauer?"

"Drop it, Karen. Please. I've already said too much to you."

Reimer lit a cigarette, the flame of a match wavering in her trembling hand. She inhaled deeply, leaned back in the chair and closed her eyes. "We went through the synthesis together twice, and I have the procedure written down, but it'll have to be trial and error because I don't have any feeling yet for the quantities involved. Right now we're looking for an order of magnitude effect anyway. I'll make up a new sample tomorrow, and we'll try it with the same L5 batch you gave to Morris. I'd like to have another run with the new neuter tomorrow after-noon. Will you run it?"

"Yes," said Karen, watching the little rat staring vacantly out of his cage. "What should I do with Morris?"

"No good for further tests, so might as well sacrifice him. Don't bother to do an autopsy; I know what's wrong with him. Use the guillotine." The death sentence was given absently, as Reimer's mind surveyed a problem in chemistry.

"I'll take care of it," said Karen, coldly. In her work she had sacrificed several rats in the miniature guillotine, fastening their little bodies in the tight lattice of metal and slamming down the razor-sharp blade to snip off their heads. Autopsy was a routine part of data analysis, a necessary part of research, but with Morris there would be no autopsy, and no justification for his death other than removal of an animal whose mind had been blown away for the advancement of science. It wasn't fair.

"Can you be here again at six? I'll have you out of here by seven, but if you want to stay and run your thesis tests that's fine too."

"I'll stay and do my other runs. I'm getting behind."

"And I'm getting tired," said Reimer, slouching in her chair. "Fortunately, or unfortunately, I am now sober enough to walk, and having gone through my evening in a hurry I'm going to go straight home to bed." She arose somewhat unsteadily, and without looking in a mirror made a feeble attempt at repairing the tangled remains of her hairdo. She stubbed out the remains of a cigarette in a Petri dish, then lit another and pointed it dramatically at Karen. "Lead me to the door," she commanded grandly.

Karen smiled, put an arm around Reimer's shoulders and guided her on wobbly legs towards the door. Her advisor's arm snaked around her waist, hand wandering aimlessly up across her breast, then down to the inside of her thigh, finally settling on a grip at her hip and squeezing gently, but firmly not once, but twice. At the door, Reimer's voice was husky in her ear. "Beddy-bye, dear," she said, and when Karen turned slightly to look at her she received a firm kiss that fell half on cheek, half on mouth. She stared incredulously as Reimer released her and staggered out the open door, cackling.

She went back to the bench where Morris sat motionless in his cage. He didn't look at her when she picked him up, holding him in her hands for a moment to think. When she put him back on the bench he didn't move, or watch her as she put on her heavy coat. She picked him up gently again and put him into the bottom of a coat pocket, leaving the flap open so he could breathe.

"Not this time," she said out loud to the drugged and confused rat. "I'll find a place for you at home." She turned out the lights, locked the laboratory and made the short walk to the library. There, she told Jack about her conversation with Reimer.

"A pretty strange lady," he said. "Sounds like she takes lousy care of herself. Probably why she isn't married."

"I don't think so," said Karen. "Drunk or not, that woman made a pass at me tonight."

"Oh, oh," said Jack. "I've got competition."

"Don't go there, Jack," said Karen, and Morris seemed to suddenly come to life in her pocket.

He was hungry, she decided.

CHAPTER FIVE

The graduate seminar was at Ten, and breakfast was toast and coffee with one shot of bourbon that steadied her nerves. There were six students, all of them potential research assistants, and Reimer listened silently while they presented their proposals for thesis research. She endured a pulsing headache the entire two hours, but managed to contribute a few helpful suggestions. Nobody seemed to notice her discomfort from the excess of the previous evening.

On the way to the Faculty Club for lunch she saw Karen at a distance, but moved quickly to stay out of view. Let the girl cool a bit, and then Reimer would make a profound apology for her behavior. It would likely be enough. Karen was not naïve about the real world, nor was she a judgmental person, and she was dedicated to her project. It was not probable she'd seek another advisor this late in her studies. Physical needs be damned, Reimer needed her for the work, and for a kind of friendship that had developed between them. And right now, Reimer badly needed a friend she could trust.

She rushed to the lab after a lunch of yogurt and fruit. Karen would be there in four hours, and two other assistants were in class. There was a new batch of neuter to make up, and some chores she had neglected for too long. Bauer hadn't done it, and now he was gone. If Reimer was next, a great price would be paid for it. Working together they had kept two sets of lab books. One set recorded early trials and failures while the other outlined solutions and final recipes for all products under three separate grants. Reimer was now responsible for all of them. The SB4 project had been the first and easiest, so far. If the modified neuter worked in Karen's testing this evening, the project would be virtually complete. One inoculation, and a whiff of SB4 would be a whiff of fresh air, with no effect whatsoever on the person who breathed it.

The disassembler project was another thing. Blocking nerves can cause sudden death. Dissolving flesh is worse. A mix of nanomites was necessary to disassemble key proteins in skin and subcutaneous tissue. Death was not the objective, only agonizing, debilitating pain. The idea had come to her in a rage against the world one day, and at times she had trouble believing she had thought it. So far she'd kept it secret. The military would jump on the proposal like wolves on a downed deer, and seven new nanomite disassemnblers later she was nearing the end of the project. Commercial interests held more promise for monetary reward. The government support had built a new lab for her, but the horror of what she was doing haunted her continually, and to deal with it she had added an addendum to the secret project. If proteins could be disassembled by nanomites they could also be reassembled by beasties with similar structures.

Karen has given her the idea in idle conversation about her thesis one day, pointing out that some proteins could be opened up by unfolding groups around the biologically active site. A molecule attached to the groups and rotating as it withdrew virtually unscrewed the structure holding the protein together. A mirror image of that molecule would, in theory, be capable of reassembling the binding structure of the protein before it had completely opened up. That single conversation, when Karen was in her second week as a research assistant, had given birth to two new classes of nano-machines. The work was split between them. Reimer worked on the disassemblers, dreaming molecular structures night after night, and feeding mirror images of her new machines to Karen for her thesis work. The girl was happy, with noble thoughts of medical applications, while her advisor worked on a horrible weapon of war in the lab next to hers. Sooner or later she would have to tell Karen what was going on.

The first disassemblers she had tested had all worked, but slowly. They would not be effective in a combat situation, but could gradually deteriorate the skin of a soldier from a rash to a purplish mess of sores, incapacitating him. Disassembler four had been the breakthrough, smaller, with shorter side chains making it look like a crab with four claws and a tail. A few molecules had wiped out a Petri dish of protein in seconds, and when she'd tried it on dead chicks and rats the skin surfaces had boiled with activity before sloughing off bone. She could not, would not test the beast on a live animal, at least for now. The thought of what she would witness was just too horrible to bear.

Karen's assemblers were still slow, but getting there at the molecular level. How to apply them as an immune agent was an open question, and not part of the girl's work. And as long as the contract managers back east didn't know about the disass-semblers, Karen's thesis was safe, and the girl would be able to publish her work.

And then there were the private interests who wanted a piece of everything. Bauer had gotten himself into a real mess, and now it was spilling over on Reimer. Report this, report that, or risk exposure. There was not one master, but three. Which one had murdered Bauer? The man had been a fool, with all his noble, rabble-rousing rhetoric about classified research. How could he not realize it would put him in danger?

As long as the work progressed and there were no final results she should be safe, for now. But she had experienced an epiphany when Bauer was killed; there are no friends in the business of intrigue, only enemies. Trust nobody, and cover your own ass is the rule.

The two sets of laboratory books were a start, and the phone number of the NSA agent now sniffing around campus. Lab notes could be faked or altered, the real ones held aside as ransom for a life. But who to trust with the ransom? There was only one, a beautiful kid who was just trying to get a degree.

Reimer made new entries in the lab book she kept stored in her gym locker, stuffed in a little pillow used on massage tables. A small flat case was stored with it. Inside were five labeled vials containing the latest samples from her investigations: SB4, neuter, and three disassemblers, all capped and fitted with a jet spray release for use in the tightly sealed glove box. Case and book went into the little pillow, which zipped shut at one end. Reimer had often thought about the sudden death so close to her face while enjoying a massage.

She made entries and zipped up the pillow, then wrote a short note to Karen and enclosed the combination of locker number seventy-four in the Field house. Making up a new batch of neuter for Karen took only twenty minutes. She locked the lab door and took the stairs to the Chemistry Department office to deposit the note to Karen in the girl's mail slot. It was sunny outside, and a two hundred yard walk to the Field house. On the way there she spotted two red berets watching her. Baby's goons, she thought, always on the lookout.

The pillow went into her locker again. She changed clothes, did a thirty minute climb on a treadmill and had a scalding hot shower that melted the tension she's been feeling. But when she went outside the red berets were still where they had been before, and when she looked at them one smiled back at her.

CHAPTER SIX

Irene Lundeman studied herself in the mirror, running both hands down her sides to feel the curvature of still firm muscles. Her hair was piled high on her head, giving what Curtis called her Helen of Troy look, and she inspected it closely for the occasional rogue, grey strand. She found one and jerked it out, looked at it with disgust and dropped it into a wastebasket. She turned around serenely as Curtis entered the room.

"You are devastating as usual," he said gallantly. "Ready for the war?"

"Ready as possible," she sighed. "You know how I hate these things; the people have nothing to talk about but crops and weather. Why can't we have a dance, or a buffet in town, instead of this silly little cakes and cookies festival in our backyard?"

"We tried a dance our first year, remember? Only a few people showed up, and even fewer got out on the floor. That's one of the hazards of living in fundamentalist territory; you must watch out for sin."

"Little cakes and cookies, and that awful sweet punch the food service brings over. Can't we even have coffee?"

"Coffee contains caffeine. Sin, sin," he said, smiling.

Irene glared at her husband, hands on hips. "If I were a bedroom mouse in this town, I could find plenty of sin."

"Any bedroom in particular?" he asked.

"No, but come to think of it I could sure use a nice roll in the hay."

His smile disappeared, and he looked away from her. "Try to

be patient with me. I've had a lot of things to worry about the last couple of weeks. It's a stress problem, and I—"

"You seem to have been under stress for a long time, dear. I'm not talking about a couple of weeks."

"Let's please not go into it now. People are already here; we've got to get downstairs for the receiving line. Later, we'll talk about it."

Irene ignored him, looked at herself in the mirror, then made a stately exit from the room with Curtis trailing behind her. When she reached the spiral staircase leading down to the main floor, her face suddenly softened with a delicate smile, and she descended the stairs with the dignity and grace of the well-schooled debutante she had been.

"Irene, you look lovely," called a steel-gray-haired woman from the base of the stairs.

"Meg, dear, here we are again. How much I look forward to this each year."

The two women embraced warmly. "Curtis, you remember Meg Everson, don't you? We don't see nearly enough of her."

"Of course," said Curtis. "Carl has been a major participant in building this university. How are you, Meg?" He extended his hand, while the older woman beamed at both of them. He put an arm around each woman as they glided through the open sliding glass door leading to a stone patio. Tables were heaped with baked goods prepared by the Faculty Wives Club under the careful scrutiny of Meg Everson, who excitedly described the international specialties there. "These are German, and this group is all Scandinavian, light and delicate, just melt in your mouth."

Irene turned to her husband, whispered, "What, no fortune cookies?" and smiled sweetly when he ignored her.

They moved to the end of the tables to set up court, standing shoulder-to-shoulder as if they could not bear to be apart, and greeting their guests as they arrived singly or in pairs. Pleasantries were exchanged with warm smiles, and touches here and there to emphasize their joy in being with their academic family on a beautiful fall evening. The deans and department chairs passed in review, a few of them escorting new faculty members who for various reasons of their own had turned down high industrial salaries in favor of a teaching life. Their faces were bright and eager. Curtis wondered how many would darken in future years with the stress and disenchantment of low raises, poor quality of students, lack of support by an ignorant public, and pressures to obtain grants and publish papers while teaching heavy loads. A few would flourish, but most would burn to a cinder or leave within a few years. Curtis Lundeman greeted them, and wished them success at Simonsen University.

The reception line slithered on: familiar faces, familiar conversations, orchestrated to win presidential favor, without much substance. Irene became fidgety, shifting her weight from foot to foot, then whispering to her husband, "I have got to get out of here, Curtis. I need a drink."

"Have some punch," he suggested.

"You know what I mean," she growled.

"All right, all right, do what you have to do, but do it quick, because I need you here. I'll make excuses for you as usual." This was all said softly, with a smile, and she smiled sweetly back at him so everyone could see how happy she was.

There were stops to chat briefly with several guests about the relative merits of German and Scandinavian baked goods. Irene gradually made her way back into the house, ascended the stairs to her bedroom where she retrieved a bottle of Black Jack Daniels from a night stand and drank three ounces of it neat from a water glass. She lay on the bed a few moments, basking in the warm glow of the whisky. For one moment her mind was blank, but then she rose again to spray her mouth with scent from a small decanter on the night stand. She descended the stairs once again. Heads turned as she came out of the house, and though she knew he was angry with her, Curtis' face only showed admiration as she walked towards him. She was the queen returning to stand by her king. She was in control again, and knew she was beautiful.

The pastries were eaten, the ice in the punch melted away, and as the sun descended below the surrounding hills there was a sudden chill in the air. The crowd thinned until there were only pairs and small clusters of people talking here and there. Curtis was included in one such group, talking intimately to grim-faced men who carefully noted when anyone else approached them. Their wives had quietly left the reception, and it was business as usual, another evening of politics and strategy in Curtis' study. Irene was left again to herself to wander the house searching out little things to do. Not tonight, she thought, and made her plan while she helped Meg clear off the tables. Meg excused herself when food service personnel arrived to complete the job; her husband had joined Curtis' entourage in the library, and informed her she should go home. Would Irene like to join her for a cup of coffee? No, she couldn't, because there was so much to do in the house this evening. Another time, for sure. Meg smiled meekly, and left alone as darkness fell.

Irene went upstairs and gulped two stiff drinks before sipping at a third, repinning her hair and spraying new scent on her wrists and neck. She added a new layer of lip rouge, stepped back from the mirror, drink in hand. "Cheers," she said, and saluted the sensuous-looking woman standing before her with flirting eyes. She swallowed the rest of her drink in a single gulp, then padded down the stairs and knocked softly on the closed library door.

"Yes?" came a sharp reply.

She opened the door a little, and peered coyly inside. Curtis sat behind his massive desk, and four men sat in chairs in front of him, turning around to look at her through the smoky haze that filled the room.

"Curtis, dear," she said shyly, "I'm going over to the main library for a while. Is there anything I can get for you before I leave?"

"Nothing I can think of, Irene, but thanks. Bundle up, now, it's a bit cold outside."

"All right, then. I should be back by ten. Have a nice evening, gentlemen." And she closed the door again softly.

"A remarkable woman," she heard one man say.

"I'm very fortunate," said Curtis.

Irene put on a heavy coat over the thin, sleeveless dress she's worn for the reception. She left the house and walked north along a well-lighted street towards the campus, turning east near its edge and north again three blocks later. She skirted the edge of campus until she reached a small bungalow set off of the street and nestled among pines on a hillside. The porch light was on, and she marched straight to the front door, started to ring the bell there, then smiled and pounded three times hard on the door jam.

The porch light went off as the door opened, but she could see his face by the light of the street lamps, and saw he was not wearing a shirt. Her heart was instantly pounding, and she snapped her arm up in a mock salute, wobbling a little.

"Private Lundeman reporting for duty, sir. Curtis is buried all night in his library again, and the private is going crazy, sir."

"You are crazy to come here," he said, opening the screen door and breathing her fragrance.

"Just give me what I need, Mister Man," she murmured, pressing against him and running a hand over his hard, bare chest.

"But this time, try not to leave any marks on me.'

* * * * * *

"There's one more thing I want to get at tonight, and that's the anti-classified research movement going on in the senate right now. I want that snuffed out, and I don't care how you do it." Curtis slapped the top of his desk for emphasis. "I have watched you sit quietly while this thing was first being discussed, as if you had no opinion. Are you waiting for me to attack it? Don't you know how that would look with me as the principle fund raiser on this campus? I need to have my deans rallying against this bill, showing how it will destroy their operations and lose

valuable faculty. I need criticism from the technical depart-
ments to offset the bullshit coming from humanities and social
sciences. Where is it?"

"If we play our cards right, Curtis, the bill will die quietly
in Senate Research Committee. The faculty knows where the
butter for its bread comes from. Without our classified defense
contracts, this institution could be closed." The man who spoke
was Carl Everson, Dean of Engineering and Technology, a large
man with floppy jowls and sad eyes who ruled his college with
quiet firmness and questionable justice, keeping rules when
they suited him and breaking them when they didn't. He was
not opposed, least of all by Curtis Lundeman, who recognized
true power when he saw it.

"Not everyone sees that, Carl. You say it to one of the big
mouths from humanities, and they'll tell you to drop the defense
work and rely solely on the state system. If I tell them the state
doesn't need another university and would dearly love an excuse
to close this one they give me a blank stare and in the next
senate meeting they're yelling again. I want them silenced, and
I want it done now."

Curtis allowed his voice to rise in pitch and intensity, and
turned towards a wiry little man next to Everson.

"Do you understand what I'm saying, David? The people I'm
talking about work for you."

David Beasley spoke slowly and succinctly, the psychologist
during analysis, the mender of human souls in a college that
primarily offered introductory courses in social science and
humanities for technical majors, himself doing little research
except in behavioral psychology. Liberal and well liked by his
faculty, David Beasley was regarded by the other deans and
higher administrators as an academic softy, and now he felt
their anger.

"You have some justification in what you say, Curtis, and I do
have some irritating people over there. All of them are tenured,
I might add."

"Tenure isn't worth shit here, David. You know that. I can

cancel a position due to financial expediency any time I choose, and I can pick who to cancel. I don't need department approval, or yours. They teach more, or play ball. It's up to them."

"You don't need morale problems, or a vote of no confidence," said David, and now his face flushed with anger. "It's not just humanities and social science people you have a problem with. Jealousy is wide spread among the physical scientists and engineers who don't have the perks from lucrative classified defense grants. They're doing good science, but they struggle to obtain the simplest supplies or equipment while money is spent with total abandon on the hill. There's a lot of resentment about that, and it's being articulated rather forcefully in the senate."

"Like Jacob Bauer," growled Carl.

"Yes, particularly Jacob," said Curtis, "but then he's no longer a problem."

For a moment there was a stunned silence in the room, and the men stared at Lundeman.

"You have to admit that sounded sinister," said Allen Klister, and he chuckled. Allen was Vice President for Academic Affairs, second in command of the university. Among the faculty members, who despised him, he was known as the Hatchet Man.

"You mean like I hired someone to take out Bauer?" said Curtis. "Well, I didn't have to; it appears a student did the job for free. Regardless of how it happened, I do not mourn the passing of Jacob Bauer."

"Neither do I," said Arthur Hilton, dean of Science and Mathematics. Arthur was a pale, squat man, and perched like a great toad in his chair. "None of you had to work with him like I did. He was a major pain in my ass, along with Judith Reimer, and I'm a little worried about how she's going to react to his death. She's not rational, that woman, and she has a drinking problem."

"Plop, plop, fizz, fizz, Arthur," said Curtis. "If she's a difficulty, do something about it, and that goes for the rest of you as well. We do not need troublemakers on this campus. You all have people involved in the anti-classified research movement, and I want them squelched right now."

"If you can't think of a reason, ask me for one," said Vice President Klister, smiling. "My office is always open for discussions with disturbed faculty."

The deans sat silently as their two chief executives smiled at the inference.

"Each of you have representatives on the Senate Research Committee," said Curtis. "Get to them right away before the bill comes up for a vote. If possible, I want that thing killed in committee. If it gets to the open senate we're going to have real trouble, because the students are there and they're not happy about having parts of their thesis work classified and unpublishable. The support they give will just encourage the speech makers in the faculty."

"We'll handle it, Curtis," said Carl. "I have some troublesome people of my own, so none of us are immune to the problem. We can take care of it, and I think it would be wise for you to keep a low profile on the whole issue. Both you and Allen. If the faculty feels pressure to vote one way they will vote the other even if they think it's wrong, then rationalize their foolishness by evoking protection of their academic freedom."

"Another dead concept." Said Klister.

"That is your opinion, not mine," said Carl, icily.

Curtis frowned. There was no love lost between the Vice President and the Engineering Dean. Both of them wanted his job.

"I think you're right, Carl. We'll keep behind the scenes on this issue unless my deans drop the ball, and I really want to believe that won't happen. I like to think I'm a good judge of leadership abilities. I hired you people because I thought you were the best around, and I still feel that way. I just think it's time for all of us to clean up our houses a bit. What do you think?"

Four men allowed themselves a faint smile. For the moment, at least, the tension had been eased.

"I think it's time for a real drink," said Carl.

"So do I. Gentlemen, the bar is now open." Curtis walked to a corner of the library, pulled back a large panel to reveal a fully stocked bar and a small refrigerator. They poured their own drinks, and for an hour made small talk, presenting ideas to show their president how valuable they would be to the future of the university. Curtis listened politely, and soon forgot everything he had heard.

It was nearly eleven when Irene returned home. Curtis had gone to bed early, drowsy from three strong drinks, but he was still awake when she padded up the stairs and into their bedroom. She turned on the closet light, undressing slowly, languidly, running her hands over her arms and hips as if caressing herself. Curtis watched from the bed, feeling a stirring within, but knowing it was unlikely to go further than that. The closet light went out, and then she was slipping into bed beside him, smelling musky and sweaty and sighing deeply as her head nestled into the pillow.

"Sorry about the meeting tonight," he whispered.

"Oh, you're awake. I got so involved at the library, and forgot the time. A couple of those red berets walked me part of the way home."

"They're out there quite late tonight."

"They seem like nice young men, but so stiff and formal, like hired guards. They frighten me a little, Curtis, and I don't know why."

"You're home safe now, and in your own bed."

"Yes."

"I'd better get to sleep. I have meetings all day tomorrow, and with the one I had tonight I'm not sure I'll be up to it. This murder has made everything so much more complicated. I feel tired all the time."

"Poor dear, you take on more responsibility than you should. I'm sure they'll find the person who killed that man. He's a student, isn't he?"

"Bauer's graduate student is missing, yes. He's a suspect."

"He'll be found, dear, and it's out of your hands. Go to sleep now." She leaned over and kissed him gently on the forehead. Her lips were moist, and a musky scent enveloped him as she rolled back on her side of the bed. She pulled the covers up before falling asleep, leaving him awake in the darkness with the first throbbing erection he had had in several weeks.

* * * * * * *

The day started badly for Joe Mott. When he got to work the foreman informed him he would have to undo much of what he had worked on for the past two days. Several errors had been found in the foundation layout; he would have to do filling, then dig several new trenches before the day was finished, all because some fuzzy-faced construction engineer couldn't read drawings. He fired up the back-hoe and had the filling done by coffee break. The new building was near the Field house, and he watched a coed touch football game over coffee and a doughnut. When he dug, the ground was soft and yielding, the machine humming under his touch, and he was enjoying himself until the hoe struck something strange, and when it came out of the ground Joe Mott started yelling because what he saw impaled by the iron hand he operated was an arm, and a leg, and a head nearly severed from a neck, staring eyes looking up accusingly at him as if resenting the disturbance. He screamed until the foreman came, and turned off the machine, and a friend took him shaking and sobbing to the site office, finally convincing him he had not killed anyone.

County Sheriff Harold Cox responded quickly to the call, roping off an area around the back hoe, and examining the body before an ambulance arrived. It was the body of a young man: early twenties, blond hair, blue eyes, very slender, wearing a thin cotton shirt and faded jeans. The head had been nearly amputated with surgical precision at tracheal level, from front to back, held to the body only by a single remaining fragment of muscle so that it flopped around easily when touched. Cox examined the wound carefully, then went through the man's pockets and found a billfold containing a few dollars, gas credit card, and student ID with a photograph. He walked beside the stretcher-born body bag and supervised the loading. "Watch the head; don't let it move around, and go direct to the coroner's office. He'll be waiting for it."

As the ambulance left, Cox walked to the site office and asked to use the phone. Joe Mott was in a corner, staring glumly at a cup of coffee in his hands.

"Good thing you dug there, or we never would have found that guy," said Cox. "Somebody expected a building to go on top of him."

Mott stared at him numbly.

Cox made a call, which was answered immediately as if expected.

"Hey, you're there already. Thanks for coming in so fast, Jake. It's a murder victim, all right. Looks like garroting; the head is nearly off. See if you tell me how long he's been dead, will you? Plus the usual stuff. Thanks." He hung up the phone, picked it up and dialed again, this time waiting several seconds for an answer.

"Lisl? Is Charles there yet? Could you put him on?" He waited a moment, whistling softly to himself.

"Charles." He said suddenly into the telephone. "Sorry to tear you away from Lisl's meat loaf, but I've got something for you. I'm on campus, where they're getting ready to put in the foundation for a new classroom building. Someone dug up a body here a couple of hours ago—yes, recently. It's a young man, fully clothed, and he had a wallet with ID in it. Does the name Leonard Dieter ring a bell for you? I thought you mentioned a suspect name Len—right, and this guy was a graduate student. No, no other cards. You mean like the ones they use to unlock doors on the hill? No. Nothing else. Look, the body is on its way to the coroner's office. Get Lisl to drive you down there, and I'll be along pretty quick. I want to secure the area, and one of the victim's shoes is missing. I'd better sift some dirt. Oh, one other thing, the cause of death is pretty obvious, unless the autopsy shows something I can't see. The guy was garroted, Charles, you know, with a piano wire or something, ranger style. Whoever did it nearly took his head clean off. Pretty ugly, and another thing; there was a screw-up here in laying out the foundation, otherwise the guy would have been covered with concrete by the end of the week. Can you believe that? Right in the middle of campus!"

CHAPTER SEVEN

Jack put on his red beret and said to Karen, "Do you want an armed escort over there?"

"No. I have to handle this in my own way. It's not a nice experience for me, but I like working with her, and now I'm a little scared."

"If she tries anything again, slap her hands and turn her in. She can get her ass fired for sexual harassment." Jack's eyes narrowed.

"We'll have to have an understanding if I continue working with her, but you stay out of it, Jack."

"Suit yourself. I've got to go to drill, now." They were sitting at their usual table, in their usual dark corner of the union lounge. Jack stood up, leaned over and planted a kiss firmly on her mouth. "Meet me here at seven?" She nodded.

Eyes followed him as he crossed the room: hard, angular body, red beret and polished jump boots accenting the camouflaged field uniform. Karen watched his swaggering gait, thinking to herself, macho, macho, you do have a nice ass.

All the lights were on in the lab when Karen arrived, but the door to Doctor Reimer's office was closed and a loud argument was in progress. There was a burst of profanity, and something slammed up against the wall as Reimer's voice became a shriek, then suddenly subsided. Karen tiptoed across the lab, put on a white smock, then sat down at a calculator to punch out statistics from the previous day's run. The work absorbed her enough that she was startled when the door burst open. Reimer's head appeared, then ducked back quickly inside the office.

"Someone else is here," she said, and Karen was desperate to hide herself. She glared at the machine, calculating furiously, but out of the corner of an eye she saw Reimer appear in the doorway with a short, fat man at her side.

"Oh, Karen, I didn't know you were here. I hope we didn't disturb you."

"Not at all, Doctor Reimer. This machine makes a terrible racket."

"Maybe we can finally get rid of it, and get something digital. What do you think, Arthur; is there money available for something like that?" She looked at the man as if he were emitting an unpleasant odor.

"I suppose so," he grunted.

"You've met Dean Hilton, haven't you Karen?" Then, turning to the man, "This is Karen Butler, my research assistant, and a very exceptional student."

"Nice to meet you, sir," said Karen. The dean's reply was a stare and a grunt, followed by something resembling a belch as he shuffled to the door and slammed it rattling behind him.

"Such an articulate man," said Reimer, smiling.

"I think he's rude," said Karen.

"Agreed. He would sell his damned soul for a bigger piece of the pie, that one, a perfect role model for the administrative lamb. When the president says frog, he jumps, and when he's told to lean on faculty who say things against policies of the royal palace, he comes in with shabby little threats about funds and laboratory space. Unfortunately for him, the bastard needs me, and knows it. Now I'm worth two people in bringing in that good DOD money he needs to keep the president off his back." She paused to light a cigarette, and inhaled deeply. For the moment, it seemed she was talking to herself.

"I don't think I should be hearing this, Doctor Reimer. I'm just a student." Karen's eyes flicked from her professor back to the calculator, embarrassed.

"I don't agree," said Reimer. "You're involved in my work,

and you might even go into academic life. I don't think you should have any illusions about it as a world of quiet study and contemplation, when in fact it's ho hum pay for a rat race of getting grants, publishing papers and teaching a lot of students who only want to survive the course. There are only a few around like you, Karen." Reimer walked slowly towards her, and Karen felt a burning sensation in her fingers as adrenaline pumped into her bloodstream.

"You are one of the exceptional people who ask questions and really want to learn. That's why you're working with me, Karen, and that's the only reason why."

Now Reimer was standing next to her, speaking softly, a cigarette in one hand, smoke making Karen's eyes burn. Panic had paralyzed Karen's voice, and she wanted to run from the room.

"About the other night," said Reimer, almost whispering. "I was having a bad time, and I was drunk. I was totally out of line. I think I scared you, and I'm very sorry about it. I promise it won't happen again." Her voice was quietly pleading. "I'll keep my hands to myself, Karen, really I will. Funny thing about booze, how it destroys the inhibitions and self control. I mean, it's not that I don't find men attractive, because I do, very much. The catch is, I find women attractive as well."

"You're bi?" asked Karen.

"I believe that's the current buzz word, yes."

"But I'm not that way."

"I know, and I respect that, but if we're going to work together you'll have to accept me for what I am."

Karen felt calmer now, looking up into Reimer's penetrating eyes, and she spoke with a steady voice. "I respect you as a teacher and scientist, Doctor Reimer, and I'll accept your other preferences as long as you don't try to involve me with them."

"Fair enough," said Reimer, extending a hand. "Friends?"

Karen clasped the hand firmly. "Yes," she said happily.

"And colleagues," said Reimer. "Now there's something else to get out of the way." She took a small envelope out of her jacket pocket and handed it to Karen. "I need you to look after something for me. My locker number and combination is in the note. The locker's in the faculty women's section of the field house, and as a grad assistant you're free to use it anytime you want. I don't get over there much anymore. You'll find a pillow at the bottom of the locker. Leave it alone, but if something really bad ever happens to me, like I get hit by a car or a meteor, take that pillow directly to the police. They'll figure out what to do with it. Can you take care of that for me?"

"Sure," said Karen, puzzled, "but why would the police want to—"

"No questions. If I feel it's necessary, I'll explain the whole thing to you sometime, but for the moment your life will be a lot less complicated if I don't tell you any more. Okay?"

Karen shrugged, then folded the envelope in half and slipped it into a pocket of her jeans. "This all seems a little sinister," she said, frowning.

"It is," said Reimer grimly. "Now let's get to work. Did you run the new neuter with the L5 version of SB4?"

"Yes, but it's still not chelating enough. Two hours after injection, the rat I used lost all motor control. He had some kind of seizure, rolled over on his side and died fast."

"Hmmm. Sounds like fright-stress syndrome, otherwise there wouldn't have been such a time lapse before symptoms appeared. I think we're close, Karen. Trial and error. A little more chelating agent and we'll be there."

"And then what?"

"Better, more controlled dying through science, my dear. Our guys go into battle pumped full with neuter agent Reimer-Butler. They engage the enemy, whoever that is these days, and planes bomb the area with canisters of L5 or SB4. The bad guys, unprotected by neuter, do a little writhing on the ground before dying, and out guys occupy the area without a shot being fired. You have to admit it's a pretty easy way to fight a limited war."

"Until the other side gets hold of the neuter," said Karen.

"Ah, but first they have to know it exists, and that can take a long time. Some interesting marketing potential there." Reimer smiled wickedly.

"When do we make another run?"

"I should have a new sample ready in a day. Let's try another one Thursday night, and I want to be here for it this time. We'll do another run with your assembler then, too. In the meantime, finish those calculations, get all the data filed away, and give me a copy." Reimer walked towards her office, chewing a finger nail reflectively, then stopped at the door and looked over her shoulder.

"I'm glad you're sticking it out with me, Karen. It's nice to have someone here I can trust."

"Thank you, Doctor Reimer," said Karen, as the older woman disappeared into her office and closed the door behind her. Karen hunched over the calculator again, the ancient machine clanking and humming to her touch.

In the quiet of her office, Judith Reimer settled herself at her desk, an old oak roll-top perforated with slots, cubbyholes and secret drawers heaped with papers and bound notebooks filled with columns of numbers, chemical equations and scrawled text. She pulled a notebook from the bottom of the heap, opened it to a blank page and stared at it intently for several minutes before beginning to write.

Quickly and steadily she summarized the neuter experiments and her conclusions regarding chemical composition, then entered the details both by volume and weight. When the entry was complete she took a piece of onion-skin paper from a drawer. Using a fine lead in an automatic pencil she made a miniature version of the entry on a small portion of the paper, and cut it out with a pair of scissors. She made a small tube out of the paper, and slipped it into the hollow shell of a ballpoint pen which she placed in the bottom of her purse, then picked up the notebook and walked to a vial-covered table where she sat down again to unlock the middle drawer.

She removed two pipettes and a small bottle filled with a blood-red fluid. Squinting in the dim light she used a pipette to measure out a small quantity of the liquid into a vial already half-filled with something colorless, then replaced the bottle and locked it up again. She shook the vial until the contents were colorless, marked 'NR6' on the glass with a felt-tipped pen, and placed the vial in a test tube stand before carefully replacing the notebook at the bottom of the pile of debris on her desk. For a moment she looked over the office, then sat down at her desk and punched several numbers on the telephone.

"Hi," she said softly, and relaxed into her chair. "I have some good news. We're very close to having an effective neuter. We might have it right now, in fact. I think it's time we get together for a marketing discussion or two—yes, right away, say tonight at my place. I can fix us a bit to eat. Of course I can cook, silly. I have many talents you don't know about. Oh yes, that too." She laughed into the phone, eyes sparkling. "You know me, I'm always eager to learn. Can you come at eight? What? No, I've got it written down and put away safely. You don't need to see that, dear. You just take care of the marketing. All right, eight o'clock. See you then."

She hung up the telephone and swiveled in her chair, smiling, then put on her coat and left the office, locking it behind her. Karen was still pounding furiously on the calculator, looking up briefly when Reimer came out of the office.

"I'm going home early, Karen. Would you believe the old prof has a date tonight?"

"Sure I would," said Karen.

"It's a guy," said Reimer.

"Oh!" gasped Karen, and both women laughed.

When Reimer left the building, darkness was near, for the sun had already dropped below the surrounding hills. Most of the students were at dining centers, but as she walked across campus, nearly alone, a pair of red berets drifted along fifty yards behind her. She noticed them out of the corner of her eye and felt uneasy at their presence. When she went into the field house the two men were standing by the entrance to the armory, and when she came out again a few minutes later they were still there, watching her. Inside the building, she went directly to her locker, retrieved the little pillow and added to the records stored there. On a shelf, a Tampon tube contained a collection of tiny rolls of paper, to which she added the paper she had written on in her office. She replaced and locked everything up. The red berets did not follow her as she crossed campus again. She walked downhill towards town until she came to a cluster of new condominiums with steep, slate roofs and large windows looking out on the valley below. She let herself in and climbed the stairs to a second floor corner unit she had lived in for two years. Putting the dead bolt lock in place behind her, she pulled drapes aside to see the town lights, and turned on a single lamp.

The room was furnished Victorian style in a bizarre array of shapes and colors. A picture of her dead mother, a stern-faced woman with her hair in a bun, sat on the mantel of a gas fire-place, and the walls were covered with ornately framed prints of bicycle riders, picnickers, and wood nymphs at play. A long hallway led to an office in total disarray. A neat bedroom had a large, canopied bed and two massive bureaus. She undressed slowly while running her bath, studied her slender body in a mirror, turned this way and that for a different perspective. A bit boyish, but nice, she thought. Still a good flair in the hips, and everything firm. She soaked in the tub for nearly an hour, then washed and dried her hair, and brushed it up into a tumbling mass before rubbing perfume into her neck, stomach and arms. She put on light makeup for color. With some effort, she squirmed into a tightly fitting black, sleeveless dress, and matching high-heeled shoes. She studied herself again in the mirror, and smiled seductively. In a half hour her table was set for a candlelight supper, potatoes were in the oven, vegetables were simmering, and two thick steaks were ready for broiling. He would be punctual. He always was, and her doorbell rang promptly at eight o'clock.

She opened the door, and he stood there for a moment, a bottle of wine in one hand. His eyes roamed over her as she posed for him.

"Hi baby. As usual, you're right on time," she said.

"I aim to please," said William Holleque.

"Good," she drawled, "so come right on in and we'll see how good your aim is tonight."

* * * * * * *

It was dark when drill was finished, and many buildings had been locked for the night. Karen had jammed the door open with a piece of wood so he could get in, and he felt his way along gloomy hallways until he found her lighted laboratory and heard the clanking of the calculator. She looked up when he entered the room.

"Your timing is perfect. I'm just this minute finished."

"That thing sure makes a racket."

"It's sort of a joke around here, but it's programmable. All the other equipment is state-of-the-art. Let's get something to eat; I am absolutely starving."

"Sounds good to me, but let's make it quick. Between football and drill, I am beat."

Karen locked up the lab and they felt their way back to the outside door, then walked across the campus and down the hill towards town. Along the way they saw two pairs of red berets, one escorting three giggling girls back to their dorms, the other standing watchfully at the edge of campus.

"The Gestapo lives," grumbled Karen.

"What?"

"That's what some people are calling them: the Gestapo. Always around, always watching. Some people don't like them, Jack."

"My God, it's an escort service, and there hasn't been a single attack since it started."

"Maybe it's the uniform, then. It makes people uneasy and it seems like wherever I go, one of those guys is watching me."

"Well, I can understand that," said Jack, smiling, "just as long as they don't do any touching. I will admit it's a strange unit, though. Eagle Squad, I mean."

"Why do you sat that when you're a part of it?"

"I can't make any friends in the unit, and people seem to come and go. Maybe three guys I actually talk to, and they hardly say anything. There are no name tags, and Sergeant Rodríguez or The Man rarely use names when they're around us. I really don't know anyone yet, is what I'm saying, and I get the feeling they'd like to keep it that way. Everyone is capable; they pick up everything fast. The training is great, and we get a lot of individual attention, but it's all very formal, and for sure there are no friends in that outfit."

"It's what you wanted, Jack."

"I wanted the training, yes, but I also wanted to be part of a team. I don't feel that way yet. Maybe it'll be different after the field exercises in a couple of weeks. I hope so, anyway."

"Whatever you say, I think some of the guys I see on campus are a little spooky."

"That's another thing," said Jack quickly. "Some of the guys on escort duty I've never seen in drill, and some haven't been in any of my classes. One guy even said he was an engineering major when I asked him. Man, we're supposed to be a special unit, and people don't know or talk to each other."

"You can always get out."

"No way. I want that training, and if I quit now it would kill my dad. You remember my call home last week. The guy is tough as they come, and he never, I mean never gives compliments, but when I told him I'd made Eagle Squad he started crying, and mom had to take the phone. There's a lot involved here, Karen."

"Okay, I was just saying either accept things the way they are, or get out."

They walked ion silence for a moment, then Jack said, "I guess I'll let things ride for awhile, but I'd sure like to look up some of those guys in the university computer and see what their majors are."

* * * * * * *

Behind the strolling couple, near the top of the hill, two red berets watched them through binoculars. One man looked at the other and said, "It looks to me like Mister Nelson is unhappy about something. Wish I could read lips."

The other man, lean and hard muscled, scowled at his partner. "That guy is too curious for his own good. I can't see why The Man let him in, except maybe to find out about the girlfriend. Nelson caught Vern in a lie about being an engineering major. Maybe now Vern will learn to keep his mouth shut. We need to keep a closer watch on this guy, and not just because of his girlfriend. He could be dangerous."

They watched until the couple disappeared inside a McDonald's restaurant, then resumed their watchful rounds.

* * * * * * *

Reimer mumbled encouragement while Karen timed the run. It had been two hours since the injections, and ten minutes since the rat had been exposed to a strong dose of L5. There had been no reaction at rest, and now the animal was under the stress of the labyrinth. Once, he stopped to sneeze, and Reimer felt her heart skip a beat, but then he hurried on until he came to three levers giving him the choice of food or electrical shock, and having made the run before he pressed one lever without hesitation and gobbled up the food dropped in front of him. When the last morsels were gone, Karen picked him up and deposited him back into a cage, where the women watched his behavior intently for several minutes.

"That's it, then," said Reimer softly. "Everything's normal, and we gave him enough to kill a human."

"There might be long term effects," suggested Karen.

"I doubt it. Any excess chelator should go right out with the urine. Be sure to do a urinalysis tonight and tomorrow morning. My guess is you'll find some chelator in the first test, and nothing in the second. It works, Karen. It really works." The excitement showed on Reimer's face, and Karen shared it in a subdued way, for what they had found was an antidote to a nerve gas specifically designed to kill human beings. Having the antidote would only make the killing selective. For the moment, there was the excitement of discovery, the feelings of accomplishment, and they were caught up in it. Reimer retrieved a tiny bottle of wine from a refrigerator, filled two paper cups and handed one to Karen.

"To science," she said dramatically, and they touched cups.

"And to Morris," said Karen. They drank the wine in two gulps.

"Ah, yes, Morris. You really made a pet out of him, didn't you? That's never a good idea."

Karen said nothing, but thought of the little creature resting comfortably in her underwear drawer in his own little box. His mind now functioned enough to eat, and groom and show pleasure at being petted whenever Karen was there. Otherwise, he slept, and lived.

Reimer partially filled their cups again, and they sipped. "You can't believe the relief I feel right now. This justifies the entire grant, and my quarterly report is going to be nice and fat. For a while there I thought the whole chelating idea was going down the toilet. I bet we could extend this to any number of nerve gases by changing the metal ion we use. I'm sure Manganese isn't the only one that will work; I think we should look at the entire transition metal series. That could be some papers for you, Karen. What do you think?" She looked at Karen expectantly.

"I'll have to think about that, Doctor Reimer. I'm up to my ears with my thesis work."

"Well give it some thought. And now, if you don't mind, I'm going to claim the rest of this wine and clean out my desk." She picked up the nearly empty bottle and went to her office, closing the door. A few minutes later she came out again, wide-eyed, and carrying a small purse.

"Too excited to work," she explained. "I'm going over to the field house for a workout. By the way, have you used my locker yet?"

"Haven't found the time, but I'll get over there. Thanks."

"Whatever you do, don't lose that locker number or combination. It's important. See you later." Reimer left the room in a hurry, banging the door behind her.

Karen remained in the lab for a few minutes, changed water bottles for the animals, then left the building and crossed campus to the union where she found Jack staring thoughtfully at figures on an engineering pad in front of him. He looked up as she sat down across the table from him.

"What's that?"

"Fluid mechanics. The problem set is due in forty minutes, and I just figured the last one out."

"Probably just as well I'm late, then," she said. "We had some real success in the lab today. I've never seen Doctor Reimer so excited, and it's catching. I wish I could tell you about it."

"More of that new classified stuff you're working on?"

"Yes."

"How can you get a degree out of that? You can't even publish your thesis."

"It's not my thesis work, but I might get a paper out of it. NDIA has to edit it first, and pull out any data or procedures that might be sensitive. Some people are objecting to that kind of thing."

"Whatever," said Jack. He scribbled two final equations on his pad, then tore out several sheets and folded then in half lengthwise. "Battle Stations," he announced.

"I'll wait here," said Karen.

"Kiss, kiss," he said, leaned over, kissed her softly and rushed away.

While he was gone she made notes on new tests she wanted to run on her reassemblers. But her mind wandered. Soon she was daydreaming, and it morphed into a full scale, mind-dumping reverie. She thought about Morris in his little bureau drawer nest, and the way he had convulsed after his final run. Without the chelator, he would probably be dead, and maybe that would have been better. She wondered if he recognized her now. Suddenly she was in the lab, feeling Reimer's hand moving across her breast, and the shock of the kiss. Even her mother had never kissed her on the mouth. Did she like it? No, but she hadn't been disgusted by it either. It certainly wasn't like when Jack kissed or fondled her and she felt on fire from head to toe. Poor woman, does she have a steady boyfriend? Everyone needs love. Reimer has a decent figure, good features. Certainly not a plain woman. She was so excited today, like a little child discovering something marvelous about the world, and yet there is a suspicious, troubled side to her that is always just below the surface, ever watchful and fearful. But don't I have my own fears, my own strangely undefined paranoia? Why do I feel uneasy at the sight of the red berets patrolling campus, when my own man wears the same uniform? Why do I feel they're always watching me? I'm acting like a child, afraid of strangers and the dark, even when Jack is with me. Now *he* is getting suspicious. Why does he worry so much about not knowing everyone in Eagle Squad, to the point where he wants to look up their majors and check out their names? That's not like him. It's as if he has an inner voice, warning him about something.

Suddenly, Jack was shaking her shoulder.

"Hey, spacewoman, come back to earth."

She looked up at him, then at her watch. For one hour she had been sitting there, daydreaming, staring at a wall. "You snuck up on me," she protested.

"Come on, let's get a junk food dinner early. Coach wants me to watch films tonight, and if I eat too much I'll go sound asleep in there."

"West dining center has pizza tonight."

"Let's go."

"I have to make a quick stop at the lab first, to pick up some notes."

"I'm right behind you," said Jack, pulling at her arm.

They left the union and hurried across a campus in twilight, purple shadows reaching across the quad. The science building was only lighted in the ground floor, where classes had let out an hour before, but two lights showed on the upper floor. Jack settled himself on a bench near the building. "You go on up," he said jokingly, "and I'll stay here to escort any girls in distress."

"Watch it," said Karen. She entered the building and went up the stairs to her laboratory floor, where she found a darkened hallway and shuffled along it carefully, keeping one hand outstretched lightly against a wall. There was a sound ahead of her in the gloom, and her heart jumped. Footsteps. More steps, someone padding down the stairwell ahead, and she sensed rather than saw movement in the darkness at the end of the hallway. "Hello?" she called, but her voice came back to her as a muffled ring, and the only other sound was her breathing.

Suddenly, her entire body seemed to go cold, and she stood motionless, pressed up against the wall. From somewhere in the bowels of the building came the sound of a door closing. She moved again, sliding along the wall and beginning to feel a bit silly. Goblins in the dark. I'm acting like a child again. Ahead of her was a faint glow, and it was coming from her laboratory, diffusing through the frosted glass in the door. She fumbled for her keys as she turned the doorknob, and her heart skipped a beat as the door clicked open. The laboratory itself was dark, but Reimer's office door glowed brightly. That was it, she thought with relief, the professor had returned to work in the office, leaving the hall door unlocked.

Karen flipped on a wall switch, squinting in the light, and hearing the excited squeaks of animals equating sudden light with feeding time. She walked to the office door and knocked on it softly.

"Doctor Reimer, it's Karen. I came back for some notes. Do you need anything?"

No answer. The absent-minded professor had come and gone, leaving her light on. Karen didn't have an office key, but jiggled the doorknob.

The door swung open.

She stepped inside, and knew immediately that something was terribly wrong.

The office was a shambles, floor covered with books, papers and broken glass. The bookshelves covering two walls had been swept clean. Pictures and a periodic chart of the elements had been torn from the wall, leaving bright, clean rectangles behind, then thrown to the floor with the other debris. Something catastrophically violent had happened here. A drunken rage? Not enough time. She had seen a sober Reimer only hours before, and she had been cheerful then.

She shuffled across the room, pushing debris aside with her feet. All the desk drawers had been thrown on the floor, and a lamp on top of it had fallen over. She reached to stand it upright and saw first a foot, near the edge of the desk, then the black dress pulled up above a thigh, and then the sad, dead face looking up at her. She gasped, started to shake as she dropped to her knees, touched the face with the sorrowful, open-eyed stare and a little tear not yet completely dried alongside her nose, mouth open as if calling for someone. The head was tilted at a crazy angle from where her spine had been cleanly snapped, the angle becoming even more severe when Karen touched her.

"Oh, my God, my God, my God," someone kept saying. Reality closed in on her. She stood up, walked to the window in a daze and opened it.

"Someone please help me! There's a dead person up here. Please come and help. Please help me!" Her voice rose to a shriek as she grasped the window sill with both hands. Boots were pounding in the hallway, someone calling her name, then the door burst open and Jack was there, staring incredulously at the body. She threw herself at him, trembling in his arms, crying as he held her tightly. In a moment, feeling more secure, she opened her eyes to look past his shoulder.

Two red berets stood in the doorway, watching them.

Without knowing why she was doing it, Karen Butler screamed.

CHAPTER EIGHT

"Things are deteriorating badly here," said Ebensack in a whisper. He'd left his cell phone in the car, and without thinking had dialed the campus phone. Lundeman's secretary had left the office to duplicate Ebensack's reports on the death of Professor Reimer and the mutilated body of one Leonard Dieter, former graduate student in chemistry. "Calling in the FBI will just muddle up the investigation. The deaths are all related, I'm sure of it, and the common tie is local: passion, or profit, there are signs of both, but I can't say for sure yet. Give me a couple more weeks, anyway. Yes, he's in the next office, quite rattled. I can't say I'm sorry for him; he's supposed to be in charge, and there's an unusual amount of dissension on the campus. We might want to reconsider some of the contracts we have here. No. I won't mention it to him, and my reports will be in the mail this afternoon. Tell Melody I'll be back in the office on Friday, and I want a meeting with the research council as early as possible."

Lundeman's secretary entered the office and gave him a suspicious glance. "See you Friday. Goodbye," he said, then listened. An instant after his call was disconnected, there was another click in the phone, then dial tone. He put the receiver back in the unit, and turned towards the secretary.

"Can this phone be used as an extension?"

"Of course."

"For what?"

"The president's office."

"No other room?"

"That's right," she said curtly.

Ebensack walked to the president's door, knocked softly on it.

"Yes?'

He opened the door and peeked inside. Lundeman sat at his massive desk, staring at a wall.

"As you heard on the phone, the situation here is serious. I suggest you get your house in order as quickly as possible."

Ebensack closed the door, and left the outer office. "Have a good day," he said to the secretary, and stalked away, angry with himself for not having waited to use his cell phone for the call.

* * * * * * *

Karen held Jack's hand, and seemed nervous. Ebensack smiled at them across the conference table he had reserved in a secluded meeting room on the top floor of the student union. A handsome couple, he thought, both tall and well proportioned, with chiseled, Teutonic features. Karen was in faded jeans and a red, knitted sweater, Jack in full red beret uniform. "I assure you anything said in this room will be held in strict confidence," he said soothingly. "You aren't suspected of anything, so please relax. Perhaps you can tell me something useful, perhaps not, but let's give it a try. Now, when was the last time you saw Doctor Reimer?"

Karen swallowed hard. "About four hours before I found her in the office."

"Did she seem upset about anything?"

"No. Just the opposite. She was so excited." Karen told him about the day, and the success of the experiment. "She was so charged up she couldn't stay in the office, and she was going over to the field house for a workout, or...." Karen's voice trailed off, as if she were suddenly thinking about something else. She opened her purse and fumbled inside it, searching for something.

"Do you know if she had any men friends?"

"I know she dated, because she told me she was having a date the other night, but I never met anyone."

"Boy, or girl?" asked Jack, smiling faintly. "She was a very liberal lady."

"She was bisexual," added Karen quickly. She pulled a small card out of her purse, and looked at it.

"Interesting," said Ebensack, writing on a yellow legal pad.

"I just remembered this," said Karen, and she held out a file card. "It's Doctor Reimer's locker number and combination in the field house, and she gave it to me last week. She said I could use the locker whenever I wanted, but she had something stored there she wanted taken to the police if anything happened to her. It was sort of an emotional moment."

"Do you know what it is?"

"She said something about a little pillow."

"Imaginative," said Ebensack. "I suggest we get over to the field house right away, and see what it really is."

"It's in the faculty women's locker room. I'll have to do it, so you might as well wait here," said Karen.

"Don't you want an escort?" asked Jack, smiling.

"No, I do not."

"Okay," said Ebensack. "I have another call to make. Let's meet back here in half an hour."

"I'll stay here and get some homework done," said Jack.

Ebensack and Karen took the elevator down and went their separate ways at the entrance to the union. It was a two hundred yard walk to the field house. Karen looked behind her twice to see if Ebensack was following her, but didn't see him.

The field house was busy, many faculty members working out after midday classes. Karen went straight to the faculty women's locker room, showed her research assistant card to the attendant there, and was issued a towel. Reimer's locker was in the back row of the room, and three women were nearby, changing clothes. Karen opened the locker and rummaged around inside it, stalling until the women left. The locker was a jumble of old clothes, and smelled stale. The massage table pillow was on a top shelf along with a Tampon tube, soap bars and a bottle of moisturizer. Karen sorted through the debris at the bottom of the locker and found nothing interesting, but when she opened the Tampon tube and saw the notes rolled up inside she felt a little shock, for Reimer had not mentioned these to her. Her shock increased as she went through them one by one, found the final formulation of the nerve gas neuter and more. There were up-to-date results of her assembler experiments, and references to a disassembler nanobot her thesis work was being designed to counter.

Karen's face flushed. Reimer had been involved in more than one molecular war machine project, and her own thesis work was involved with it. There would be no thesis publication, no papers in open literature, nothing to use in jump-starting an academic career, unless...."

A part of Karen she would later feel guilty about suddenly took charge. She carefully rolled up all the little papers concerning the neuter work and replaced them in the tube. The nanobot papers were folded in half and went into the coin pocket in her purse.

The pillow had a zipper at one end. She opened it and went rapidly through the contents. Two of the three lab books, all including final tests, were dedicated to the nerve gas studies. Only the third was about nanobots. Karen skimmed through it, felt a terrible horror, and put it in her purse. The others went back into the pillow. Now she was nearly in tears. A part of her knew her actions were wrong, but she was driven by something she only felt and didn't understand. Only the neuter results were final, and the murders would likely be connected to this work. Everything with nanobots was preliminary, could not possibly be relevant to Ebensack, so why bring it up?

The little box with a rack of storage tubes came next. SB4, L5 gases and the neuter samples were there, as recorded in the lab books, but the other three samples were not recorded. Labeled nano 1, 2 and 3, they had to be up-to-date samples of the disassemblers Reimer had been working on. Karen took those three tubes and put them into her purse for testing. She could always argue later she had found them in the laboratory, along with another notebook.

Everything she declared relevant went back into the pillow. She zipped it up, closed and locked the locker. Ebensack intercepted her when she was halfway back to the union.

"Got it," she said, and gestured at the pillow.

In a minute they were with Jack again, the little pillow sitting on the table before them.

"There was nothing else?" asked Ebensack.

"Nothing," said Karen. "Gym clothes, shoes, stick deodorant, soap bars and a towel. This is what she told me to look for."

"Well, then, you do the honors," said Ebensack, gesturing at the pillow.

"I've already seen what's inside," said Karen. She picked up the pillow, unzipped one end and spilled the contents onto the table.

"The books have complete notes on the gas and neuter work, and there are samples of the products in these tubes." She picked up the tampon tube and opened it, used a fingernail to pull out all the small flimsy notes inside. "These are final results and formulas for all the L5 and SB4 experiments, including the last one that gave us the neuter. It was the inside paper in the roll; that's why she left the office so quickly, to store this record before—" Her voice suddenly cracked.

"What do you mean, neuter?" asked Ebensack.

"An agent to neutralize the effect of the gases. That's all we'd been working on for the past few days."

"I don't think I'm supposed to hear any of this," said Jack.

"Jack doesn't have a security clearance, Mister Ebensack."

"I'm not concerned with that, since this conversation never took place. Karen, have you ever read the original research proposal submitted by Reimer to NDIA two years ago?"

"No, sir."

"There was no mention of developing a neuter agent in that proposal, only work to determine physical effects at very small dosages of L5, or SB4, as the Pentagon calls it."

"Oh, that was all finished before my involvement," said Karen. "I think the neuter idea started with Doctor Bauer. My advisor practically said that a couple of times."

"The chemist who was killed earlier?"

"Yes," said Karen.

"He wasn't even on the original proposal, but I know he did some of the first work on L5. That was before he became so disenchanted with classified research in a university setting. Did you know his graduate student, Karen?"

"No. Has he been found, yet?"

"I'm afraid so, but I can't give you any details."

"Must be the body they dug up where the classroom building is going in," said Jack matter-of-factly. "The head was nearly cut off."

"Oh, God," said Karen, putting a hand over her mouth.

"And how would you know that?" asked Ebensack.

"Two Eagle Squad cadets I know saw the body when it came out of the ground. There was a lot of screaming."

"You red berets seem to get around a great deal, Jack. I'd like to talk to you privately about that in a few minutes."

"Yes, sir," said Jack, suddenly alert and ramrod straight in his chair.

"Karen, if you were to search Doctor Reimer's office, could you say whether or not anything was missing? A lab book, or chemicals? It's possible whoever murdered the lady wanted the formula or composition of the neuter to L5, and I'm concerned she never mentioned this work in her last two quarterly reports."

"Maybe she wanted to wait until it was finished. I remember her saying something about reporting it, and even writing a new proposal."

"No, standard procedure is to report all work in progress, even if it wasn't a part of the original proposal, and all patentable or potentially marketable devices and methods are property of the NDIA. Certainly you can see how marketable the neuter would be. Imagine you're a petty little dictator with access to L5, which is readily available, now. Imagine your military and political advantage when you have a small army shot-full of neuter, and a small air force to disperse the gas. Formidable."

"You think she was trying to sell it?"

"I'm saying it's possible, that's all, and if she had a greedy partner it could explain her murder. Having successfully developed the chemical, her usefulness would be over. If Bauer was involved, this might explain his death as well. It's all conjecture at this point, but it makes sense. What I'm missing is someone who would have the connections necessary to market the neuter."

"A military person?" suggested Jack.

"Possibly, but more likely someone involved with international business, particularly military hardware. In this country, it's legitimate business, and lucrative, all in the interest of balance of trade. There may be several people involved, but what I need to know right now is whether or not the murderer has found the composition of the neuter. From the shape of Reimer's office, I think not; the mess looks like the result of blind rage and frustration to me. Could you tell if any key items were missing?"

"I watched her record a lot of things in the lab books, and these little papers here are probably exact copies. I could check to see if all the lab books are there, but I didn't help her with the chemistry, so I'd be guessing there."

"Even a guess might help," said Ebensack.

"Well, I'll do what I can," said Karen, "if I can get in the lab."

"Officially it's sealed off, and the lock has been changed. I'll get you a key. Please let me know when you'll be in the lab."

"Why's that?" asked Jack.

"I want to be called the instant she finds anything. I'll give you a number to call, and I'll be waiting when she's searching the lab."

"I'll be there with her," said Jack, frowning.

Karen bristled. "That's very macho, Jack, but I don't need a bodyguard."

Ebensack laughed. "Whatever you do is fine with me, but it's wise to be cautious. Now, Karen, I'd like to have a few words alone with Jack, if I may."

Karen gave him a dark look.

"It has nothing to do with you, and I promise we won't discuss bodyguard duties."

She smiled, then arose and marched to the door, turning to glance haughtily at both men. "I'll be right outside," she announced, and banged the door behind her.

They sat at the table for a long moment, silently studying each other.

"Karen is both intelligent and independent," said Ebensack, finally.

"I agree," said Jack, and then there was silence again. Ebensack turned a few pages of the yellow legal pad in front of him.

"You think she's in danger, don't you?" said Jack.

"It's possible. She's the only one left who took active part in the experiments."

"I wasn't kidding. I'm sticking close to her wherever she goes, even if she doesn't like it."

"I'm counting on that," said Ebensack, "but it's not what I wanted to talk to you about."

"If it's not about Karen, it must be about Eagle Squad," said Jack. Eyes hard, he sat at a brace in his chair.

"You're quick, too. That's exactly what I want to talk about, particularly the people who are in it."

They talked for several minutes, Jack giving names of the people he knew, and his concerns about those he never seemed to see outside of drills.

"You get me names, and I'll check them out with the registrar," said Ebensack. "What about the red berets who work for the escort service? Do you know them?"

"I've worked that service myself, and I pretty much know everyone, but there' at least one pair of guys, maybe more, but two of the guys I can't remember seeing in drill."

"Did you see them the night Doctor Reimer died?"

"No, only Bert and Allen, the guys who went upstairs with me when Karen yelled. I've taken classes with both of them. Poor guys, Karen screamed bloody hell when she saw them. It was embarrassing."

"Why would she do that?"

"I'm not sure. Sometimes she thinks they're following us, or watching what we do. Maybe they are. It's the guys I don't know who bother her the most. There are times I feel we're being watched, too, and I like to think I'm fairly levelheaded. It's sort of an instinctive thing, a crawling in my stomach, you know? I mean, a lot of guys look at Karen when we're out, and that doesn't bother me, but you can spot that kind of look a hundred yards away. A couple of times, red berets I don't know have been hanging around, looking at everything except us, even when there were no other people around, and it felt weird. A normal guy will glance at Karen every chance he gets."

Ebensack smiled. "She is certainly a lovely girl. I must admit I'm concerned about her. In fact, I'm concerned about both of you. Jack, there are several things I'd like you to do for me. Much of it is just information gathering, but there is a small element of danger, and I'm not going to minimize that. You'll need to keep as low a profile as possible, and talk to no one about what you're looking for. That includes Karen, I'm afraid. Are you willing to do that?"

"We're already in some danger, aren't we?"

"I believe so."

"Then I'll do what you want." The voice was flat, monotone, the eyes grey in the bright light of the room. Ebensack felt discipline, determination and something else, a kind of danger, subtle, a burst of warmth touching him briefly, then withdrawing to a hidden place in the young man who sat rigidly before him.

"Good," said Ebensack. "Now here's what I want you to do."

A few minutes later, Ebensack arose from his chair and walked to the window looking out over the quadrangle below. A huge flag waved cheerfully from a pole in the center of the area, beds of flowers radiating outwards like the spokes of a great wheel. Students lounged on the grass, talking or reading in breeze-carried scent of the flowers. He opened the window, inhaled deeply. He watched as Jack and Karen came out of the student union entrance below him and strolled lazily among the gardens, arm in arm, deep in conversation. He watched until they were halfway across the quad, then started to close the window, looked down as he did so, and felt a sudden flutter in his chest.

On the sidewalk below stood two red berets, looking up at him.

One of them was grinning.

* * * * * * *

Madge Proctor sat at her desk, shuffled paper and generally looked busy as the screaming went on and on behind the closed door of the president's office. Voices rose to hysterical pitch, falling to muted mumblings as accusations were exchanged and argued. Finally, there was silence, and when the door opened the deans came out in single file, hunched over and red-faced, marching past her desk without a sideways glance, and straight out the door. Vice President Allen Klister followed them to the door, shut it loudly behind them, then came over to her desk and put down a handwritten list of names in front of her. She looked up at the arrogant, scornful expression on his face, and reminded herself that in her twenty years as a top level secretary in academe, she had never disliked anyone as much as the man, or the influence he had on a president whom she regarded as a good person facing a terrible series of problems and setbacks.

"Get on this right away, Madge," he said crisply. "Pull the files and resumes of these people, and schedule half-hour slots for them to meet here with the president and myself by the end of the week. If they ask what it's about, tell them we want to discuss their future with the university. Classes are no excuse; if they have to reschedule classes to make a meeting, so be it. If they don't make the meeting, they're out. Tell them that, Madge."

She bristled suddenly, anger showing in her eyes, but Lundeman spoke to her from the doorway in a tired voice.

"Please do it, Madge. Be as gentle as you can. I know it's a dirty job, but it's going to be even harder for me."

He looked exhausted, standing there hunched over, eyes red in a gaunt face. She guessed he's had no rest for days, from the pressures of a world crumbling around him. His look was pleading, and she was suddenly terribly sorry for him.

"I'll take care of it," she said, glancing fleetingly at Klister, who looked very pleased with himself.

"Thanks, Madge," said Lundeman, softly. "I know it's a cliché to say it, but I really don't know how I could get along without you."

Her heart was warmed, her existence justified, even though she knew deep down inside that people get to be university presidents by knowing how to say the right thing at the right time. The two men went back into Lundeman's office and closed the door. Madge looked at the list, and the familiar names. She had heard them many times before. They were good people with families and mortgages, and little upward mobility left in their chosen professions. They were serious teachers, and passionate in their opposition to classified research that had become the financial backbone of the university. They rationalized on the grounds of academic freedom, and open dissemination of research results. Idealistic, ivory tower hermits, her president called them, and closed his mind to their complaints. Could they possibly be right? She picked up the telephone to make her first call. Right or wrong, it made little difference at the moment.

The purge was about to begin.

* * * * * * *

The front door was open, but the entire building was in darkness again. Karen fumbled along a wall while Jack stood in the doorway, squinting after her.

"Why don't they put light switches down here?" she complained.

"Keep down the light bill, of course. I heard a janitor bitching once about how faculty people can't seem to get their work done during the day. I bet the vice president for finance agrees with him. I don't suppose you have a flashlight?"

"Not funny, Jack."

"To hell with it, let's go upstairs. Here, take my hand." He reached out, and found her cold fingers.

"Nervous?"

"You'd better believe it. The last time I was in here, I found a dead person. Ouch!" She stumbled on a step and squeezed his hand hard. "What are you, a cat? I can't see anything in here. I remember a feeling someone was moving around in the dark ahead of me last time. I don't feel that now."

"You search the office, and let me watch and listen. One more flight, right?"

"One more," said Karen, and they climbed upwards again, hands sliding on the banister, feet rising in fixed cadence from step to step. Faint light from outside the building was diffusing through frosted glass in hallway doors. Ahead of them, in the dim light, nothing moved, the only sound that of feet sliding on polished wood. Karen found the lab door, unlocked it, and reached inside to turn on the light.

Nothing happened.

"Oh, Jack, I don't like this."

"Stay behind me," he growled, and pushed the door wide open. He led her to the door of Reimer's office, and twisted the door knob. It opened. Karen reached past him and sudden light exploded in their faces, their pupils contracting quickly as they saw the room was as they had seen it before, filled with debris.

"Relay must have gone off. Go ahead and look around. I'll stay here at the doorway."

"Try my desk lamp," she said. "I should feed the animals while I'm here." She stepped gingerly towards Reimer's desk.

Jack felt his way back across the room towards where he knew Karen's desk was. There was a curious silence he did not expect, and when he turned the lamp switch, light spilled over empty laboratory benches.

"Karen!" he called out. "The animals are gone. There's nothing on the benches here."

She came out of the office in a rush, and went straight to her desk, opened it and checked all the drawers. "Nothing missing," she said reflectively. "the department could have moved the animals to make sure they'd be fed, but without telling me? And now an experiment has been disturbed. I don't like it, Jack. Doctor Reimer would have been furious."

"Better check it out," said Jack.

"You bet I will. I still need a urine analysis from one of those animals, the one we used in the last neuter test."

"Could anyone get a handle on the neuter composition from that rat?"

"I don't think so. Once in a bloodstream, any free neuter is only stable for an hour or so; all anyone could find now would be sub-units or byproducts. Even a good chemist is unlikely to figure it out from that."

"You need to find that one rat, anyway."

"Tomorrow, Jack. I'll ask the chairman." She went back to the office, and Jack followed her inside, standing patiently while she sifted through the piles of paper and other artifacts left by the late Doctor Judith Reimer. She put aside three laboratory record books, after carefully skimming through them. "Early experiments," she explained. "Not very useful, but I don't want them to get lost." On her hands and knees, near the desk, she wrapped something up in a handkerchief, and handed it to Jack. "Put this in your shirt pocket, and button it up. It's breakable."

"Is it important?" he asked.

"Very," she said, without expression. "Please don't ask me what it its."

He had never seen her so serious, so stony-faced, in all the time they had been together. Here was Karen the scientist. He preferred Karen the warm and vulnerable, knowing well it was an ego issue he had to work on if they were to have a happy married life together. For the moment he accepted her as she was, but he wanted desperately to protect her.

The search went on while Jack waited at the doorway, alert for a sound, odor, or even a breeze that might mean movement within the building. Twice he thought he heard something, looking up and down the gloomy hallway, seeing nothing while Karen, oblivious to his concern, continued her rummaging. She had piled up a small stack of laboratory notebooks, and then there was the little bundle Jack had in his pocket. He patted it occasionally to make sure it was still there. "All the experiments are recorded here," she explained, "but all the key formulas and compositions are only on those little papers we found in the locker. Only the older compositions, like the one used on Morris, are here."

"Morris?"

"My pet rat; the one in my room."

"The one who sleeps in your panties," said Jack, grinning evilly.

"Why Jack, I think you're jealous," she said in amazement, then seriously, "There's nothing else to find here. Let's go." She stood up, scooped the laboratory notebooks into her arms. The floor creaked.

In the hallway, there was another sound.

The hair on the back of Jack's neck rose to attention, but he said nothing. Karen started past him on the way to the hall, and he put a hand on her arm. "Turn out the lights, and let's wait here a minute so we get used to the dark and don't fall over something." He flicked off the desk lamp as Karen hit the wall switch in Reimer's office, plunging them again into momentary, inky blackness. Their eyes adjusted quickly, the doorway faintly glowing in light from a window.

"I still wonder why the light in this lab wouldn't go on," he whispered.

"Who knows? Let's go," she said impatiently.

"Hold it a second, while I check the hall."

"Why are you whispering?" she whispered. "Did you hear something?"

"Just being careful," he said. "Stay right behind me. Where's your hand?"

"It's helping me hold a ton of books. Go on, now. I can see you."

Jack peered around the doorway, both ways along the hall. The walls were in deep shadow, polished floors in the center, glowing faintly. They stepped out into the hall and stood for a moment, listening. Total silence, except for a faint humming somewhere in the building, and the sound of a car driving past outside. Jack centered himself in the hall and moved forward slowly with Karen pressed closely behind him. "This is definitely creepy," she whispered.

The humming faded, and Jack relaxed. The stairway downwards was just ahead of them. He turned to take Karen by the arm, and saw a faint red light the size of a saucer, several feet above the floor and moving up behind them. The light descended, bobbing and weaving, and illuminated weakly below it was a muscular, human arm. Jack grabbed Karen and pushed her sprawling to the floor.

"Stay down!" he shouted, as two dark figures hurtled towards him out of the darkness. Jack came up out of a crouch, slamming his shoulder into one of them. The impact was blunted by something soft and spongy. He drove the attacker up against a wall and heard something snap. There was an agonized groan, then an arm was around his neck, cutting off his air so abruptly that fireflies in green and red danced before his eyes. He slammed his palms together behind his head, heard a grunt and felt soft rubber, then twisted his body and brought both elbows down and back in one motion with a hard instep kick. He was gratified by a howl of pain, and the return of his breath.

He turned to grasp his assailant and swung underhand, bringing up a claw into the crotch area, and then stepped forward to smash his head into a face. Plastic, plastic everywhere: a nut cup, yet, and some kind of goggles over the eyes, shattering with the blow.

Behind him, Karen was yelling, "Let go, you bastard. Let go. Jack. Jack!"

He twirled into a roundhouse kick, made contact with a rock-hard stomach and the man went down, bounced off a wall and came up running towards the stairwell, two other figures following him.

Karen screamed, "Jack, they've got the books!"

He could hear the attackers ahead, taking stairs in giant leaps, and then the door on the main floor banged back against a wall. His throat was sore, and he felt dizzy. Suddenly he was angry with himself.

"They're gone," he said despondently, and then Karen was in his arms, squeezing him so tightly he could barely breathe. "Damn, I blew it," he moaned.

"They only wanted the books," Karen said. "I dropped them on the floor when you pushed me down, and then this guy was all over me, pushing my hands away and grabbing for the books. I was fumbling blind, but I swear that guy could see in the dark, and I ended up trying to pull things out of his hands."

"They used infrared light," said Jack. "I think I broke a rib in one of them. I felt something give, and then he yelled."

"Ugh," said Karen. "Let's get out of here, Jack, before they come back."

"They won't be back. What for? They got what they came for, and I let them get away."

"Right. Three guys to one, and you allowed them to get away. Come on, Jack, you kept us from getting killed."

They left the building and walked quickly across an empty campus. Their eyes searched bushes and trees, and saw nothing. Karen's apartment building was well lighted. She let them in, and they ascended a flight of stairs to her rooms. She unlocked the door, and Jack pushed his way in ahead of her, body quivering. They turned on all the lights, finding everything in place. Karen went to the bathroom, and turned on the light there.

"Jack," she called softly.

He went to her, found a cloth Raggedy Ann doll hanging by its neck from a shower curtain rod, a perfect hangman's knot tied in a piece of clothesline. A note, scrawled in pencil on lined paper, was pinned to the doll's chest. It said: 'Karen, if she talks.'

"The door was locked," she said incredulously.

"That doesn't seem to make any difference around here these days."

"Jack, we've got to call someone."

"No, not now. Let me take care of it."

"Well at least we should tall Mister Ebensack."

"Please, Karen, I'll take care of it."

There was something in his voice and the way he looked at her that made her stop and think. He thought she was badly frightened. He was taking care of her again. Finally she said, "All right, you think you can handle it. I'm going to bed, and you're going home now."

"In that order?"

"Tonight, yes. I have two friends next door who will stay with me tonight. Oh, I need the vial you put into your shirt pocket. God, I hope it wasn't damaged."

Jack fumbled in his pocket and pulled out the rolled up handkerchief, unrolled it, exposing a small bottle filled with clear liquid. "Looks okay," he said, handing it to her.

"Wouldn't they give anything to have this?" said Karen, amused.

"What?"

"The neuter. This is another sample of it. I recognized the label from the last experiment. This is the stuff that worked, and it doesn't look like anything has precipitated out yet."

"We'd better get it to Ebensack."

"Tomorrow. I want to keep it around awhile. Let me take care of it, Jack," she said impishly, teasing him.

"It might be dangerous, Karen."

"Do I look scared?"

"No, but you should be. These are bad dudes we're playing

with."

"I was scared earlier. I saw your face when we came out of the building. You were smiling, Jack. You enjoyed pounding on those guys, didn't you?"

"I don't think enjoyed is the right word."

"That should scare me, but it doesn't," she said.

"Oh?"

"I love you too much for that." She walked to her bureau, pulled open the top drawer and peered inside. "Hi, sweetie," she cooed. Jack looked over her shoulder and saw Morris the rat curled up in his box on a pile of cotton panties and blinking at them painfully in the sudden light. At one end of the box was a food dish half-filled with grain, and a water dispenser was screwed to a side panel. The little white animal uncoiled, lifted his head and closed his eyes as Karen petted him with a finger. "He likes to be petted," she said. "Otherwise, he just sleeps and eats." She put the neuter vial under panties in a corner of the drawer, then slid it partially shut. Jack put his arms around her from behind, kissing her neck, cheek and mouth. "Go home," she murmured, running a hand across his face.

"You'll be okay tonight?"

"My jock girlfriends will be here. You would be too much distraction. I've had my warning, and I don't expect them back. Meet me for breakfast?"

"I'll be here," he said, walking to the door. She went with him, arm encircling his hard body, head on his shoulder. At the door she kissed him long and soft, releasing him with an evil smile. "Night, night," she said, and closed the door, leaving him there with flushed face, pounding heart and a painful throbbing in his groin.

Karen watched him until he was a hundred yards away, then picked up the telephone and called Ebensack.

Jack jogged all the way back to his dormitory without seeing anyone, and went straight up to his room.

Someone had been busy there.

He got off the elevator and stepped across the hall towards his room, freezing in place when the door burst open and the bulk of Arnie Kant was filling the doorway. Arnie was breathing hard, and his face was contorted in anger, a most unusual state for the big man.

"Finally you get back," he said. "Can you please tell me what the fuck is going on here!"

Jack edged past him and looked at the chaos in the room. "Oh, shit," he grumbled. The room was a shambles: drawers pulled out, book shelves cleaned, furniture overturned. It had been a quick, sloppy job, but thorough.

"There's a love letter for you in the bathroom," said Arnie. He followed Jack there, where someone had scrawled a message on a mirror with red lipstick. It said: 'Keep your mouth shut, or you're dead meat.' Hanging on a towel rack next to the mirror was a pair of panties he knew must be Karen's, with a lipstick tube wrapped in it.

"This sure has nothing to do with me," said Arnie, "but I think I have a right to know what's going on when my stuff gets dumped all over the floor."

"I doubt if the stupid assholes stopped long enough to realize I had a roommate," said Jack. "I just came from Karen's, and they were in her room, too."

"Terrific," growled the big man. "Now what's it all about?"

"Some bad dudes we ran into at The Plumbing shop. This should be the end of it."

"Bullshit! You don't go to bars!"

"Stay out of it, Arnie. It's over, now."

"Come on, Jack. I'm in this, too. Take a look around you."

"Yeah. Sorry about me, and my big mouth that irritates drunks. Come on, I'll help clean this up, and let's get some sleep. I'm beat."

* * * * * * *

Across campus, two men sat behind tripod-mounted binoculars focused on the window of Jack and Arnie's room.

"Ten bucks says he's telling him everything, so now the big jock is involved. You shouldn't have tossed his room, Len."

"So what?" said Len. "It just means one more guy to kill. You told me to go over there, Tom."

"What I told you to do was search his bedroom, not mess the whole place up. Those were the colonel's orders, and that's the way I told it to you. Now you can explain it to the Colonel. I'm sure he'll be very understanding."

"You said we should scare them."

"I said, and the Colonel said, we should scare the girl, and I did what he ordered to the letter. Nelson is only an irritant. You made a mistake on my watch, so I'll have to take my lumps too. Let's get it over with. I wish Nate could go with us."

"He's at the infirmary by now," said Len. "That rib of his is either cracked or broken."

"Then he's the lucky one," said Tom.

They folded up the tripod and made the walk to the armory, where their master awaited them.

CHAPTER NINE

The purge lasted two weeks, a blitzkrieg that attacked the heart of the anti-classified research movement and scattered pieces of it to the four winds. One by one, key antagonists were called in to the president's office to face their two chief executives. Academic records were examined and discussed at length, with emphasis on research productivity and grants received. It was made clear to all villains that the fundamental issue was open opposition to classified research, and such opposition would no longer be tolerated. Faculty without grants were threatened with a cutoff of funds. Those with grants were threatened because they weren't teaching enough, and those with good teaching records were threatened because they weren't publishing enough.

Madge watched them come and go: ashen-faced, beaten down, humbled by fear. A bill to ban classified research on campus died a quiet death in the Faculty Senate Research Committee, and debate on the issue was suddenly no longer interesting, being replaced by a controversy over whether or not to increase student parking fees.

Certain consequences would be forgotten with the passage of time. There was the case of Doctor Linus Oswald, Associate Professor of Philosophy, aged fifty-six. Oswald had written two books on ethics in his thirty year career, slowly evolving into an active campaigner against military research on a university campus. After a three hour session in the president's office, Doctor Oswald was exhausted and went home early, where his wife of thirty four years, Doris, fixed him a hearty supper. It was just the two of them, their three children all having left home to start families of their own, and there were four grand-children scattered around the country. After supper, Linus lay down on the front room couch, not feeling well at all, and Doris covered him with a warm blanket. She moved quietly around the house until it was time for her to go to bed, and then she went to wake Linus. She found him on the floor by the couch, quite dead from a heart attack. At a large funeral attended by many faculty member, president Lundeman held the widow's hand and gave her soft words of comfort.

A more bizarre case was that of Doctor Richard Dick, physi-cist and political activist, who quickly developed a severe drinking problem after his meeting with the president and vice president. He became increasingly belligerent and abusive with everyone around him, not regarded in itself as unusual behavior for the man. But one day he terrified his colleagues by openly carrying a .357 magnum on one hip during his seminar on catastrophe theory applied to critical phenomena in solids. The audience had listened with more than rapt attention that day. And one night, his distraught wife called the police after Dick arose from his bed, loaded his pistol, and shot to pieces the two toilet bowls in their ordinarily quiet house. He was arrested, examined by a psychiatrist, and sent to a private rest home near Phoenix, Arizona to amuse himself writing unusual and often pornographic poetry.

During the purge, Ebensack continued his investigation quietly, keeping in touch with Jack and Karen through a message drop arranged with Jack during their meeting at the Union. The drop was a book titled Poultry Farming Today, gathering dust in a dark corner of the library. The book had never been checked out, and one could only speculate as to why it had ever been ordered for a high-technology campus.

Jack left messages inside the book, and Ebensack replied on the same piece of paper, In this way, he coordinated their activi-ties, and made sure they had some sort of contact in situations he considered dangerous, even though they had demonstrated they were not helpless in such cases.

As news of three murders faded to the back page, Ebensack reviewed faculty files, using the unlimited resources of his office in Arlington to provide further background, and helping him to build a scenario that seemed more and more realistic as the weeks went by. Occasionally he relaxed, attended a play or took a long walk in the woods. Once he encountered Jack and Karen in a pizza parlor; it was if they had never met, no eye contact being made, but in the league championship game he sat in the stands on a cold, blustery afternoon, cheered on the Cougars and watched Jack make six unassisted tackles. But Simenson University lost to Concordia College thirteen to ten, with a last minute kick sailing forty yards in strong wind to make the difference.

All too soon, winter came to the north country, with snow, bitter cold, and howling winds plunging civilization into the labyrinth of tunnels and caverns beneath ground level on campus. For three months, only the adventurous or the masoch-istic walked the frozen surface of the local planet, puffed their way along on snow shoes and skis, or scampered between the trees on snowmobiles.

It was a November Tuesday, and the wind was blowing hard. The wind chill had dropped to minus fifty when Jack pulled on the hood of his parka to make a tunnel he could see out of, and trudged through snow drifts across a deserted-looking campus to the library. Inside, he stamped the snow from his boots, went upstairs to read more about poultry farming, leafed through the book until he found a yellow, postcard-sized piece of paper. The message said, 'Carter and Mason are not registered students', and was signed 'E'. Jack read it without surprise, wrote, 'thanks. Nothing new' on the back and replaced note in book on the shelf. Adjusting his hood once more, he crossed campus to the armory just in time for one of his two weekly sessions in the rifle range. Sergeant Rodríguez gave him an irritated glance as the last student to arrive.

There were ten students in class, and ten positions on the range. One of the students was Thomas Mason: tall, sinewy, hard eyes, and long hands. Jack had just been told this man was not a registered student, yet there he stood, uniform and red beret, presumably the scholarship that went with them, waiting his turn at the line. Jack worked his way through the others so he would be Mason's neighbor on the firing line.

The subject for the first in twelve sessions was the hand gun. Rodríguez lectured to them about stance, grip and breathing, then ordered them to the line. On a table at each position lay a Hi-Standard Victor target pistol, and a box containing fifty rounds of .22 long rifle ammunition. Following the directions of their Sergeant, each student loaded a clip with five rounds, took a stance, then thrust out an arm, moving a back foot to bring the natural aiming point in line with the target fifty feet down range. The procedure was repeated with pistol in hand.

Altogether, Jack made three adjustments in his stance, but Mason, to his left, picked up his weapon and aimed it only once. They fired two strings of five rounds, and changed targets. This time only a plain piece of paper was there, without bull's-eye. The exercise was to force them to look only at their front sight, and not the target. During the lull, while they reloaded clips, Jack looked over at Mason and smiled.

"I haven't seen you around," he said, tone friendly. "Are you an engineering major?"

The man smiled, but with a sinister curl of thin lips. Jack looked back into the man's shark eyes.

"None of your fucking business," said Mason.

Jack's mouth dropped open in surprise. "Well, excuse me," he drawled.

"Ready on the left!" screamed Rodríguez. "Ready on the right. Ready on the firing line. Fire!"

In ten seconds, fifty explosions echoed in the range. They brought their targets back, Jack looking at the scattered shot pattern on his with dismay. To his left, the man named Mason looked without expression at his circular pattern of five shots, the size of a quarter, dead center on the paper. Rodríguez checked targets, nodded to Mason and slapped Jack on the back.

"What's the matter, Nelson? You're jerking your head and changing focus. Keep it on that front sight." He moved to the next man. Jack felt his face heat up, and Mason gave him another venomous look.

The rest of practice was mercifully short, leaving Jack frustrated and angry with himself. Cleaning up cartridge brass with a push broom, Jack looked up in time to see Mason slip out the door.

"What's the matter, is he too good to sweep up?" he said to Rodríguez.

"Mason? He has another class, now. What do you care?" Bullshit, thought Jack, keeping silent because Rodríguez was looking at him curiously, now. There are no classes scheduled at five-thirty, and that's now. Where the hell is that guy going?

"I asked you a question, Nelson." Rodríguez moved closer, frowning.

Jack was suddenly aware of his own mood: irritable, and childish. He was making himself look bad.

"No problems, Sergeant. I've just had a lousy day."

Rodríguez relaxed. "Don't be so hard on yourself. If you relax, you'll shoot better. Pistol is the toughest weapon to master, Nelson. Give it some time, think ten, and keep positive pressure on the trigger. It'll come." He winked at Jack.

* * * * * * *

The students had been gone for nearly an hour, and Rodríguez was going over equipment inventory cards in the range when the door eased open and Colonel Holleque sauntered into the room.

"Working late tonight," The Man said, approvingly.

"Just paper pushing, sir. I'll be finished here in a few minutes."

"Everything go well this evening? Can the kids hit the paper yet?"

"Pretty well, sir. Mason is a natural, and he's already shooting in the two eighties. The rest of them are having the usual problems, but I'm sure their patterns will tighten up pretty quick."

"How do they get along with each other?"

"Fairly well, at least good enough to function as a squad in the field exercises coming up."

Holleque smiled. "There are some talented people in that group, but I'm asking if there are personality problems or feuds going on yet."

Rodríguez thought for a moment, hesitating to point a finger, then said, "Yesterday, I would have said no, sir, but today Mason and Nelson had a head-bump of some kind. Nelson asked Mason what his major was, and Mason told him to blow off. I don't think they even know each other, but it didn't sound friendly."

"I don't understand that," said Holleque, concerned. "Mason's in political science, I think. Yes, I'm sure he is, and Nelson's in some kind of engineering. Sounds like it's Mason who's upset by something, so I'll have a talk with him. I want those people to be able to work together, Sergeant."

"Yes, sir," said Rodríguez, and he went back to his cards as the colonel turned away. While the sergeant finished his work, Holleque rolled two targets down range, then retrieved his personal pistol, a Browning target model with aim-point sight for competitive target and night shooting. Adjusting the light intensity in his sight, he proceeded with four strings of slow fire, punching a tight grouping of holes in the dime-sized ten rings of both targets, then switched to timed and rapid fire as Rodríguez quietly left the room for the night. Holleque had fired nearly a hundred rounds when there was a knock on the door, and he opened it to silently admit six men, uniformed and with red berets, carrying travel bags. They were grim-faced, somewhat older than the usual students. One of them was Thomas Mason. Holleque gave him a hard look as he came into the room.

"Take a place at the line, people, and use your silencers, please."

Each man moved to a point on the firing line, where a small table remained. Each removed a pistol identical to Holleque's from his bag, screwed a long tube at the end of the barrel to muffle the muzzle blast, and loaded two clips. Holleque walked up to Mason, and without looking at him, spoke in a whisper.

"You antagonized Nelson today, and we don't need that problem."

"He's snooping, sir."

"I don't care. No trouble. Get along with him, unless I say otherwise. And another thing, if anyone asks you what your major is, it's political science, do you understand?"

Mason smiled. "Yes, sir. I understand, sir."

"This will be rapid fire, five shots in ten seconds. For your first string of rapid fire, with five rounds, load."

The slides of six semi-automatic pistols came forward with a synchronous snap. Seconds later, there were muffled coughing sounds in the room, as all weapons accurately spewed forth their messengers of death, and Holleque watched with fatherly pride the hard core of the thing he had created.

Eagle Squad.

* * * * * * *

Heavy hangs the head that wears the crown, someone had once told him, and Lundeman thought it was amusing at the time. Not now. The day had been hell, and he filled a highball glass half-full of scotch before splashing in a little soda with it. It would be nice if Irene could stay home long enough to share a drink, cuddle on the couch, and just talk to him, but she was at her hairdresser's again. That meant she was bored. A friendly voice was what he needed, a person who understood what he was up against and what he was trying to build. A little tenderness, a little love. He needed a little love, after a day filled with hate. The deans had been stoically silent during the budget meeting, motivated only by fear, and he saw it in their eyes. He did not want that, had never wanted that. They tiptoed around him like frightened puppies now, isolating him from their problems, no longer asking his advice. Robots, all of them, watching their asses, making no waves, keeping in line with the system or whatever damned thing it was called. At the senate meeting it was even worse, no discussions or arguments, a collection of issues so trivial he wanted to leave the room. No eye contact. Nobody looked at him, even when he spoke. Fifty pairs of eyes found a wall or a rug to study while he made a comment or asked a question. And all because he had crushed a movement that threatened to destroy the university. Didn't they understand that? Heavy hangs the head that wears the crown, and his crown had thorns in it. He took a long drink, then refilled his glass quickly when the telephone rang. He answered it, suppressing an urge to hang up when he heard the rough voice on the line.

"You're not supposed to call me here."

"No problem. I saw your wife downtown, and figured you'd be alone. No mistress or anyone, right?"

The Man was amused, probably a little drunk, and Lundeman felt disgust. "Say what you want to, and get off the line."

"That's not friendly, mister president. Partner. I just want to give you a progress report. It's been a while since we've had a chat."

"So get on with it. Have your hired thugs killed anyone else lately?"

"Now, now, don't get dramatic. What was done had to be done, or we'd both be in jail now."

"Even your own woman? I know you'd slept with her."

"Just another piece of ass, my man. I have a lot of women." There was the sound of ice tinkling in a glass. "You really ought to try it sometime."

"All right, so what do you want to tell me, Holleque?"

"I think we have what we need, now, but we'll have to make some tests. I'm arranging that on my own. What you want to hear is that I have a buyer, and money is not an issue with him. How does ten percent of seven million dollars sound to you?"

Lundeman gulped. "It sounds good," he said, "and incredible."

"I knew I'd make your day. Told you it would be big. Tax

free, in a Swiss bank or wherever you want it. A nice retirement supplement, right?"

"We don't have the money yet," cautioned Lundeman.

"Soon, soon. Give me a few weeks, and keep the faith."

"Anything else?"

"No, that was it. Wanted you to hear the good news. Oh yeah, there is one more thing. You know that hairdresser your wife goes to?"

"The one in town, yes. She's there now."

"That's him. Well, I don't like gossip, but scandal is even worse, and I'm hearing some interesting things about that guy. It seems he has a very good pair of hands, and his fingers are finding their way into dark, moist places in several of his customers, including a prominent lady we both know. Better'n a vibrator, I hear." More ice tinkled in a glass, the voice raspy, taunting. "Though maybe you'd like to check it out."

The laughter was a cackle, evil and painful, and then the line went dead.

Lundeman finished his drink, made another. A warm glow engulfed him as he sat on the plush couch in his living room, staring at an empty chair. After a few minutes, his breathing became normal again, and he felt in control. He thought carefully about what he should do, deciding the situation was far too important to overlook. It would have to be dealt with in a clear and forceful manner. One should not diddle a university president's wife without fear of consequence, he thought.

He knew the hairdresser and his dubious status in the community, a status keeping him safe from nobody. There were young punks available who, for fifty dollars, would break both legs and perhaps an arm, but that was so impersonal, so low-class, and thugs were unreliable. There was a risk, but he had been taking risks all his life, never failing to accomplish what he wanted to do.

The drive to town was short, the street nearly empty as people enjoyed their evening meal. He found a parking space in front of the beauty parlor, noted the curtains pulled over the windows, and the 'Sorry, we're closed' sign hanging in the front door. The warm glow was still there, brought a smile and a serenity he rarely enjoyed. At this moment he knew the feeling of being totally in charge, with the very lives of people in his hands.

He went to the door, and tried it. The door was locked. He knocked, calling out, "Irene, this is Curtis! Come out, please." Beyond the door there was a scuffling sound, and in his peripheral vision he saw the edge of a curtain move. "I know what you're doing in there, dear. Let's go home, now." His voice was calm, soothing, with no sign of irritation, yet his answer seemed not to be forthcoming.

He had seen the four garbage cans, empty and shining brightly in orange twilight by the shop. He chose the largest of the four, carried it around to the front of the building and set it down on the sidewalk with a bang. "Stand back, please!" he called out, swinging the can around in a wide, horizontal arc and seeing, at the instant of release, a pair of wide staring eyes looking at him out of a pale, fragile face at the edge of the curtain.

The entire window shattered into a thousand pieces. It's all in the wrist, he thought.

He stepped to the door, but the pause was only momentary because someone was already clawing at the lock, screaming, "Crazy sonovabitch, crazy bastard! I'll sue your fucking ass, and have you—"

The door flew open, ejecting forth a slender young man with hate in his face and claws outstretched, reaching for his eyes. Lundeman kicked him expertly, with great force, in the solar plexus. The man dropped to the ground in a writing heap of sorry humanity, gagging and wretching up what looked like the remains of a recent pizza dinner. Irene appeared suddenly in the doorway, looked at the creature on the ground and then at her husband as if she had just seen the hand of God writing on a rock.

"Get in the car," he said firmly.

She moved past him cautiously, hair in disarray, exuding a musky fear that made him suddenly quite horny, and she saw it in his face. She got in the car and shut the door without a word, while her husband jerked the gasping, famous fingers man to his feet and pushed him back inside the shop. They stood looking at each other a moment. Lundeman smiled. The pretty one shook with pain, fear and anger, and then he did a foolish thing. He lunged for a pair of scissors, and would have made it except that Lundeman, grinning wildly now, hit him in the navel and the crotch simultaneously, and dropped him to the floor again. The man shrieked. Lundeman grabbed his long hair, pulling his head back with a snap. The pretty face was so close it was drowning in alcohol fumes, and spittle was raining down on it.

"If you ever touch my wife again, I will kill you," said Lundeman, "and if you say anything to the police or anyone else about this, I will make sure it is done scientifically and slowly. Do you understand me, sweet thing?" Still smiling, he helped the man agree by slamming his head sharply against the floor three times, then stood up and walked quickly to the door, pleased with the whimpering sounds he heard coming from behind him.

The drive home was quick, and in total silence. Irene was still sitting in the car when her husband entered the house, poured himself a generous drink, and went upstairs to lie on the bed and read a magazine. A few minutes later, she entered the bedroom, carrying her shoes, moving cautiously as if he might come at her any second. The thought of enduring pain, or an injury that would flaw her beauty had brought her to the edge of hysteria. She sat on the end of the bed, near her husband's feet, and began to weep softly, looking down at her lap, hurt, full of shame and anger, yet at the same time strangely attracted to the man who buried his face in a magazine and sipped his drink. Time seemed to stand still, she could hear her heart beating, the faint rustling of magazine pages, and a radio playing far down the road. She swallowed hard.

"I don't know what to say, Curtis. I'm so very sorry. You have every right to be angry, but—" Her voice trembled, then broke. The magazine moved. He was watching her, now. "You're always so busy, and I needed someone to talk to, to touch, or hug, to make me feel like a woman. I wasn't looking for sex, but Allen told—Allen told me I was beautiful, and he made me feel good. I didn't go to bed with him."

"I hear he has marvelous hands," snapped her husband, eyes like setting suns on the horizon of the magazine.

"I didn't go to bed with him," she repeated, tears streaming down her face. "I—I just wanted to be loved by someone."

The fire in those burning eyes seemed to suddenly go out, and he lowered the magazine, frowning at her as she began to weep again. She pulled her legs up onto the bed and crawled towards him, and as she came close he held out his arms to her, still frowning, enveloping her shuddering body in a crushing embrace of fragrant warmth. He drew her into him until she moaned and began pulling at his shirt, then his belt buckle as his hands moved over her. In a moment they were undressed, moving together on top of the covers. Irene made little grunting sounds and clenched her teeth as he drove hard into her, suddenly filling her up as she cried out with a pleasure barely remembered with her man. Her own man, her husband, the only one, well, not the only one, but the one she loved, the one she really wanted, and now he was in her, and she felt wonderfully warm and married and secure. In only a few moment, entwined together, they drifted into a dreamless sleep.

* * * * * * *

Curtis had left for work when she awoke, warm and naked in their bed. He had covered her up, adding an extra blanket. Still drowsy, she fixed her hair and began to dress, happy until the telephone rang and an all too familiar voice broke the spell.

"Hubby gone to work?"

"You know he has."

"Thought I'd check to see why you didn't come over last night."

"I was with Curtis."

"How dull."

"Not so dull. We made love, and it was very nice."

"Really, he finally got it up, huh? No much comparison, of course."

"You only think you know Curtis, and that could get you into trouble someday. By the way, how did he find out about Allen? Are you looking in windows now?"

"The little queer who hand jobs the ladies? Oh, I guess I told him. So what?"

"This must be one of your manic days. I don't want to see you anymore."

"Hey! Just because I told on your little sex slave?"

"Curtis beat him up last night, and smashed the window in his shop. I think it's safe to expect a lawsuit over that."

"Settle out of court, for Christ's sake. My God, Curtis my man, you've been reborn. I'm proud of him. Now you've got two real men, lady."

Irene's voice was precise and cool. "I think you've missed a point here. I love my husband, and I don't ever want to see you again, under any circumstances."

"That's going to be difficult."

"Believe me, I can arrange it," she said firmly. "I've been considering this eventuality for quite a while. Surely you can find another plaything."

"Just like that, you think you can blow me off with a wave of your hand. It's in character, Irene. Don't you realize I could destroy your marriage with a few words?"

"And your business at the same time. Somehow, I think money is more important to you than sex, and certainly more than any kind of real relationship. Anyway, I'll take the risk."

"Very noble, Irene, but you're risking far more than you think."

Irene Lundeman suddenly felt a chill.

* * * * * * *

It was not enough to read a brief note scribbled in haste. Karen had to see it for herself, and Jack would be in the armory for at least two hours tonight. All of the red berets would likely be there with him. Indeed, she saw none of them on her way to and from the field house, the little rack of storage tubes nestled safely in her purse.

She had dismissed the idea of sacrificing a rat for the tests, and settled on a package of fresh chicken breasts from the grocery store in town. She put chicken and tubes into the glove box, closed it up and purged the interior with nitrogen before letting in air again. Working slowly in the gloves, she unwrapped and laid out three chicken breasts and lined up the storage tube samples labeled Nano One, Two and three. The tubes were under pressure, and produced a fine spray. A small lever at the top of each tube released the spray when depressed. The gloves were too awkward for that, so she used the base of a pair of tweezers to do it.

There was no surprise until the final test. When she sprayed chicken breasts with Nano One and Two, nothing happened right away, so she waited several minutes. Nano Two eventually produced only a purplish discoloration of skin on the breast, and nothing on the meat beneath. The notes seemed to be an exaggeration of the effect for that sample. Nano One did nothing at all. Karen was disappointed, and unprepared for what happened next.

Using the tweezers, she pressed hard on the spray release lever for Nano three. The surface of the chicken breast glistened wetly for only a heartbeat before the meat seemed to explode right next to her gloved hands. She jumped back, pulling her arms out of the gloves. A white vapor filled the interior of the box. She looked inside, saw a purplish, bubbling mass of flesh eroding away to nothing before her eyes, steaming as if cooked. Beside it, the other two breasts had small patches of rapidly eroding flesh, and over the next ten minutes those also disintegrated to a fine ash residue.

Karen watched in horror. When the chaos had ceased in the

glove box she purged the system twice with nitrogen and wiped everything inside clean with first acetone and then alcohol. Sweat beaded her forehead when she opened the box to remove the storage tubes. She waited for an itch, a burning sensation, anything that might tell her the nanobots had invaded her flesh, Her hands were steady, but she had never been so frightened in her life, and she was alone in the lab, far from help. When the tubes were back in the rack, Nano Three wrapped in its own little plastic envelope, she put the rack in another sealed bag, and only then did she feel safer.

All the way back to the field house she was conscious of the nightmare nestled in her purse. In a moment it would be hidden away in Reimer's locker, but Karen had already made a decision.

This was one weapon of war that would never see the light of day.

At least, that was her intention at the time.

CHAPTER TEN

The noise level in The Plumbing Shop had reached pain threshold for most of its occupants, but nobody seemed to notice. Strobe lights in red and blue flashed to the deep, husky disco beat of a Tina Turner tune as couples crammed together on the tiny dance floor. Weaving, jerking, twisting like snakes, the guys looking cool, gals slinky and sensuous, all were having a great time. Willy Niven sat at the bar, nursing his third beer of the evening, and watched a little blond writhing around in a tight, sleeveless dress. The guy she was writhing with looked like something out of a Playboy ad, and he was certain she would go home in a Corvette or Porsche Turbo tonight. Money do make the world go 'round, Willy, Willy, he thought, and you got none, well, maybe enough for another beer or two. He had that, at least, after striking out with the women. Five times he had asked for dances, five times he had gotten only giggles, so screw it. Let them have their Corvettes, and the wimps who drove them. Fuck them all. He drained his glass, and the bartender was magically there to fill it again. He checked his wallet, found enough there for one more beer and a phone call. He sipped the new, cold beer, and ran a hand over his mottled face, tenderly touching two of the flaming eruptions there. Wasn't acne supposed to go away when you hit your twenties? Not for Willy, old zit face, high-school dropout, living on unemployment, with a talent for making women giggle.

Someone brushed by him, and he turned as a guy in his twenties slid onto a stool and ordered a Windsor coke. Sharp features, crew-cut and big hands. That's what he especially noticed, the big hands. The guy sipped his drink, then suddenly turned and said, "Hi."

Willy nearly dropped his teeth, because people never, never initiated a conversation with Willy Niven. He was surprised, and pleased.

"Hi," he returned, cheerfully.

"I've seen you here before," said the guy. "You're Willy Niven."

"How do you know that?" asked Willy, suspicious now.

"Oh, a lady friend of mine. A friend of hers is hot to meet you, but she's kind of shy."

Willy's eyes darted around the room.

"They're not here tonight," said the guy, "but I'll get you two together sometime. Hey, I'm Pete Howard." He held out a hand, and Willy shook it, so pleased with himself he hadn't even felt the hook go in.

"Glad to know you, Pete. You from around here?"

"Yeah. I work up at the University. Research assistant. Pay's not so hot, but the work's nice, and I don't have someone looking over my shoulder all the time. How about you?"

"No job right now," said Willy. "Had one until two months ago, running a saw, but then they shut down the mill at Bayer Lake until lumber prices come up again. Laid all of us off."

"A guy's gotta be glad just to have a job, now," said Pete. "How do you make it?"

"Unemployment, and I had a little saved. That's about gone, now, but I don't need much. No family, or anything. Just me. Get me some beer money, and I'm okay."

Pete sipped his drink for a moment, then thought of something and put a big hand on Willy's arm. "I think I can get you a hundred bucks."

"What?"

"Hey, I'm serious. Listen. The guy I work for does tests with drugs, behavior stuff, like how a medication influences the way you think or act. Mostly mild stuff: antihistamines, cold medicines, tranquilizers. He has a big grant from the government and brings people in all the time for tests. I've watched him do it. He gives them a drug and they take a written test of some kind. I don't know what he asks, but it's over in a few minutes and then he hands them a hundred dollars cash. The guy's rolling in money. Interested?"

Willy thought, but mostly about having a hundred bucks in his pocket. "Does it hurt?" he asked.

"I never heard anyone complain," said Pete. "In fact, one guy told me he felt pretty high on the stuff he took. Said he could answer questions like, you know, it made him smarter. Most people don't seem to notice much effect. Roy, I mean Doctor Elton, he's the guy I work with, he says the effects are small, and show up in the answers on the written test. He's still in the lab, and runs tests all the time, even late at night. If you want, I can give him a call right now."

Pete looked at him, seemed expectant. Willy felt uneasy and hesitant. Pete put a hand on his arm, confiding in him. "Tell you what. If you do it tonight, I'll buy the beers until the bar closes. There's twenty bucks in it for me. Like I say, the guy is rolling in dough."

Willy smiled. Scratch a friend's back, get a hundred dollars and free beers all night, and what have you got now, Mister Niven?

"Sure, make your phone call," he said.

Pete was back in less than a minute. "Yep, he's there. Said to come in quick, because he has somewhere to go. You got a car?"

"No."

"No problem. After the test, we'll close the bar tonight, and I'll take you home."

"Thanks," said Willy, feeling really good about his new friend who didn't seem to care that he had no job or money.

They left the bar. Pete had a black BMW with 'Simonsen University' stenciled on the driver's side. The drive to the campus was quick, without conversation. Nearly all the buildings were dark, except for one surrounded by floodlights at the top of a hill. At the base of the hill, as the road swung upwards, was a small, one-story brick building with a giant metal ball like a propane tank beside it. All the lights were on inside, and a car was parked in front. Pete pulled up behind the car, and parked. It was quiet when they got out. Now Willy had a stomach full of butterflies, and sweat on his forehead. Pete smiled, and slapped him on the back.

"Follow me, and we'll see what the good doctor is up to." He opened the wooden door, and Willy followed him inside, butterflies and all.

The whole building was a single laboratory room, with white polished floors and stainless steel furniture, reminding Willy of the hospital emergency room they had taken him to after his nose had been broken in a fight with some Indian from Canada his first day on the mill job. There was a young man in a surgical gown bending over a table at the far end of the room. When they got closer, Willy could see he was dissecting a cat, working on the brain, and all the convolutions were visible, just like in pictures he had seen. Willy's stomach turned over a couple of times before the man extended his hand and introduced himself.

"Roy Elton." He said cheerfully, and pumped Willy's hand with an iron grip. "I understand you'd like to make some quick money and help science at the same time?"

"Sure," said Willy, trying to get his hand back.

"You understand you can do this only one time, because once you've done the test you'll remember it, and I can't give it to you again? It's a one shot deal," he said, then matter-of-factly reached into his pocket, took out a roll of money and handed a crisp one hundred dollar bill to Willy.

"There you go." Roy replaced the money roll in his pants pocket. "Tax free," he added, "so now let's get started."
Roy picked up a notebook lying near the staring eyes of the dead cat, and opened it up. "A little history, first," he said, pen poised over the paper, and then he asked a bunch of questions: age, height, weight, childhood diseases, the asthma trouble he'd had as a kid, his diabetic uncle, and a persistent mother who had

tried suicide three times before finally succeeding when he was twelve. Willy didn't like to talk about that, but the young scientist said it was important he know the entire family medical history. Finally, he seemed satisfied.

"I'm going to give you a shot, now. You shouldn't feel anything unusual, but if you do I want to know it immediately. Roll up your left sleeve, and make a fist." Roy took a vial from a table and unwrapped an insulin syringe. He stuck the needle into the vial top, holding it upside down, and carefully drew a clear liquid into it.

Willy made a fist of his left hand, veins popping out all over his forearm. Roy looked at them approvingly. "Hold it like that, and don't look."

Willy looked for Pete and saw him bent over a table in a far corner of the room. He wasn't scared anymore, but still felt uneasy. It was the ages of both men. Can't be much older than me, and they don't look like scientists, he thought. More like jocks: hard, muscular bodies, and short haircuts. But then he thought about the hundred dollar bill in his pocket, and whatever was burning in his left arm at the moment. He looked up to see Roy put the syringe back on the table.

"Feel anything?" asked Roy.

"Just a little burning."

"That's normal. We'll wait a couple of minutes, then put you in isolation and give you a written test that will take only a few minutes. Easy, huh?"

"Yeah," said Willy, relaxing even more. Pete smiled at him from the corner.

"I'll be finished here in a bit, and remember we're closing the bar before I take you home," said Pete.

Willy smiled, too. The evening was turning out just fine.

They waited several minutes, and Willy felt nothing except a prickly sensation in his left forearm. Roy looked at him occasionally, and Willy shrugged his shoulders. Nothing new here, man. For a while, he watched Roy carve on the cat's brain, but it made his stomach queasy, and it seemed like the cat was looking right at him, trying to say something. He turned away, and wandered over to Pete, who was loading glassware into some kind of oven, and then Roy called him back.

"That's enough time, Willy. Over here." Roy opened a door and ushered Willy into a tiny room with a table and chair, blank walls, a single TV camera pointed at the table and a ceiling grate, from which flowed cool air. A folder lay on the table, upside down, and a pencil beside it. Willy sat down on the chair, and reached for the folder.

"Not yet," said Roy. "I'll tell you when over the intercom, so I can time you. Now concentrate, and do the best you can."

Willy nodded, and Roy left the room, closing the door behind him with a loud snap. Suddenly, the room seemed very small, and the butterflies were back, playing tag in Willy's stomach. He sat bolt upright in his chair, feeling cool air flowing past his face.

"You okay?" asked a disembodied voice. It was Roy.

"Yeah, but I felt a little closed in there for a second."

"Just relax, and breathe deep. You can start the test anytime, now." There was an audible click as the speaker went off, leaving Willy alone again with his heartbeat and looking up at the TV camera.

He opened the booklet in front of him and breathed deeply. In boldface type, he read, 'Stanford-Curtis General Interest Evaluation' at the top of the first page. One hundred questions. Fill in the little circles of your choice, using the pencil provided. An interest test? A dollar a question? He started down the first page, filled in circles with little thought, bent over the table. The air conditioner went on, spilling cool air over him. He didn't hear the hissing of gas coming from a tygon tube placed downstream from the compressor, didn't notice the musty odor, or the moth that suddenly dropped to the floor near his feet. He breathed deeply again. His throat seemed dry, scratchy, a little sore. He swallowed, and it was difficult, like his tonsils were swelling up. Another circle filled, he turned the page and it slipped from his fingers. A numbness in his fingertips moved quickly into his hands, and up both arms. Sweat burst forth on his face and forehead, he tried to speak, and heard a strange croaking sound. The glass eye of the camera looked down on him without emotion. He croaked again and tried to move, the numbness now in his chest and legs. The chair rattled once against the floor, then was silent. Willy's head flopped over against his shoulder, a little smile on his face as if amused by the wall he was staring at. The smile was an artifact, because by now Willy wasn't amused by anything; his brain had ceased to function above a primitive level. The reptilian complex was now in command from the base of his skull. Willy stared at the wall, recorded nothing: camera watching, air conditioner reversing to draw air from the room, the opening snap of the door, or the two men who entered to inspect their work.

"Shit," said Roy. "That dose should have protected an elephant."

Pete shook his head. "Not enough, I guess. The instructions must have been wrong. Either that, or the stuff isn't any good. We're not responsible for that. Straight from his mouth, Roy. He can't blame us."

"First, let's get rid of this," said Roy.

The two men lifted Willy like a drunken friend and carried him out to Pete's car. They drove through town and into the north woods, chatting as they traveled. Willy showed no interest in the conversation as he stared at the road ahead, chest slowly rising and falling. Roy looked back at him.

"The guy's still alive."

Pete chuckled. "That is a matter of opinion. Anyway, there'll be no doubt in a few minutes. He needs a bath; I nearly puked sitting next to him tonight." He called to Willy over his shoulder. "What do you think, pal? Time for a dip?"

"Where?" asked Roy.

"Burford Creek hit flood stage two days ago. County twenty is close ahead, now."

"It's spooky, Pete, the way the gas killed his brain, but not his body, you know what I mean? The junk I shot him up with did something right, I guess, but man, he has no brain! Next time I'll double the dose."

"Better do it fast, or we are going to be in big trouble," said Pete seriously. "The company has deadlines to meet." He turned the wheel sharply as they left the paved highway. Gravel crunched beneath tires, and birch and aspen trees were a canopy above them.

"I don't give a shit for deadlines, and I'm not taking the heat if they put us onto the wrong stuff. I'm no damn chemist, and neither are you. I've got enough left for double tonight's dose, and that's it, If that doesn't work, we've got the wrong stuff."

"Back to the bar," said Pete, and he braked the car to a halt at the edge of a steel bridge arching out before them. Twenty feet below, clear, cold water roared in cascades over boulders of granite, headed for the Mississippi river some sixty miles to the south. The bridge was open-framed, with one narrow walkway and a waist high hand railing. Spray filled their nostrils as they hauled Willy out of the back seat and dragged him over to the bridge, his toes making two little grooves in the gravel road. They leaned him against the railing like a wooden board while they retrieved the hundred dollar bill from his pocket, rested a moment, then Pete said, "Well, let's get on with it."

"Right," said Roy. "Bye, guy."

In one quick motion, they lifted Willy by his legs and flipped him over the railing, watching his slow forward gainer as he fell towards watery chaos, and then the explosive pop as his head hit a boulder, showering the rock with red and grey matter. His body slipped quickly beneath the water, and a few seconds later a foot bobbed briefly above the surface, already thirty yards downstream. The goo that had once been Willy Niven's dead brain quickly washed from the rock, leaving the environment clean and pure. Satisfied, Pete and Roy got back into the car, backed all the way out to paved highway and headed south.

They drove in silence for several minutes, then up ahead in the lights of the car was a figure walking at the edge of the road, heading in their direction. A kid: old clothes, light jacket on a cold night, hair down to his shoulders. Pete looked at Roy, smiled, and pulled over next to the walker.

"Need a ride to town?" asked Roy.

"Sure," said the kid, tired and bleary-eyed. "You're the first car I've seen for an hour." He climbed into the back seat, smelling of pine and sweat, and they took off again. Roy talked while Pete drove. Mike Dill, a runaway from Manitoba, no job, no food, no friends. Mike Dill was out to seek his fortune, which is hard to do with or without a work permit when you're fifteen years old.

Roy nodded sympathetically. "No money, huh Mike?"

The kid agreed. "gotta get enough somehow to get to Minneapolis or Chicago. Should be plenty of jobs there."

"Maybe we can help out," said Roy. "Do you know what I'm thinking about, Pete?"

"Sure," said Pete, as if he'd suddenly remembered something. "Hey, Mike, how'd you like to make a hundred bucks for just an hour's work?"

Mike thought that sounded pretty good.

CHAPTER ELEVEN

It was unseasonably warm for late April, the jet stream settled comfortably in Canada and pulling up warm air from the south. The lawns around the dormitories were littered with sunbathers, and even the most studious minds had paused to experience the blood-thawing warmth of a new spring. New couples walked together hand-in-hand across campus. Grass appeared with sudden green life, and birds staked early claims on old nests in the trees. For most people it was a time of happy anticipation: summer sports, fishing, boating, and the packing away of heavy winter clothing. For Karen Butler it was a pensive time. Something disquieting gnawed persistently at her stomach as she paced nervously back and forth beside her car.

Jack appeared at the dormitory door, wearing his khaki camouflaged uniform with cap and jump boots. A heavy-looking duffle bag was slung over his shoulder. He walked jauntily towards her, grinning at her grimness.

"All set, if your heap can take the weight. It is a six block drive."

Karen smiled weakly at his joke and opened the door of her little car. Jack crammed the duffle into the back seat and climbed in, banging the door shut with a tinny clang. They drove silently down the hill and through an awakening town bathed in the orange glow of a clear morning sun. They turned a corner, and the bus station was a block ahead when Karen broke the silence with a deep sigh.

"God, I feel awful. My stomach is tumbling all over itself."

"Too much pizza and beer last night," said Jack.

"That's not it. I'm apprehensive, like I'm about to take my doctoral exam. I know what it is, Jack. I'm afraid something's going to happen while you're gone."

"It's several weeks since any trouble," said Jack, and then he lied because it seemed right for the moment. "I hardly hear from Ebensack anymore."

"But after all this time, the people who stole the lab books must know the neuter formulas they have don't work. They must have tested them by now." The car had slowed to a crawl as they inched towards the bus station.

"Maybe they threw it away, and moved on. How could they know you found a neuter that worked? You only tested it once. I know, and so does Ebensack. Who else?"

"Doctor Reimer might have told someone."

"Possibly, but otherwise I don't see how anyone else could find out about it."

"If they did, Jack, they'd come after me, and they'd wait until you weren't around. That's what I'm nervous about."

Jack sighed. Ebensack's people were watching them constantly, and still she worried.

"You sure know how to wreck a guy's trip. Now I'll be thinking about you all the time. Well, I do that anyway, so I guess it's no problem."

"That's okay," she said, then pulled the nearly stopped car over to the curb and put the gear in neutral. "I want you to think about me." She leaned over and slipped her arms around his neck and kissed him until both of them were breathing hard.

Jack nuzzled her neck while she clung to him. "I don't think there's any room for you in my duffle bag, but we could try it."

"Call me, Jack. Please call me as often as you can."

"I will. We can't take cells, but I know there's a phone at the camp, and we'll have some free time. Call Arnie if anyone gives you trouble. He makes jokes about it, but that guy would gladly break bones for you, Karen. One call and he'll be over at your place in a minute. I mean it. If someone threatens you, call Ebensack, too. There are lots of people here to help you if you yell for it."

"I'll still miss you," she murmured.

"That's good," he said, and they kissed again. "On the other hand, if we don't hurry up you won't have to miss me because I'll miss my bus and be kicked out of Eagle Squad."

"Party pooper." She pouted, then released him and started the car. A fifty yard drive, and they reached a bus marked 'Charter' surrounded by young men in camouflaged uniforms and jump boots. Among them strolled a tall, slender man with grey hair and a tanned, chiseled face. He smiled, slapped an occasional shoulder, adjusted a collar or a button here and there like a hen inspecting her brood.

"Oh, who is that with the grey hair?"

"That is The Man. Colonel William Holleque," said Jack, making no effort to hide the admiration in his voice.

"He is a hunk," said Karen.

Jack chuckled. "He's old enough to be your father."

"I don't care. He's still a hunk, and, oh, God, he's coming over here!" Karen began adjusting her hair. Holleque had started towards the car in a precise, military stride. He came around to Karen's side of the car, leaned down and smiled at her before glaring at Jack.

"Pushing it pretty close, Nelson. Get your gear in the bus pronto. We're ready to leave."

"Yes sir," said Jack sharply, and he grabbed for the door. Karen looked at him, rolling her eyes in warning.

"Oh, sir, this is my girlfriend, Karen Butler."

"Nice to meet you, Miss butler," said Holleque, face close to hers. "Does this guy treat you properly?"

"Oh, yes," she said.

"Good," he said, and looked straight into her eyes in a way that made her forget to breathe for a moment. "I expect all my people to be gentlemen. After all, it's the women and kids we fight the wars for. Isn't that right, Nelson?"

"Yes sir," said Jack, suspecting that underneath the iron mask face, Holleque was having a good time with Karen, who seemed momentarily mesmerized, lost in a fog of musky aftershave.

Holleque stepped back when Jack came around to give Karen a goodbye peck on a warm cheek. "I'll call," Jack whispered, and she nodded with a smile that faded as he turned away. As he walked towards the bus, Holleque beside him, Jack heard the car start again and move quickly away.

"A very pretty girl, Nelson," said the Man, then almost as an afterthought, "very pretty indeed. A delight for anyone, I think."

Later, Jack decided it was the tone of Holleque's voice that had bothered him so much.

* * * * * *

The quick drive home was a mixture of loneliness and excitement for Karen, muddling her mind so much she nearly ran over a bicycle rider who slowed down ahead of her. His left arm was pointing to the side to make a left turn, and he pumped hard and fast to get out of her way.

Ignoring his angry shout she drove on up the hill to her apartment and went inside, opening curtains and a patio door to let in fresh air and sunlight to break up the gloom of empty rooms. She changed Morris' water bottle in the new cage she kept him in during the day, and played with him a while, pleased with his response to her petting and teasing. Just maybe his brain was continuing to heal, or was that wishful thinking? For the moment she felt as if all she had in the world was the little white rat, as he arched his back under the gentle caress of her fingers. Tears leaked onto her face, first a trickle, then a sobbing torrent. In a moment it was over, and her mind seemed to clear. She felt a little foolish, a grown child afraid to be alone, pining for her lover. How juvenile.

And the way she had reacted when Colonel Holleque leaned close to her. Surely he saw something in her face; she'd been shaking all over. Those blue-grey eyes saw her naked soul, she was sure of it, and his odor wasn't just cologne. It was the odor of a real man: dangerous, alive, ready for action. Oh yeah.

Karen giggled out loud. Jack's right; he is old enough to be my father. I don't care; he's still the most sensual man I've met lately. She put Morris into his box apartment in her panty drawer for the night, then went to the bathroom and stripped off her clothes. Jack's bus would be on its way by now. Yoo-hoo, Jack. See what you're missing? She inspected herself in the mirror while water ran in the tub, and liked what she saw. The air filled with steam, and she soaked herself languidly in the tub, nearly falling asleep before the telephone rang, and she suppressed the urge to answer it. Let it ring; this is my time. It rang ten times, then stopped. She added bath salts to the water and soaked some more, feeling slippery all over and very, very sexy. Finally she dried herself and put on a short terrycloth robe, then sat down on the little sofa in the living room to do her nails.

The telephone blared again, and she answered it.

* * * * * * *

Jack lay on his back, hands behind his head, and listened to the creaking and groaning sounds of old wood under stress as the barracks settled in for a cold night. Everyone had gone to bed soon after the bus arrived in pitch blackness, and they had silently followed the beam of Holleque's flashlight to their temporary quarters. On the bus, the colonel had announced a principal rule of the camp; they would not speak to each other in idle conversation during training, responding only to their officers when called upon to do so. They would learn to listen to every sound in the day or night, particularly night, and interpret each sound. The next week would be one of observation, concentration and stealth, as they learned the ways of covert warfare. Walking was forbidden, except on maneuvers. They ran everywhere they went. When they'd arrived at the camp they saw only dark silhouettes of fir trees and one tower, like a forest fire watch post, all of it inside a steel-mesh fence topped by rolls of barbed wire. Boy scout camp was never like this. They were herded straight into cold barracks headed by an even colder Sergeant Rodríguez, and now Jack lay on his back, staring at the ceiling and remembering the look on Karen's face when she met Colonel Holleque. The image kept him awake until three o'clock the next morning.

They were awakened at five.

One week can be a terribly long time when you are driven to the point of physical and mental exhaustion eighteen hours a day. The barracks was luxury accommodations, and they slept in it only two nights. The rest of the time they slept, when allowed, in wet underbrush swarming with biting insects, or down in muddy spider-traps with worms and millipedes waiting to strike the enemy which was themselves. They stalked each other in groups, day and night, setting up ambushes, learning to disperse in flanking counterattack units, and running routes designed to draw attackers away from predesignated targets. They ate cold food, drank brackish water, and learned to wipe their asses with dirty fingers when required. They worked in total silence, using only hand gestures, learned to listen for and interpret the slightest sound or odor, getting in touch with senses underused in a world of verbal and visual communication. They were all young, hard, finely tuned athletes dedicated to a military career. In three days, they were miserable.

On their third night maneuver Jack was on point for a group of seven students. Sergeant Rodríguez trailed along behind as observer. They had split up into three groups, Holleque taking one and the other led by a man Jack had never seen before. They had left the camp at dusk, going in different directions with orders to make a silent rendezvous at a point ten miles south at midnight. There they would bivouac before continuing exercises the following day. At twenty-three-hundred, Rodríguez had sent Jack out on point to locate a permanent rope bridge fixed over a creek ahead of them, and he was fifty yards ahead of the group when he heard a clicking to his right. He dropped into a crouch, turning in that direction. There was a muted popping sound, a flash in the trees, and a rushing of wind past his head like a small bird had flown close, then silence. Not quite. He listened hard, rustling leaves nearly obscuring a rhythmic crunch as someone scurried away among the trees. It suddenly occurred to Jack that whoever it was had just fired at him. What do I say? Hey, Sarge! Somebody just took a shot at me! Right, Jack. Didn't I tell you? This is a real war we're in. Now get back on point! He imagined the harsh voice, and was still in a crouch, adrenaline pumping. The squad was coming up behind him.

Jack lurched forward again, staying low, and forced himself not to run along the narrow trail lit ahead of him by occasional moonlight as clouds drifted overhead. In a minute he heard water tumbling over rock and quickened his pace, leaving the squad fifty yards behind. The trail ended in thick brush; he crashed through, and teetered on the edge of a small gorge filled with racing white water roaring in his ears. Jack glanced left, then right, gasping with surprise and some anger as he saw the rope bridge and the black figure crouched over low, moving catlike across it and disappearing into the brush on the other side of the torrent. He tiptoed along the edge of the gorge until he found a small beach just below the bridge, and jumped lightly down onto it. He pressed himself up against an embankment to stay out of the moonlight. His breath came in short, whistling gasps as fear tried to grab him, but there was little time for fear. At that moment the brush above him crashed forward and Sergeant Rodríguez was glaring down at him.

"What the hell are you doing down there, mister? We nearly walked off a god-damned cliff when we followed you back a ways." The voice was a whisper, but the anger was loud and clear.

Jack winced, and thought fast.

"Staying out of the moonlight, Sergeant. I thought I saw movement on the other side."

"That's crazy, Nelson. It's an hour before rendezvous, and we still have a quick-march to do. Get on it, now. Get across that bridge."

Oh, shit.

As he stepped onto the quaking bridge, Jack could imagine his body glowing like a candle-flame and centered in the electronic cross hairs of a sniper scope. The bridge swayed lightly beneath his feet, and he could feel the eyes of the squad examining his back. Get going, chickenshit. You're a beautiful target standing here.

He ran.

The bridge bounced in a crazy rhythm. The trail snaked up a steep embankment, disappearing at a dark edge with stars above it, and the bridge bounced again as the squad trotted across behind him. He moved up the trail, keeping low as he neared the top of the slope and then crawled a few yards in tall grass before chancing a look.

In front of him a buffalo-grass-covered hill ran gently downwards to a rectangular valley crisscrossed with shelter belts of birch, and in the center was a single light. In an instant, Jack knew it was the rendezvous point, and then he saw a second light strobing on another hill rising from the ridge he was on, two hundred yards to his right. He signaled with his flashlight, and two short flashes came back to him. Holleque's group. How long had they been waiting?

Rodríguez crawled up beside him, and grinned.

"Okay, mister, what now?"

"Down the hill."

"Wrong. Moon's behind us. We follow this ridge with our heads just below the top until we reach that gully over there, and then we follow the trees down. That way we don't get dead. Move it out."

Jack gave the hand signals and started a traverse just below the top of the ridge on their forward slope. They moved out quickly in a line, and reached the gully in a few minutes. Jack gave a hand signal, and turned to move downhill.

"No," said Rodríguez. "Keep going to the gully ridge, then follow it down."

Jack hesitated, puzzled.

"A little game the Colonel and I play, Nelson. Do it."

They traversed the gully, up to a scree ridge and over it, then downhill with Rodríguez shoulder to shoulder with Jack, the others trailing behind in blind obedience. When they were near the bottom, Rodríguez motioned to stop and moved them silently up to the ridge where they flattened out and looked over the edge to where the gully ended a few yards below them. Beyond the rocks was the trail Jack had started to take downhill, and behind each boulder, scattered along the wash beside the trail, there was a man waiting quietly. Jack turned towards Rodríguez, and saw only white teeth shining in the moonlight. The Sergeant signaled for them all to stand, and as they did he said in a loud voice, "Bang, bang, y'all are dead!"

There were cries of surprise below them, then nervous laughter. They met at the boulders, the midnight rendezvous of Eagle Squad. Colonel Holleque appeared at the edge of a shadow, death mask face blackened with grease. He walked up to them, looked first at Rodríguez and then at Jack. His thin lips drew back over teeth in a smile.

"Looks like I buy the beers tonight," said the Colonel in a friendly voice, but Jack felt a sudden, panicky urge to jump and run.

In his entire, young life, Jack Nelson had never seen such a dangerous expression on the face of any man.

* * * * * * *

It was a man, but his voice was an echo, somehow artificial, distorted. It was no human voice Karen had heard before.

"May I speak to Karen Butler, please?"

"This is she speaking."

"Ah, I'm glad I caught you so soon. We've never met, Miss Butler, but I've seen you around campus with Jack Nelson and, well, I know he just left on a military science field trip for a week, so I thought this would be a good time for us to have a little chat."

"Really? Who is this?" Karen asked coldly.

"Names aren't vital. And please don't hang up on me, Karen. It's important that you hear what I have to say."

"One foul word, and all you'll hear is dial tone."

"This isn't a heavy breather call, if that's what you think. It's business, for both you and Jack." The metallic voice was calmly serious.

"I'm listening," she said quickly.

"Good. I'll get right to the point. I'm a regional representative for a group of international businessmen who have a wide range of interests, particularly in emerging nations with relatively untouched natural resources. They are naturally concerned with the political stability of these countries, and often supply the weapons necessary to maintain this stability. It's often a disagreeable business, Miss Butler, and we have product delivery deadlines that must be met to avoid dangerous consequences. What I'm calling you about is one deadline that has not been met, and unfortunately you are involved."

"I don't know what you're talking about," said Karen sharply.

"Ah, but I think you do. You have something that belongs to us, and we have a nervous customer waiting for it. That something, as you might know, is a neutralizing agent for a nerve gas known as SB4. It was synthesized and tested successfully by you and your thesis advisor, Judith Reimer, who then sold it to us at a handsome price. We're requesting delivery of the product. Does this sound unreasonable to you?"

"You're the ones who attacked Jack and I in the hallway that night, aren't you? You're the ones who stole the notebooks. What nerve for you to call me."

"A regrettable incident, Karen, but it seemed necessary to obtain our property, and for a while we even thought we had it."

"You killed Doctor Reimer."

"Nonsense! She was a business associate. You'd do better to check up on her lovers; she was a most promiscuous woman with both sexes, as you might know."

"I don't know anything of the sort!" Karen said angrily.

"Whatever. The fact is she told us about the successful test right after it was performed, and then someone killed her, and now you have hidden both the neutralizing agent and its correct formulation, all this after we have paid for it. Surely you can understand our position? We only want what is ours."

"It isn't yours. The lab is government funded; everything belongs to them, patents, everything."

"A fine point, I'm sure. Doctor Reimer took our money, and now we want the neutralizer."

"But you have it. The formula was in the notebooks you stole."

"Please don't trifle with me, Karen. Testing of the formulae in those books has taken three human lives to date. Would you like us to continue?"

"Oh, my God," she said softly.

"We are serious people, you see, and there is a great deal of money involved. Please give me a time and a place for delivery."

"I can't do that," she said weakly.

"I beg your pardon?"

"It's not yours. I don't believe anything you've said to me, and besides, the government has taken both the formula and the small sample we had left over after the testing."

There was a long pause at the other end of the line, and Karen could hear rapid, shallow breathing.

"I have every reason not to believe you," said the man quietly, "but let's suppose for the moment that you have told me the truth. Let's suppose that you're not a foolish person; you really don't have the formula, or a sample. This leaves us in a very difficult position. You're the only person left alive who worked on the project with Doctor Reimer. It follows that you could use your skills and intelligence to reproduce the formula and a tested sample, and deliver these in the near future, say two weeks give or take a couple of days. I think we could even find it in our hearts to pay you a substantial sum for your efforts. I assume, of course, you weren't aware of our deal with Reimer. We appreciate accurate, fast work, Karen. Doctor Reimer was a valued associate, and I assure you we had nothing to do with her death. If you cooperate, in fact, I think I can find out who did kill her, and why. Can we work together on this?"

His voice was soothing, though tinny and somehow inhuman; she wanted to believe him very badly because she was alone and a little frightened, but she said, "I don't know why I should believe an unidentified voice on a telephone."

"I wish there was a way we could meet," he said quickly, "but I'm afraid I must remain a disguised voice to you. My clients prefer I keep a low profile in matters like this, but I do have authority delegated to me. For example, I can offer you ten thousand dollars to reproduce the formula for us. That's cash. Used bills. If you agree, I can have the money sent to you by tomorrow."

Karen gulped. To a research assistant, one third of that amount would keep her in groceries for a year. Do you remember what meat tastes like, kid? A new knot in her stomach reminded her of the hallway attack, a sad face looking up at her from a pile of debris on an office floor, and her anger returned with a rush.

"It would take me weeks to do what you want, and I have no reason to trust you." She could hear the weakness in her own voice.

"Twenty thousand dollars," he replied calmly. "I'll give you twenty thousand dollars for two weeks work, half now, the other half on delivery of the product. This is a most generous offer, Karen. Please consider it."

Her throat seemed paralyzed, and she made a little sputtering sound into the receiver before catching her breath enough to form a recognizable word. What she said was, "Please leave me alone. I can't help you."

"Think about it a while. It's a surprise, and Jack isn't here, and I'm sure it all sounds very mysterious to you. On the other hand, it's straightforward business to me, and I'm anxious to conclude it. I'll call you back again tomorrow afternoon, when you've had a chance to relax and think more clearly. Goodbye, Karen."

She hung up the telephone, sat down on a sofa and closed her eyes. In less than a minute she was nearly asleep, then suddenly sat bolt upright and rushed again to the telephone, dialing a number from memory.

Ebensack answered the call himself, chastised her for calling directly and reminded her about the library message drop. She told him about the caller, and they discussed strategies for several minutes. Finally he said, "Are you going to be all right? I can increase the watch on your apartment."

"No. They might spot that. Your people are good. I've never noticed them."

"They're close by, but not too close. You and Jack are always vulnerable, so keep your eyes open and don't use the phone in the future. It might get bugged."

"How do you know it isn't right now?"

"We checked your apartment out while you were at the bus station."

"Oh."

"Does that bother you?"

"No, not really. Right now, I feel better with big brother watching me."

Ebensack chuckled. "Take it easy, and use the library," he said, then terminated the call.

The rest of the day passed routinely with apartment cleaning and the washing of clothes, followed by three hours at her desk working on the first draft of her doctoral thesis. Karen felt some bitterness about work she didn't dare include. Wasn't a university a place for open research and public disclosure of results? A factory for new knowledge? It was until the results could be used by the military, and then the rules changed.

Had Reimer really sold out to someone? Maybe more than one customer? A double-cross? I don't think she was worldly enough to even conduct business that way. Ebensack seems nice enough, but his people came in here and went over the apartment. I know they will do anything necessary to get what they want, too. I wish Jack were here.

She mused the afternoon away, hunched over her desk. She turned on a lamp near dusk, and finished a chapter in her thesis before she slept.

The next afternoon, her telephone rang again.

It was the same voice, hollow and artificial like a computer talking, but a speech pattern somehow familiar as she listened to it again.

"You've had some time to consider my offer, Karen, and I'd appreciate a decision now."

"I still don't know," she said. "I have to talk to Jack, because this involves both of us. I can't make this decision without him."

"I wouldn't expect that from an independent woman like you, Karen. You disappoint me."

"Well, that's the way it is."

"I've explained my deadlines, which I must pass on to you. I don't like it, either, but delays of any kind are most undesirable."

"I still have to talk to Jack, and he's not here. Your timing is lousy."

"I know, I know. Just a moment."

There was a long pause, with background noise like static, or paper crinkling before the man spoke again. "I have a number here. Start calling it Tuesday evening, and keep trying until you get someone." He gave her a curious number with twelve digits. She wrote it down without question.

"They will put you in touch with Jack, and you can discuss this. At the same time I fear a warning is in order, because I detect a definite reluctance on your part to cooperate with us, and you are vital to what we want."

"Are you threatening me?" she asked curtly.

"Not you, not now, but someone else. Yes. Someone you love dearly, I'm afraid."

"Jack," she said softly.

"Just a warning, this time, and there will only be one. You can talk about all that on Tuesday, or you can decide to work with us now and nothing will happen. Which is it, Karen?"

He had pressed too hard, and now she was angry again. Her

answer was instinctive, from the heart, and not well thought out.

"You can go to hell!" she said. "Jack and I will make the decision, and if you even hurt him you can forget about my ever helping you."

"Now, now," he said soothingly, as if speaking to a child. "I think you should sleep on that, and look at both sides of the issue. This can be very profitable for you and Jack if you'll let it happen. Please think of it in positive terms, Karen, because we really want to work with you, and there's nothing illegal about making money with science, is there?"

"You will have to wait," she said through clenched teeth.

"Very well, until Tuesday night, then. We all have to live with our decisions. Goodbye, Karen."

As the line went dead, she wanted to call him back, her anger subsiding as fear, anxiety, and a terrible feeling of guilt flooded over her, but it was too late. Whatever they did to Jack would be her fault, and what could she do to prevent it without giving in to their demands? She dialed the number the caller had given her, again and again. At first it was busy, but then there was no answer.

She put down the telephone, and burst into tears.

* * * * * * *

In a large stone house four blocks from Karen Butler's apartment, Curtis Lundeman sat alone in his bedroom, talking on the telephone. When the call was finished, he turned off the amplifier and multiplexer units he had used to disguise his voice, then placed a call to Holleque. His instructions were specific: something subtle, but enough to provoke fear. There was to be no physical harm of any kind. It should be done before Tuesday. Yes, she would call that evening. Any call before that should go unanswered. Let her sweat a little.

He hung up the phone, and sighed deeply. He hated working with thugs like Holleque. Giving pain and fear to people was not pleasurable to him, going against everything he had been taught by a God-fearing mother who also believed in the dignity of human beings. Why didn't she also teach him to avoid the big and the powerful, the money-makers? He was caught up in something from which there seemed no escape, but something that could make him very wealthy, and after a long, poorly paid academic career he wanted that badly enough to even sacrifice the principles he had learned as a child.

He sighed again, then opened the briefcase that sat on the floor next to his desk chair, and took out a yellow legal pad. There was some scribbling on the top page, and he stared at it for a while, frowning and writing marginal comments. He looked up when there was a soft rapping at the bedroom door.

"Curtis? Can I bother you for a moment?"

"Certainly. Come in."

Irene glided into the room; a shock wave of perfumed air proceeded her by a yard. "the girls wanted to see the brooch mother gave me last Christmas; you know, the big cameo?" She rummaged around in her jewelry box until she found the piece. "They're quite taken with this," she said in amazement. "I don't have the heart to tell them I think it's horrid."

Curtis laughed. "When will this hen party be over?"

"Very soon," she said, watching his eyes move over her.

"Join me for a drink?"

"Champagne would be nice, in here."

"Whatever madam wishes," he said.

She left the room, closing the door behind her. Curtis moved the legal pad in front of him on the desk. The speech to The League of Women voters was only a week off, and he was just getting around to it. He had decided to summarize his views on the need for military research in a democratic society. He thought for a moment, then leaned over the yellow pad and began to make notes.

CHAPTER TWELVE

They set up their tents in an open field by the rendezvous point, and went to sleep. In no time at all, Sergeant Rodríguez was kicking at the tents, telling them to have everything torn down and packed in fifteen minutes. Without the moon it was even darker than when they had gone to sleep.

When the sun peered over the horizon, they had already marched eight miles and were resting in a grove of birch trees, silently eating a cold meal of something that looked like sand and tasted like grainy cheese. "Up and on!" yelled Rodríguez, and they moved out in the same groups as the night before, diverging from a line heading towards the morning sun.

The sweating, and the biting flies, began.

They made a forced march of eight miles without a break, rested fifteen minutes, then did another six miles. Rodríguez moved without effort, regarding with silent distain their pain and agony. They said nothing, pride and ego forcing them ahead until their feet were shuffling heavily over the ground, and there was no feeling remaining in their arms or shoulders. Eyes stared vacantly at the dust ahead, faces of zombies moving together to a silent drum beat until finally, at a swampy grove of maple and birch trees at the base of a grassy hill, Rodríguez motioned them to stop.

"Ten minutes. No smoking, no talking. Keep your eyes open," he said, and his eyes were darting around the perimeter of the grove as he spoke. Jack sat on his haunches, watching the man's eyes, ready to jump. Beside him, a kid named Jerry flopped down luxuriously on his back, then sat up and started tugging off his boots.

That's when the shooting began.

It sounded like firecrackers going off up on the hillside, but then small tree branches began falling, and there were explosions on the ground all around them.

"Holy shit!" shouted someone. That's live ammo!"

"Shut up, and take cover!" screamed Rodríguez, and he stood like a monument in the middle of chaos, bodies flying in every direction, bullets ricocheting near his boots, his hands on hips, snarling.

"Go, go, go, go!"

Jack landed in the swamp face first, hands buried in slimy vegetable matter and mud. He wanted badly to puke, but when bullets tore up the water around him his face was quickly back in the slime and his hands were digging frantically. This seemed to go on for a long time, although later he realized it was only for a few seconds, and then there was sudden silence except for coughing and water splashing, and someone mumbling loudly.

"Get me a loaded M-16 and I'll kill those mother-fuckers."

Jack peered out of the water like a crocodile and saw Rodríguez standing in front of him, back turned, looking carefully up the hill with binoculars. When he turned around, he was frowning angrily.

"All right, girls, it's over. On your feet. Nelson, Evanson, and Ash, good instincts, good cover. The rest of you are dead meat. When fired upon, you do not present a profile by hiding behind bushes or a small tree. You get down flat, people, even if it's mud or swamp, or a lake of shit. Do you hear me?"

"Yes, Sergeant," they screamed in unison.

"In combat, many of you would now go home in a pine box, and I would have to write letters to your mothers and girlfriends. I don't like to write letters!"

The chewing out went on for another minute while they sat there wet, cold, and shaking. So it had been a drill, thought Jack, but the bullets were real enough, and for a moment they had been very close to real death. He remembered being told that students had been killed in the past. Was this how it happened? A wrong move, at the wrong time? Our apologies, Missus Nelson, but your son died sucking swamp water in a class on how to be a soldier. No more birthday parties. Sorry.

Later, when they climbed the hill, Jack saw concrete-lined dugouts and fixed gun emplacements from which controlled fire had been directed at them. The emplacements were empty when they passed by.

They never saw the people who were shooting at them.

Two hills and a short march later, hard ground turned to orange rock with purple shadows. They came to a paved, winding road ending at a cluster of wooden buildings surrounded by a twelve foot cyclone fence with a metal sign announcing 'U.S. Government property. Keep Out.' To emphasize this message, two uniformed, armed guards accompanied by sleek German Shepherds patrolled the perimeter, watching carefully the exhausted people who passed their positions. For one glorious, fleeting moment, Jack thought they might spend the night in real beds, but they kept moving until they reached a small plateau overlooking the buildings, and Rodríguez screamed at them to set up their tents. In fifteen minutes they were flopped on top of bed rolls to air out aching feet, dozing.

Jack was drifting, drifting into a warm, pleasant land filled with the odors of barbequed steak and baking bread, but then someone started kicking the bottom of his feet. His feet! He came back reluctantly, opening his eyes a crack, and there was Rodríguez thumping away at him with a boot. Thump, thump. "Nelson, wake up," he said softly, but then more thumping.

"We moving out already?" Jack asked groggily, and the Sergeant smiled.

"No, but you have a phone call."

"A phone call?" Jack was wide awake, now. "Where?"

"Down the hill. Go to the gate, and give your name. You're expected. Your daddy a general, or something?"

"My dad's a farmer."

Rodríguez shook his head. "Well, somebody knew how to get hold of you out here. Better get going, before they hang up."

Jack scrambled from the tent and shouldered past the dark-skinned man who looked like he wanted to ask another question, but had decided to postpone it. Even as he walked away, he felt the human presence behind him. Ahead, the way was illuminated by flood lights that had been turned on inside the compound. Gravity pulled him in lengthening strides down the hill and to the gate, a sentry, a name tag, a dark look. A large, silent dog held firmly on a short leash regarded him with yellow eyes. Jack gave his name, the man pointed to an open door, brightly lit beyond, and as Jack went through the gate he felt as if bugs were crawling all over him. In the heavy silence his boots made loud crunching sounds on loose gravel. He looked nervously around him, and caught a glimpse of a face at a window, a startled look turning away, gone. Tom Mason? Where the hell has he been hiding?

The room was an office of some kind, with file cabinets around the walls, a desk and three chairs. Nothing more except the single bare light bulb hanging from the ceiling, and on the desk a telephone. No field phone here; the line must be underground. No books, papers, pictures, even a pencil, anywhere. He sat down at the desk and picked up the receiver.

"Hello. This is Jack Nelson."

He swallowed hard when he heard her voice.

"Karen! How in hell did you find me? I was going to call you later in the week."

"Oh, Jack, are you all right? I've been going out of my mind with worry, and they wouldn't answer the phone. Has anything happened to you?"

Her voice was nearly hysterical, which frightened him, but he heard himself laughing nervously at her.

"Well, I've marched a hundred miles, slept in a swamp and been shot at, but otherwise everything's fine. How about you?"

In a torrent of words, she told him everything.

His smile faded, lips stretching into a grimace. There was a shooting pain in his head as he crushed the receiver against an ear. He heard her words, and felt anger, guilt, remorse, tenderness, love, then anger again, all in an instant.

"Hey, hey," he said softly. "I'm okay, really. Nothing has happened, but I'm pooped. The training is realistic and tough, like I knew it would be. And I'm learning stuff."

"You're sure? You're not holding back something are you, Jack? I'm not a baby."

"No, no, everything's fine here. Look, it was a threat to make you cooperate. Why don't you do it?"

"What? Make a new sample? Why would I—"

Oh, baby, I hope you're thinking clearly.

"Really. The money's good, and anyway, we don't have the formula. Ebensack took everything. You know the chemistry to figure it out, if they'll be a little patient. Give 'em what they want."

There was a pause. He could almost hear the gears turning in her head. Karen had scribbled copies of the formula in several places, one sample of the neuter still stored in Reimer's locker along with the other chemicals for her thesis and the nano studies. She had indeed given a large sample to Ebensack, along with all the remaining laboratory books she had. The bad guys had undoubtedly arranged this conversation, and had to be listening to it. Someone in eagle Squad or its organization must be involved.

"But I called Ebensack," she said, "and he—"

"He's a federal cop, Karen. Good thing he isn't listening to this. They want the neutralizer all to themselves, and for what? So the feds can sell it! Where's your capitalist spirit, and how will they even know if someone else has the formula? For all we know, the secret is already blown. Sell it while you can."

Silence at the other end of the line. Oh, God, let her understand, he thought. And when she spoke again, she was calm, as if she had finally decided on a course of action.

"Maybe you're right. I can't do it in two weeks, but they might give me more time if I'm close to finishing. He'll call me back sometime tonight. I could ask."

"There you go! Hey, we can have a time with twenty thousand dollars." Jack chuckled.

Her voice was flat, her words precisely spaced. "I've been silly about this. It scared me, that's all. I'm glad he gave me the number so I could talk to you, Jack. It all seems okay, now, but I miss you. Hurry back to me."

"I will, kitten. I love you." And I am so proud of you, he thought.

"I love you, too. I'll get to the lab tomorrow, and start the chemistry I can remember. If I work real hard, I won't miss you quite so much. See you in a few days."

The sentry and massive dog watched him sullenly as he left the office, crunched across the compound and climbed the hill to his camp. As he walked, Jack thought of a flash in the night, a rush of wind and, later, bullets churning up the water around him. A warning? Or did someone also want him to be dead?

Despite exhaustion, he slept poorly that night.

* * * * * * *

Rodríguez watched the night, and smoked a cigarette. The camp had been quiet since Nelson returned, and the exhausted young people now slept. He strolled between the tents until he reached the edge of camp, where a large command tent had been set up. The entrance flap was pulled to one side, and he could see Holleque sitting at a wooden table, working by the light of a kerosene lantern. He stepped up to the entrance and cleared his throat before leaning forward into the light.

"Can I bother you for a minute, sir?"

Holleque looked up sharply. "Come in, come in, Sergeant. I was just finishing up. Like a cup of coffee?"

"Thank you, sir."

"Trade me a cigarette for it?" The colonel reached out a hand, and Rodríguez handed him the pack. Holleque lit the cigarette with a wooden match, handed back the pack and exhaled luxuriously. "So, how was your day?"

"Pretty good, but there's a lot of tired young people out there tonight. All in all, they're coming along. They can be men when they have to be. Funny thing tonight, though; I guess Jack Nelson's girlfriend can't get enough of him. She called him about an hour ago."

Holleque looked at him curiously. "Which phone?" he asked.

"Down in the compound. One of the guards came up to get him; said it was his girlfriend."

Holleque smiled. "Have you seen her?"

"Yes, sir," said Rodríguez, grinning back at him. "I wonder how she knew the number to call here?"

The colonel dismissed his question with the wave of a hand. "Who knows? Maybe the department secretary gave it to her. Did he seem okay when he got back to camp? Worried, or anything?"

"Nothing I noticed. He went right to sleep."

Holleque poured two cups half-full of coffee from a thermos bottle, and handed one to Rodríguez. "Hot, and black. Want something in it?" He gestured at a full pint of Jim Beam next to the thermos, and the Sergeant nodded. Holleque added a splash of bourbon to each of their cups, then leaned back in his chair and took a sip. "Sit and relax, Sergeant. You look tense tonight."

Rodríguez sat down. "Not really, sir. A little worried, though. Something's been on my mind most of the day." He sipped his coffee and bourbon thoughtfully, hesitating to say more.

"Part of my job is listening to people's problems, Sergeant. Spit it out."

It was quiet, and they were two friends sharing a drink in a warm, dimly lit tent. The thought had nagged at Rodríguez all day, and he needed to dump it.

"Well, it's about the drill at the swamp this afternoon, hill fourteen, where we put in the auto-fire pattern at tree level."

"Yeah, I worked that location the last time out. What about it?"

"There are only two manned emplacements on that hill, for

directed fire, and one of them nearly killed Jack Nelson and me today, sir."

Holleque's eyes narrowed. "Which one?" he asked softly.

"Number two, up high, with twin M16's, but only one of them was firing. I checked the duty roster, sir. Tom Mason was on that position today. His fire was too close, and too sustained. He was banging away after the autos had shut down, and his fire was directed at Nelson, who was face down in the swamp. He didn't stop until I looked up at him, and I was in his target area."

"Did Nelson complain?"

"Not a word, sir."

"Good. Don't say anything to him about it, and I'll have a talk with Mason. Some of the pro-boys get a little gung-ho at times, and I still want to keep them away from the students. Is that being enforced?"

"Ever since you cut the order, sir."

"No contact at all?"

"Not even by sight. The regulars are confined to barracks while we're here."

Holleque nodded, smiling over his raised cup. "People problems," he said. "Another drink?"

"No thanks, sir. I'd better get some sack time myself, so I can run them good tomorrow." He stood up, put his cup on the table, then saluted sharply. Holleque returned it slow and relaxed.

"Good night, Sergeant."

"Good night, sir." Rodríguez turned on a heel, and walked into the darkness.

The colonel poured a last cup of coffee, added a generous volume of bourbon to it, and drank it down quickly. He stared at the darkness for several minutes, then retrieved a commando knife from his field pack. Both edges had been honed razor sharp, and he kept the weapon in a custom-made Teflon-lined sheath. He shoved sheath and knife into his right boot, then put on a light jacket and slipped out of the tent into the quiet and serenity of a starlit night. He padded through the camp, knees bent, staying on soft ground until he hit gravel near the gate at the bottom of the hill. The young guard at the compound gate suddenly saw and recognized him. The gate opened, and Holleque stopped close to the guard, breathing fumes on him. "That was a slow reaction, mister," he said between clenched teeth. "You could be a dead man."

The young man swallowed hard, and stared at him. "Yes, sir," he said, voice quavering.

Holleque glared at him, then crunched gravel to the office where Jack had made his phone connection. He went inside, turned on the bare light, crossed the room and unlocked another door with a skeleton key. Inside a closet-sized space he turned off a recorder monitoring all phone conversations, rewound it for several seconds, then plugged himself into the machine with a pair of earphones and turned it on again. He listened to the entire conversation, and chewed thoughtfully at his lower lip as he rewound the machine once more. He went to the phone and dialed a number. Lundeman answered immediately.

"The girl called this evening," said Holleque. "I'm sending the recording to your machine."

"Did she sound scared?" asked Lundeman.

"See for yourself. She seemed to recover pretty quick. These are smart kids. Better be careful with them. I have a gut feeling they might be stalling for time. This is taking too long. When are you going to let me handle things?"

"Probably never," said Lundeman. "All you know is brute force. Just stick to customer relations, Holleque. I'll do the rest."

"Better do it quick. Our customers are getting nervous, and I'm the first one they'll come after if you screw up. I won't wait much longer."

"You'll all wait as long as I tell you to do so," said Lundeman. "Now. Send me that recording, and remember your place in this organization."

The line went dead. Holleque took a pencil from a table, snapped it neatly in two, and ground his teeth together. Arrogant prick. Didn't Lundeman realize that he and his bitch wife could be snuffed out in an instant?"

Holleque saved the recording to another disk, then PC, and sent it wireless to Lundeman's office at his home. He smoked a cigarette, switched the recording machine back to record, locked it up and turned out the lights before leaving. The cigarette was snuffed out between his fingers and placed in his pocket.

Outside again, in shadow, he took a deep breath and exhaled slowly. When he moved between buildings there was no sound, even on loose gravel. He moved to the door of a building, and opened it silently in one motion, closing it behind him in the darkness as irises expanded to collect light reflected onto the fifteen sleeping men there. He moved over the open floor space between the bunks until he reached a place beneath an open window where a young man with sharp, Teutonic features lay on his side, snoring softly.

Holleque stepped up beside the bed, leaned over to slide the knife from his boot. He sat lightly on the edge of the hard mattress, and touched the man's jugular vein with the point of the blade.

"Tommy," he whispered, and the man's eyelids flickered. "Wake up, Tommy."

The eyes opened. The man saw and felt both the blade and the glinting cat's eyes in the dark form above him.

"Don't move, Tommy, or you'll bleed a lot. You've been a bad boy, you know. You haven't followed orders again, son. You need to concentrate harder, listen harder, so you won't foul up."

The blade tip punched a tiny hole in the flesh, and blood began to ooze from it. The man winced, but made no sound.

"Oh, that's good. Good control. I won't kill you, Tommy. Not now. But if you foul up again, I'll ship you back to your Nicaraguan colleagues in a trash bag. When I tell you to scare Jack Nelson, you will scare him and not try to kill him, and you will not endanger the life of my aide ever, ever again." Holleque lifted the blade from the man's neck.

"Sweet dreams," he said, then floated into the darkness, and there was a quick flash of light as the door opened and closed.

The man who called himself Tom Mason lay on his cot,

rubbing two fingers across a sore neck. He put them to his mouth, and tasted salty blood, then relaxed and contemplated his good luck in still being alive.

Outside, Holleque moved in shadows between the buildings towards the back of the compound, then sprinted to the fence in full floodlight and went over the twelve foot obstacle without a jingle, using an overhang strut to bypass barbed wire at the top, and doing a forward roll as he hit the ground. As the guard adjusted the collar of his dog, whose ears had suddenly gone up, the founding father of Eagle Squad sprinted up the dark hill beyond the lights of the compound, grinning with the pleasure of his exertion and skill, and padding back through the darkness to his tent.

Nobody heard him, and the guard wondered what had become of Colonel William Holleque that night.

CHAPTER THIRTEEN

Cold Wind turned to warm breeze from the south, and new sounds burst forth from the north woods. Rock music blared from loudspeakers hanging from dormitory windows to entertain the worshippers of the sun. As Karen crossed the campus, a Jell-O-wrestling contest was noisily underway at the center of the crowded quad. Two lithe coeds in bikini remnants grappled on and off their feet in a giant plastic tub of orange goo, and within a few minutes representatives of fraternities had joined them while the crowd screamed encouragement. Karen watched for a few minutes, and a clown with white face and big feet gave her a balloon on a long string. The balloon was orange, with black letters spelling out SPRING BLAST, and she let it drift along with her to the chemistry building. She tied it to a bicycle rack before going inside. The building was dark and empty. It was a Saturday morning, and spring, and beautiful. She trudged up the stairs, thinking about Jack. Another day and a half, and he'd be back. She was confident of that; they wouldn't do anything to him now, unless they wanted to reproduce the formula on their own.

The calls came every day at the same time, while she was at the lab. The money had arrived as promised the morning after she had talked to Jack, with a friendly note explaining the call had been monitored. She was not surprised, and deposited the money, all used twenties, in a new account. Ebensack had been informed about it, and she had also recorded her conversation with him. She had begun to feel that she and Jack were only pawns in a dangerous game, and she no longer trusted the federal man with their safety. She'd remembered the correct chemistry even before checking her scattered notes, had made up a large batch of tested neuter and stored much of it in falsely labeled bottles on laboratory shelves. The rest of the time was spent on her own thesis work, now nearing completion. She had retrieved the rack of chemicals stored in Reimer's locker in order to use the samples of nano-assemblers it contained from her earlier work. She stored it above the ceiling panels at the end of each day. And the debate on what to do with Reimer's horrible nanomite disassemblers had already begun in her mind.

Karen kept the lab door shut tight, hid all her chemicals above one of the ceiling panels in Reimer's old office where she did much of the work. She hoped they would all underestimate the powers of a thinking woman, and as it turned out they did not disappoint her. Absorbed in her work, she forgot about how much she missed Jack, until the end of a long evening when she would return to the silent apartment to play with Morris while she listened to sad and lonely music.

The next day was the same routine, with the same call at four in the afternoon.

VOICE: "Do you have it yet?"

KAREN: "I'm getting close, but it's still not working right. The gas causes a moderate paralysis, but it's not killing."

VOICE: "I can get you some help."

KAREN: "It will only slow things up. I don't have time to train an assistant."

VOICE: "Good news. I've been authorized to give you another two thousand if you deliver within the week."

KAREN: "That's fine with me. It'll be soon."

VOICE: "It's nice working with you, Karen. Maybe we can work out a permanent arrangement."

And then on that Saturday afternoon, before Jack returned, she was startled by a second call, this time from the chairman's office. The chairman wished to visit with her right away, if it was convenient. Oh God, she thought, while hiding all her chemicals above the ceiling, they want to know what I'm doing in here. My thesis work is nearly finished, along with everything else I have to do for the degree, and here I am, working day and night.

She thought about cover stories as she walked down the dimly lit hallway. There had been some anomalies in an experiment, so she was doing a statistical treatment of the data. Or, some of the rats had developed erratic behavior weeks after supposedly successful tests, so she was doing a new synthesis to see if that could be improved. That made more sense, because anyone could smell the chemicals she was using.

She entered the department office, but it was empty. The secretary had left a note for her, which said to go into the conference room and wait for a few minutes. She did so, closed the door and settled herself comfortably at the end of an enormous, oak table.

A moment later the door clicked open, and a familiar face peered into the room.

"Good afternoon," said Ebensack, smiling coyly. He saw the quick anger in her eyes, and in the curl of her mouth.

"I was supposed to see the chairman," she said curtly.

"And so here you are," said Ebensack, settling himself in a chair next to her. "We need to talk, and this room is secure. In a few minutes you'll be back at work for whoever it is you're working for. Wouldn't it be nice if we knew who it is? Actually, I have a pretty good idea who your regular caller is, but the scrambler he's using will make voice print identification subject to devastating debate in a courtroom." He smiled, looking pleased. "One of the many challenges of my job."

"You've tapped my phone," said Karen, "without telling me."

"Of course. We wanted your conversation to be natural, uninhibited, particularly with Jack. I think he has been a very lucky young man on this field trip. He was quite guarded on the phone, don't you think? Didn't want you to worry about him. Of course you're helping them now, so there's probably no danger to either one of you for the present time. Jack did tell you to be cooperative. Are you making good progress?" The man leaned back in his chair, resting his chin on folded hands, awaiting her answer.

"I don't even know why we're having this conversation," said Karen sullenly. "You seem to know everything that's going on."

"Perhaps," said Ebensack, "but I'm not certain about that. Karen, I'm trying to catch the person or persons who murdered your thesis advisor. You want that, don't you?"

"Of course," she said angrily.

"I just want to be sure we're working in the same direction," he said softly, but his expression was that of concern, and he began to drum fingers of one hand on the table.

"I'm doing what Jack told me to do," she said. "Why don't you talk to him about it?"

"I will, Karen. My concern is that you'll panic, and help the other side. My hope is you'll trust me and my organization to protect both of you until these people are rounded up."

"You can help by giving me back some of the neuter that didn't quite work. You have the records for that. The good stuff was easy. They might think I'm stalling them, and then there could be bad trouble, and I don't think you'll be able to stop it. That's what you can do."

Ebensack looked at her thoughtfully for a moment. "You reproduced the correct formula?"

"Yes, I did."

There was a long silence, with Ebensack looking straight into her eyes, and she exerted all her willpower to keep from looking away from him. Finally, he said, "I'll see what I can do. Tell Jack there will be a message for him Monday afternoon."

"What does that mean?"

"He'll understand."

"You have some kind of an agreement with Jack, don't you?"

"Now Karen."

"Why can't I know what you're telling Jack?"

"Please trust me."

"Oh, shit," she said. "I'm going back to work." She stood up, and started towards the door.

"We'll be watching," said Ebensack.

"I bet you will," she snarled, and slammed the door behind her. Fuming, she marched down the hallway and rattled the glass in her laboratory door when she slammed that too. Glaring at an animal cage, she asked a startled rat, "Can you think of anything worse than a condescending man?" The animal looked curiously at her, and twitched his whiskers.

She worked the rest of the afternoon and early evening, and made some progress on her new assemblers. That night she took the rack containing her thesis products and Reimer's terrible creation home with her, and put it behind books on a shelf in her apartment. She was certain that Ebensack's people had searched her apartment, but not her lab yet. The work represented in that rack was hers, not the feds, and she intended it to stay that way.

* * * * * * *

Karen watched from her car when the bus pulled in, and a line of tired young men filed out of it. Jack was near the end of the line, looking rumpled and bleary-eyed. She honked the horn; he saw her, and waved. Colonel Holleque said something to him, then smiled at Karen over his shoulder, and a little shudder oscillated up and down her body. How can a man be so sexy and evil-looking at the same time? And from a distance, yet.

Jack threw his duffle into the back seat, then slid in beside her and kissed her long and soft until she was humming. As she started the car, he collapsed back into the seat. "God, I am so tired. I'm going to sleep for a day."

They pulled away from the bus, and Karen saw Holleque watching them. "You guys looked like zombies coming off the bus."

"Yeah, but we were in step," he said, smiling and looking

over at her. "How're you doin'?"

"Fine, now. I've been worried about you."

"I was a little worried about me, too," he said.

"Oh, Jack, what have we gotten into?" Her knuckles turned white as she gripped the steering wheel.

"Nothing we can't handle."

"Oh, right. What happened on the trip, Jack? Did you really get shot at?"

He leaned back, closing his eyes. "Twice. Probably just part of the exercises."

"And you think we're in control of the situation?"

"For now, yes. They need you to get the formula, but once they have it we've got a new ballgame."

"Well, they don't have it yet, because I've been ordered to stall them in the lab, and the guy keeps calling, and then yesterday Ebensack snuck up on me at work and practically accused me of collaborating with the enemy. God, that made me mad."

Jack frowned. "He said he wouldn't contact us directly again until everything was over."

"Of course not, since he has his private contacts with you," she said sarcastically. "By the way, I'm to tell you there will be a message for you Monday afternoon. You will know what that means; I'm not mature enough to be given such important information."

"He doesn't want to worry you," said Jack defensively.

"Naturally. I might get hysterical, and hurt myself. Isn't that what you mean?" When Jack sat bolt upright in the seat, she knew she had his attention. "Well, let me tell you, Jack Nelson, when I have to I can handle any situation this ridiculous world can throw at me." She turned to glare at him, but didn't when she saw his smile.

"All you're doing is turning me on," he said gently. "You can be soft and dependent, like a little girl, but you're something else when you're pushed."

"Is that one of your subtle compliments?"

"Yeah it is. I like you that way. It takes some of the pressure off of me."

They drove in silence for a moment, and then Karen said, "I never thought about it that way." Jack, nearly asleep, regarded her with half-opened eyes, and then they were pulling up in front of his dormitory, and he was kissing her again.

"Pick me up at six, and I'll buy you a pizza."

"Sounds good," she said. "Now, go to sleep."

"Yes, missy," he said, then got out of the car and pulled his duffle out through the open window. She drove away, and watched him in the rear-view mirror as he dragged the duffle forlornly up the walkway to the dorm, and a soft bed. Part of every man is a baby, she decided.

The drive home was quick, and as she opened her apartment door, the telephone started ringing.

* * * * * * *

"Another call," she said to Jack over the giant combo-pizza in front of them. "And this time, the guy didn't sound friendly. He said I was stalling until you got back, and that he'd better get delivery in the next couple of days."

Jack talked with his mouthy half-filled with pizza. "No threats?" he asked with difficulty.

"No. That will probably happen in a couple of days. I have what they want, Jack. What do I do now?"

He chewed thoughtfully, then said, "Keep working at the lab, and I'll see what Ebensack has to say tomorrow."

But a waiter suddenly appeared at their table, and put down two sealed envelopes in front of them. "The world is getting weird," he said. "Some little kid just gave me five bucks to give these to the young couple in the corner. That's you."

"Thanks," said Jack, shrugging his shoulders. The waiter stuffed the money in his shirt pocket and walked away smiling. There were names on the envelopes, and Jack handed one to Karen. "One for you, and one for me."

They opened the envelopes, reading the contents in silence.

"Ebensack," said Jack.

"He worked fast," said Karen, surprised. "This will really help." She held a sheet of paper close to her face, studying it. "It's close. Jack, I've got to get to the lab."

"Hold on. Hold on. Listen to what he says here." Jack read his note in a near whisper.

"Jack: I've given Karen a version of the neuter formula dangerously close to the real thing. I'm going to start pressing buttons, now, so be careful, both of you. Forget the library drop. Any trouble at all, call me at 285-2236. E."

"Let's go," said Jack. He crammed one last slice of pizza in his mouth and paid the check. Karen drove them the three blocks to the edge of campus, where they found a meter space for free on a Sunday evening. They hiked across campus to the chemistry building. Karen let them in with her key, and in a minute she was scurrying around the lab looking for chemicals, while Jack watched passively from a chair by Reimer's old desk.

"Is there something for me to do?" he asked.

"Just keep me company," she said excitedly, and all the time she worked, hunched over the laboratory bench in Reimer's office, she was mumbling to herself. The mad scientist at work, thought Jack, but he loved this one. He amused himself by rummaging around in the desk, found nothing more exciting than two candy wrappers and an unopened roll of antacid tablets. Karen left the room briefly, and returned with her purse. At the bench, she put something into it, snapped it shut, then poured a cloudy but colorless liquid into a small vial and held it up to the light. "Doesn't look quite right, but how can they know what it's supposed to look like?"

"Whatever you say, Doctor."

She picked up the vial and her purse, and walked to the door. "I'm going to run a live test on this stuff. Please stay here while I do it. Okay?"

"I'll be right here, thinking deep thoughts, Doctor."

Karen rolled her eyes, and closed the door behind her. She remained in the outer laboratory for nearly an hour while Jack dozed in the chair, and when she opened the door again she was scowling.

"Anything wrong?"

"I don't know," she said. "Come see for yourself."

Jack yawned, and arose slowly from the chair. He followed Karen to where she had been working inside a glove box. She tapped a finger on the thick-glass window of the box. "Inside," she said.

Jack looked, saw a yellow light, an open cage with a very alive rat eating food pellets, and around the outside of the cage, scattered bits of broken glass. "I see a live, hungry rat," he said, as if bored by it all.

"Very much alive, which is fine except that I gave him one heck of a dose of nerve gas nearly an hour ago. Surely Ebensack doesn't want us to give these people the right stuff?"

"He said it was close. Maybe they won't bother to wait for results like you're doing. They'll set up a demo for a customer, quick test, quick sale."

"With a human subject for sure. They'll test it on a person, Jack. I don't like it."

"Wait and see what happens," he said.

They watched the rat off and on for two more hours, and when they left the animal seemed alert and hungry again. When they returned the following morning, they found it twisted pathetically in a puddle of its own excrement, quite dead.

* * * * * *

"I finally got it, last night," said Karen on the telephone. The call had arrived at the usual time.

"You're certain, are you?" asked her caller. Again, there was something familiar about the way he arranged words. Where had she heard that before the phone calls?

"I've done animal tests: all positive, no paralysis. I have the formula, two ounces of material, and a dose rate according to body weight made up. When do you want it?"

"I'll check on that, and call you at home tonight."

"I'll be there."

"Good, and there will be another two thousand dollars for you on delivery. You'll find us most appreciative of good work, Karen. Our salaries are more than competitive with those of industry or academe. Perhaps you and Jack might consider positions with us after this transaction."

"Jack?"

"Oh, yes, a fine young man, an engineer with a military mind. We definitely have a place for him."

"You'll have to talk to him," she said.

"Until then," said the caller, and broke the connection.

Karen looked at Jack, and Ebensack, who had listened to the caller over a conference speaker. Jack was grinning, and Ebensack looked as if he had just smelled something foul. "Don't you ever believe those people," he said. "Once they have the formula, they need you for nothing."

"Still, it's nice to be wanted," said Jack, jokingly, but Ebensack ignored him.

"Try to be serious, Jack," Karen said icily, and then immediately regretted saying it when she saw the hurt in his eyes.

"Don't worry, Karen," he said evenly. "I understand what's going on."

Karen sighed.

"We'll be on the line when he calls tonight," said Ebensack. I want you with her, Jack. If they tell you to go somewhere, just go. My people will be right behind you, but don't look for them. I'm not after arrests just yet; I want to know who's involved, all the way to the top. I want video and pictures, and we can get them at a distance, so you needn't worry about these people finding anything on you. Just play your parts, and deal. Don't jump at any recruitment offers. They won't believe you. If the situation gets dangerous, we'll move in, but only if your lives are threatened."

"Terrific," said Jack. "We could be dead before you make a move."

"We're not beginners," Ebensack assured him.

"Neither is the guy on the phone," said Karen feebly. "I'm only doing this to get Doctor Reimer's killer. Protection is good, but I'm not helpless either."

"That makes two of us," said Jack, and looked darkly at Ebensack.

"Better get going," said Ebensack. "I'll sit here in the dark for an hour or so, and leave by the service dock door. Be cool."

"Be cool?" said Jack, grinning again.

"Or whatever they're saying these days," said the older man.

After Jack and Karen left, Ebensack sat in growing darkness, smelling the scents of unknown chemicals and listening to the squeaking of the rats. A ringing telephone shattered the stillness. It rang three times, then stopped. Ebensack looked at his watch, and a minute later the phone rang again. He picked it up immediately. "Thank you for calling," he said, then patiently waited a moment while his voice print was verified.

"Yes, Tom. Did you get it?"

He paused, a smile growing on his face.

"But can you say in court the call definitely was traced to his number? Good, then all we need the video for is to show him using the scrambler. Let him explain why a university president needs one of those, eh? Thanks, Tom. Go ahead and make your call. Your crew has done a great job."

He hung up the phone, breathing a deep sigh of relief. "Got you, you son-of-a-bitch," he said out loud, "and your boss is next."

* * * * * * *

When Curtis Lundeman hung up the telephone, he felt a strange mixture of elation and fear. The elation he understood. Karen would make delivery, and he was at least temporarily off the hook. The fear was another thing; somewhere deep in his gut was a kind of apprehension, a feeling of something wrong, illogical, out of place, and he could not bring it into focus.

He locked the scrambler in an attaché case and put it in the bedroom closet along with two empty cases, then lay down on the bed to relax and think. In a few minutes he was at the edge of an uneasy sleep, heart pounding, and sweat gushed from every pore on his face. Christ, he thought, and sat up suddenly. I'm having a panic attack. He padded across thick carpeting to Irene's bathroom, and found her tranquilizers in the medicine chest. "What the hell," he said softly, then popped two tablets in his mouth and swallowed them dry.

The medication relaxed him, and he slept a while, dreaming he was sitting on a narrow, wooden beam near a high ceiling. There were many people on the beam with him. It was getting too crowded, and someone bumped him, and he began to topple off, terrified because it was fifty feet to the floor below. He started to scream.

The telephone was ringing, and when he answered it he heard the voice of a young man, perhaps a student. He was formal, and succinct.

"President Lundeman?"

"Yes."

"I'm an associate of Charles Ebensack, sir, and I have some information and documents I'm sure will be valuable to you. You'll be amazed by the amount of material we've been able to put together in the last two months."

"I know Ebensack, but otherwise what are you trying to say, please?"

"Oh, I'm talking about your business, sir, the one you and your partner have run so successfully for the past several years. Very innovative. I don't think we've seen anything quite like it before now. All those people doing free research for you, government funding, military connections at your fingertips, and all you do is keep your mouth shut and share equally in the profits."

"If this is a fraternity prank, I suggest you consider the consequences. What you are saying is libelous."

"Oh, but it isn't, sir. We have all the data. We have copies of letters from guerrilla groups in Central America, and packing slips for canisters of nitrous oxide which are really filled with SB4 nerve gas, and defoliants, and bacterial agents developed in the marvelous facilities of your university. We even know the numbers of the Geneva accounts you people opened, and the name of the man who provides papers for the revolutionaries who study military tactics on your campus. You must admit this is very important information, certainly enough to put an end to your private enterprise, and lock you away from society for a long time. The only question is how much, in a mercenary sense, this information is worth to you?"

He could hear the humor in the young man's voice, the little spider playing with the big fly. Well, this fly could bite. "I'd better hang up, now, before I really get angry and bring myself down to your level, and I don't want to do that."

"Well, sir, I do believe in civilized discussions, particularly about money, but I really must rush you a bit. You'll want to contact your partner before we begin any negotiations. My tastes are simple, and I'd like a quick deal. Please tell him I'll turn over the data I've mentioned for twenty-five thousand dollars cash in small, used bills. I'll get back to you in two days."

"Of course you will," said Lundeman. "The moon will be full by then, and you'll be able to come up with something even more insane than this. Goodbye."

Lundeman hung up the phone, and every nerve in his body seemed to fire at once. His body shook, and he wanted to scream. He stumbled forward, and found he edges of a table with his hands. Holding on grimly, he closed his eyes a moment as a wave of nausea passed over him. He lurched into the bathroom and threw up first in the sink, and then the toilet. The stench was immediate, foul, and in his sweat. He threw up until there was only green bile coming. For a long while he remained on his knees by the toilet bowl, breathing deeply as his offended stomach twisted and turned. Finally, he arose and looked with disgust at what he had done. He cleaned up the bathroom, and sprayed a scented air freshener around when he was finished.

For several minutes he sat on the edge of the bed, head in hands, then picked up the telephone and made a call. No answer. He hung up and dialed again, this time getting an immediate response.

"I didn't expect you to be in the office so soon," he said. "We have to meet right now, and we can't discuss it on the phone. Delivery is settled, but I just got a threatening call from a crazy man. I'm going to walk downtown, now. Meet me there."

He slammed the receiver down with finality. Enough moaning, Curtis. It makes no sense to sit still while other people tear your world apart. Take charge, and get rid of them.

The sun was at the tips of fir trees on the western ridge when Curtis walked down the hill towards town. He smiled at students who waved to him from their bicycles and Frisbee games. A crushing problem had been newly inflicted on him by forces he had no direct control over. Surgery would be necessary, a process he'd despised since the incidents with Bauer and Reimer, but isn't it supposed to get easier by the third time?

He entered town, and passed the boarded, broken window of the closed hairdresser's shop. What was his name again? No matter. He wasn't fucking Irene anymore, having moved out to seek greener, safer pastures. He crossed the street and entered the pharmacy, certain he was being watched. It was thirties style, with a soda fountain and six booths in the back. He sat down in the last one, back to the door, and waited. A young kid wearing an apron came over to him, looking tired and bored.

"What'll it be, Doctor Lundeman?"

"Alka-Seltzer in water, and a cup of tea, Les. Thanks."

The kid walked away as the front door banged shut, and there was a familiar voice. "While you're at it, bring me some coffee, kid."

Lundeman looked up as William Holleque slid into the booth with him. "Well, now, how's it going, Mister President? You sounded a bit green around the gills."

"Let's say I've had a mixed day. Would you like the good news first?" He looked up and coughed, clearing his throat as the waiter returned with their orders.

"Alka-Seltzer, yet. You have had a bad day," said Holleque.

Lundeman ignored the sneering tone of voice, and told him about the conversation with Karen Butler. "Well, what do you think?"

"It's a little sooner than I expected. I suppose she remembered enough to do the job quickly. She's quite bright, that one. But I don't like it."

"What do you mean?" asked Lundeman.

"I don't like the whole deal. It doesn't fit the characters of those two young people. Both of them are straight-arrows if I've ever seen any, and I don't see them selling out at any price, especially Jack Nelson. A professional soldier, maybe, but a mercenary, never. Flag and country all the way, and here he is, in a scheme to defraud the government. It doesn't fit, Curt."

"I agree," said Lundeman quietly. "It has bothered me from the start, but I was also feeling deadline pressures."

"I'll bet Ebensack is somewhere in on this."

"I haven't seen him for weeks."

"Means nothing. He has an organization working for him. Remember that."

Fear stirred in a dark corner of Lundeman's mind. "I got another phone call this afternoon, and that's the bad news," he said, sighing.

He described the threat, and the twenty-five thousand dollar demand. As he talked, he frowned, smiled, then frowned again.

"And here we are, meeting together, right after the phone call. Not once did he mention any names, and here we are, you ass-hole," growled Holleque.

"I wasn't followed. I'm sure of that."

"Listen to me. It's a setup. There's no way in hell they could know all those things. They're guessing."

"How about the Geneva accounts? Is that guessing, too?"

A match scratched, and Holleque blew smoke into his face. "For a smart guy, you are so naïve. Don't you see Ebensack in this? Do you really believe everyone will sell out if the price is right? There are no Geneva accounts, or any other accounts. It's fifty-fifty, cash on the line. You've seen the books."

"I've seen a set of books, yes."

"Shit. Look, we've got to move fast on this. When the guy calls again, tell him we agree to his terms, but if he keeps copies of stuff he's a dead person. Set up a meeting, and I'll handle the rest."

"You'll handle it? Does this mean another murder?"

"You don't reason or bargain with these people, Curtis. You kill them. Set it up, and get back to me."

"Just like Bauer and Reimer. No anger, hatred, no emotion of any kind. It's so easy for you."

"Remember that," said Holleque, and Lundeman felt cold.

Lundeman shook his head. "I don't know how I could have become so involved with a person like you."

A chuckle, low and resonant. "Because you like money, my man."

And Lundeman knew it was true. "What do I do about getting delivery of the neutralizer? Forget it?"

Tell Karen to bring Jack along when we meet. We want to talk about jobs, right? We'll call at Karen's apartment tomorrow evening, and tell them where to go. I'll take it from there. "And?"

"I'm going to arrange my own testing of the neutralizer. If they're trying to con us, the results should be fun to watch. All that twitching, I mean."

Lundeman laughed nervously, and twisted his fingers together on the table. Holleque smiled nastily at him.

"Oh, dear, have I offended your sensitivities again? Well, this is what it's about. It's not all fun and profit, and when we don't deliver we can have angry customers who send bad people to break our bones or worse, and I really don't think you're ready for that. I don't think you're ready for ninety years in a federal prison, either, and that's where we can end up unless a few people are put out of the way. You do what you're told, and we'll get out of this. God, are you scared!"

The booth groaned as Holleque leaned over the table and then the nightmarish face was there, glaring down at Lundeman with predatory furor. "You're pathetic. Welcome to the real world, sweet cheeks, and hang on to daddy," he snarled. "Stay cool, call the girl and arrange a delivery time, then go home to your books and fancy wife. And when you talk to whoever is trying to get twenty five grand out of us do not, I repeat, do not mention my name. Partner is fine. Are we communicating?"

"Yes. I'll get it done."

"Good, then I can leave. You took me away from something delicious, and I wouldn't want it to get cold."

Holleque's look was venomous and vile. Lundeman couldn't look at him, and stared at the dregs in his tea cup. The man laughed, and walked away, as Lundeman began to shake again.

It was at that moment, as the two men parted company, that each man decided to kill the other.

* * * * * * *

Across the street from the pharmacy, and behind a rack of paperback books in a grocery store, curious people watched a young man with video camera and shotgun microphone changing powers on a thousand millimeter zoon lens. As they watched, he also adjusted contrast to highlight the faces of two men having coffee together. "Just a class project," he explained to his audience.

CHAPTER FOURTEEN

"First we're in a rush, and now you're poking along. The guy said seven, Karen, and it's five-thirty this minute. Let's get something to eat."

Jack paced nervously back and forth in the laboratory as Karen, hunched over a table, carefully filled a tiny vial with a colorless liquid.

"Tell your stomach to wait," she said irritably. "This isn't the most stable compound in the world, and we have to demonstrate it."

Jack shoved his hands deep into his jeans pockets. "I don't see what I'm going along for, except as shotgun for you."

"I told you they want to talk about a job. Ebensack advised me to say you wouldn't be interested. I did. They want to see you anyway. Did you call Ebensack?"

"Yeah. He said someone would be watching. I don't find that comforting, and I told him so."

"We have to trust him, Jack."

"Trust, hell. We're worms on a hook, and we're expendable. What do you want to bet?"

"Then trust us. We're not stupid people." Karen took a metal vial from the table, opened her blouse at the top and pushed the vial down between her breasts. She wiggled an eyebrow at Jack as she buttoned the blouse up again, then held up a second vial in front of her, stuck it with a hypodermic syringe with a short needle in it, and drew up some liquid. Satisfied with the amount, she sat down on a stool, grabbed a piece of flesh on her thigh, and plunged the needle into it without wincing.

"What the hell?" said Jack, taking a step towards her, but she looked up and smiled at him sweetly.

"Hush, now," she said softly, then pulled out the needle and rubbed the offended place on her thigh with an alcohol-soaked cotton ball. She capped the needle, snapped it off and threw it in a red wastebasket, then pulled out another and filled a syringe as before. Jack looked on silently. She squirted some liquid up in a little fountain, then walked towards Jack and raised an eyebrow seductively.

"Okay, hero," she said invitingly. "roll up your sleeve. This is insurance."

* * * * * * *

They left the building shortly before six, intending to walk back to Karen's apartment where they would be picked up, but they didn't make it to the street. A Chevette with university markings pulled up in front of them. A square-jawed young man with a butch cut pushed open the front door on the passenger side and gave them a country-shucks-style grin.

"Hey, Jack and Karen. Hop in, and I'll take you to the chemistry demonstration. We decided to move it up a little."

Jack started to protest, but Karen pushed past him and crammed herself into the back seat of the little car, holding her purse tightly against her chest. "You sit in front, Jack," she said. "You'll never fit back here." So Jack got into the front, where the young man held out a big hand. "Hi. I'm Pete. It's only a little ways."

They moved out, made a U-turn and drove around the quad. Jack said, "A university car?"

"Why not?" said Pete. "This is official business, of a sort."

He laughed richly, lightheartedly, a man with a sense of humor. Pete gave an admiring glance at Karen in his rear view mirror, then looked at Jack and rolled his eyes. He was young, but not real young, maybe middle twenties, perhaps a graduate student like Karen. He had the body of an athlete, and exceptionally large hands. Jack particularly noticed the hands, and the heavy calluses, peculiar for a university employee. They circled the quad, then turned sharply and went down a narrow street leading to the Gordon Science Center above campus, but just as they reached the hill Pete turned quickly into a little parking lot by a red brick building next to a huge storage container for liquid nitrogen.

"Here?" said Karen. "This is the gas liquefaction building."

"There's a little lab here, too," said Pete, "and it's a lot more private. Roy's car isn't here yet, so we'll have to wait a little. Come on, let's go in."

They went inside and waited for nearly a half hour before hearing a car stop outside, and then the door opened and another young man entered the room. He looked around, and smiled at them.

"You're late, Roy," said Pete.

"Meetings, meetings," said Roy, then to Karen, "You mind if we don't use last names?" and Karen shrugged.

"I believe you have something for us?"

Karen took a vial and a wallet-sized spiral-bound notebook out of her purse and handed it to Roy. "The sample is good enough for twenty people, and everything else is in the notebook."

Roy smiled, held up the vial and shook it delicately. "Pete, get the lady's money and put it where she can see it." He opened the notebook, and thumbed a few pages.

Pete fumbled around in a desk drawer, then came over to them and plunked a thick stack of twenties on the table in front of them. "Two thousand, cash, tax free," he said, grinning.

"Of course we've got to test this stuff first, don't you think, Pete?"

"Naturally," said Pete, still grinning.

"I ran several tests with rats," said Karen, "and they all did okay."

"Really? Hey, that's great, but you know it isn't enough. I

mean, we have to know how it works on people, Karen, and you too, Jack. We're doing something for people here, after all, protecting them from a lethal nerve gas. That's important in our business, protecting the troops, you know. It's a big money item, too. Especially when both sides have the gas. Provided by us, of course."

"It's good business," added Pete, "and you can both be a part of it starting right now."

"We can talk about that later," said Jack. "I haven't made up my mind."

"Oh, but we're not asking you to decide anything, Jack. You're going to work right now. Isn't that right, Pete?" said Roy.

"It certainly is," said Pete. He raised his right hand, and there was a 9mm Browning automatic in it, pointing at Karen. "You've made the team, Jack." His mad eyes twinkled with amusement.

"I don't get it," said Jack, tensing. "Put the gun down."

"Can't do that, good buddy. Roll up your sleeve. You too, Karen, and you can do the honors. Stick with the dosage to weight ratios in the little book there. We want a fair test, and then, if you're still alive, you get your money, and we can talk about your future. Fair enough?"

"I think that's very fair," said Roy sagely.

Jack took a step towards Pete, and the gun swung around. "Go ahead, make my day," drawled the young man with the big hands, and all Jack could see was the black maw of the pistol.

"You see too many movies, Pete," said Roy. "Jack's going to help us, aren't you, Jack? A little needle never scared you, a big football star and all around solid American guy."

"Take it easy, Jack," said Karen lightly. "We know the stuff works."

He turned to look at her, and she seemed so calm, confident and serene.

Quite suddenly, he understood.

"All right, all right, but back off with the gun. You don't need it." Jack rolled up one sleeve past the elbow.

"Oh, what a big muscle," said Pete, but he lowered the still cocked pistol so it pointed at the floor. Jack had no illusions about how fast it could come up again.

Karen carefully drew up a dose and shot it into Jack's triceps. Great, he thought, now I have two sore arms. She sat down on a chair and gave herself a shot while Pete and Roy watched admiringly, then put vial and notebook back on the table and stood up. "Now what?" she asked.

"Right this way, brave lady," said Roy.

"Pretty, too," said Pete. "You go with her, Jack." The big gun was leveled at them once again.

Karen took his hand in hers, and they followed Roy across the room where he ushered them into a closed, windowless space with only a chair, table, and a small television camera mounted on one wall. There was an odor of disinfectant in the room, and a gentle breeze was blowing from a vent in the wall.

"This'll only take a minute," said Roy, smiling, and he closed the door with a snap.

"Not a good place for a claustrophobic," Jack said uneasily.

"Try to breathe naturally," said Karen. "They won't keep us in here long."

"How right you are," said a disembodied voice from one wall, and then there was a hissing sound. For an instant, Jack saw something like white mist spurt forth from the air conditioning vent, and there was a putrid odor in the room. Karen's eyes widened. She grabbed the edge of the table with both hands, and breathed deeply. "God, I feel like Doctor Jekyll," she said.

"What?" Jack felt something, and then it went away. It was as if a giant hand had grasped his throat hard, and released it in an instant, leaving him with a metallic taste in his mouth, and a buzzing in his ears. He started to sweat, and looked up as the television camera swung around to face them.

"Hey, you guys are looking good," said Roy. "The Man will be pleased."

The Man?

They waited for several minutes, and there was a rushing sound as air was sucked into the vent, followed by return of a cool breeze. The process was repeated twice before the door opened, and there was Roy, grinning at them, motioning for them to come outside. Even Pete was smiling, and the crazy glint had gone out of his eyes.

"You really did it," said Roy. "Here I thought you were bullshitting us, and all along you really knew what you were doing. Pete, give the lady her money while I call the boss and give him the good news."

"Sure," said Pete. He put down an open flask of liquefied gas he's been moving across the room, and handed the stack of twenties to Karen, who now looked quite pleased with herself. Jack looked into the flask next to him on a bench, saw the bubbling surface of clear liquid, felt the icy vapor coming from it. Nitrogen gas, he knew, liquefies at seventy seven degrees above absolute zero. That works out to minus three hundred and twenty degrees Fahrenheit. A human cell exposed to that temperature can explode, so keep your fingers out of the flask, Jack-boy.

Karen was counting money, and everyone seemed happy and relaxed, even though minutes before, death had been close.

"There could be a place for you guys in the organization," said Roy enthusiastically.

"I thought you worked for the university," said Karen.

"Oh, no," said Roy.

"Just passing through," Pete added.

"I'll get the boss over here to talk some business, and then we'll go out to eat. Pete, shut down the cryogenerator, will you? We've made enough liquid nitrogen for ten shipments already."

Roy dialed the phone while Pete went to a corner and fiddled with the machinery which chugged rhythmically there. Karen and Jack stood next to each other at a bench where the vial and notebook had been placed, and Karen was shoving money into her purse.

Roy was animated in his conversation, but then he suddenly changed, glanced uncomfortably at Karen and Jack, and talked in muffled tones. Then it seemed like he was arguing a point, but soon he was quiet and only listening to whomever it was they called The Boss. He hung up the phone slowly, and when he turned to face them there was disappointment in his eyes. Pete came back to meet the three of them at the bench.

"Well?" asked Jack. The tenseness was back, twisting around inside his stomach.

"Sorry, folks, all bets are off. Who knows why. I just follow orders. Pete?"

"Huh?" Pete was looking at Karen, and hadn't been listening carefully.

"Kill them, Pete," said Roy coldly, and he stepped back to get out of the line of fire.

"Why—?" began Pete, his right hand moving slowly towards the pistol stuck in his waistband before the command had even registered in his conscious mind. Pete's mouth opened in surprise as his big hand grasped the automatic and pulled it free, the crazy gleam returning to his eyes with a new opportunity to kill. But Jack twirled smoothly, sweeping up the liquid gas flask in both arms as Karen's hand darted to the bench to grab and throw a glass vial in one motion. As his one hand lifted the flask while the other tipped it, Jack saw the vial strike Roy above the right eye in a burst of red. Roy stumbled left towards Pete, whose gun was leveling, trigger finger working, but he had put the slide safety on to keep from blowing his balls off, and nothing happened. His thumb moved to the safety as Roy crashed into him, and Jack swung again, emptying the unbelievable cold contents of the flask into both their faces.

Karen clapped both hands over her ears as the hideous screaming began. Both men dropped to the floor writhing and kicking. Pete's gun slid across the floor, struck a baseboard and discharged loudly but harmlessly. Jack swept it up as he headed towards the door in flight, but Karen kept her head, stopping to jam her hands into Pete's pockets and jerk out the car keys from his writhing body. She glanced at vial and notebook on the table and floor, but left them there and followed Jack out the door.

Even as they got in the car they could hear the screaming.

Karen banged a key several times on the ignition switch before getting it in, starting the car with a roar and a lurch. Rear tires spit gravel against the building, and then they were racing along the road back to the quad, and both of them, sitting there wordlessly, were beginning to shake.

"Oh, shit, did we blow it. We really blew it. They didn't believe us, and I thought it was looking so good."

"Jack, they were going to kill us. I'm sure it was something said on the telephone; they were ordered to do it."

"I don't get it. The stuff worked for them."

"It worked, Jack, and they bought it. I've got the money right here." Her fingers were snow white on the steering wheel as they neared the quad.

"We've got to call Ebensack. He was supposed to be watching us," said Jack, calmer now, but angry.

"We'll swing by my place first, then go to the lab and call from there if we have to," said Karen. "He might be watching my apartment, wondering where we are."

"Terrific," said Jack.

They reached the quad and swung left, swerving to avoid a university car driven at high speed by Colonel William Holleque, who gave them a horrified look and made a screeching turn onto the road they had just left.

"Boy, is he in a hurry," said Karen. Jack was silent, full of a sinking feeling about a man he admired.

Why was he so surprised to see us?

* * * * * * *

Holleque heard the moans even before he pushed open the door and saw the two figures on the floor. Their eyes were closed, paper-white faces covered with enormous blisters that seemed to grow second by second, and Holleque felt a rare, fleeting sensation of pity. These were good men. Conscious or unconscious, they moaned their agony and didn't seem to know he was there. He found the notebook on a bench, thumbed through it, put it in a pocket, then the vial, on the floor, cracked but not leaking, labeled RD4, AGENT N. He searched the room for anything else. Pete's gun was missing, and his targets had escaped in his car. Roy's car was still outside. He tried to talk to the men, but got no response, and the moaning made him jittery. He took their wallets, their dog tags, and Roy's keys. The LN tank was full, he had all the building keys, and the building rarely had visitors. The freezer in the back of the room would do for a while.

He stood over the men, mourning a little because it seemed fitting, then pulled his nine millimeter Beretta service automatic from a waist holster, and chambered a round. Pete cried out, and Roy turned over, lifting his mutilated face towards his Colonel, trying to talk with a destroyed larynx.

"Help me," he said.

"That's what I'm here for, son," said Holleque, and then he aimed his pistol and shot both men carefully in the head.

* * * * * * *

They drove past Karen's apartment three times, fearing there would be a trap waiting for them. There were no observers in parked cars along the street. Jack was still angry, and had to talk to Ebensack right away, so they drove downtown to the drugstore where Jack made a call while Karen waited in the car with the motor running. In a few minutes he came out again, lips compressed to a thin line so she knew he was truly pissed even before he slammed the car door so hard there was a ringing in their ears.

"That son-of-a-bitch is mad at us!" he screamed. "Claims we should have stalled, gotten back to your place where he had someone waiting. Jeezus, he's blaming us for nearly getting killed! The man is a flake!"

"What are we supposed to do now, Jack?" Karen put a hand on his arm, trying to calm him down.

"He says go to the department conference room where we

talked before, and stay there. I wanted to call the police to pick up Pete and Roy, and he nearly got hysterical, said to stay out of it and leave it to him. He said an operation is underway, and hung up on me. I don't think he knows what he's doing, Karen."

"Maybe the local police are being kept out of it, Jack. Ebensack must have some reason, but I don't trust him either, not now." *And not for some time*, she thought to herself. Karen drove quickly back towards campus while Jack slumped in silence, exasperated. Near the edge of the quad, they saw President Lundeman walking down the hill towards town, carrying a black briefcase. Fifty yards behind, a pair of red berets followed, faces coppery in the setting sun. Jack looked puzzled, but said nothing until Karen drove into the visitors' parking lot.

"You're parking here?"

"They'll look for the car by the chemistry building. We'll walk from here, go through the heating plant and take the elevator off the loading dock. I have a key."

Jack shook his head. They locked the car, walked quickly across the street and along a winding walkway to the large brick cube with towering stack and open iron ladder that was the heating plant. Fraternity members had climbed the two hundred foot ladder to decorate the tower with Greek letters. They went through the quiet building, past both coal- and oil-burning furnaces, inert for the summer. They saw one maintenance man at a distance, then crossed a narrow street to the loading dock of the chemistry building and ascended in the slow freight elevator to the third floor.

They opened the door to darkness. "Uh, oh, I think we've been here before," said Jack. "Why don't you guys ever pay your light bill?"

"The office is left, on our side," said Karen.

They felt their way along the wall until they were touching glass and looking at a spot of orange light. "This is it," said Karen, and she fumbled again with her keys. "Looks like someone left the coffee-maker on." The door opened with the third key she tried, and they turned on the light in the conference room.

"God, I'm getting hungry," said Jack.

"I'll see what's in the fridge," said Karen, and she left the room.

"Right," said Jack, dripping sarcasm, but in a few minutes she was back again, holding up something wrapped in wax paper.

"Would you believe half a birthday cake, and all the coffee we can drink?"

"Time for a party," he said. They closed the door and stuffed paper towels under it to keep the light from showing outside, even though there were no security guards ordinarily inside the building. You never know, argued Jack, and it somehow made them feel safer. After they had eaten, Jack looked up at the bookshelves lining the room around the conference table.

"This is great," he said. "Cake and coffee, and time to catch up on all my back reading in chemistry."

"Is that all?" said Karen, teasingly.

Jack looked at Karen, and then the conference table. "I know it's not the right time for this, and we'll have to take off our shoes."

Karen turned out the lights.

* * * * * * *

The call had come earlier than expected, twenty-five thousand dollars in small bills to be delivered to an address in town where he would find all the material he was paying for. He would take said material and leave the money, knowing he was being watched. Any short-changing, and he would be dead within an hour, along with his lovely wife Irene, for whom the process would be slow. He didn't really believe that, not for twenty five grand

Somehow, as he walked along the street, briefcase swinging gently from one hand, Curtis Lundeman knew he was dealing with amateurs, or at least with people cursed with a naïve attitude regarding the innate ruthlessness of human beings engaged in the business of death. And Lundeman was indeed an agent of death. The meeting had lasted only ten minutes in a brick building on the edge of campus. Holleque had shown him the plastic explosive, and the detonator activated by a photocell. The briefcase had a combination lock, not set, and could only be opened in the zero position. In that position only, the combination wheel closed the battery-driven photocell circuit, arming the detonator. Holleque had closed the briefcase, and handed it to him with a smile. "Good hunting," he had said.

So here he was, a university president on a mission to kill, a bomb in his hand, and it somehow seemed natural. I've become one of them, he thought. The spies, mercenaries and crazies, with or without causes, the professional killers who disrupt the peace of the world with their terrorist acts, I'm a part of that, and all for money. There's only one person I want to kill, and that's William Holleque. And I only want to do that because I know eventually he will try to kill me. I'm not a violent man, but—oh, yes, I am a violent man. I am a very violent man, and soon I will be a murderer.

He walked briskly, oblivious to traffic or people, the little car racing by with Jack and Karen, the two red berets who followed him from a distance, or the little man who watched him from a parked car as he reached an old, board house with a white picket fence at the edge of town. A sign stuck in the weed-overgrown front yard announced the house was for rent, and gave a phone number to call.

Three people watched him cross the street and walk up to the front door. The porch creaked loudly as he tried the door, which opened to blackness. He stepped inside and closed the door, breathing shallow because the air was foul, as if there were a dead animal nearby. The room was bare, except for a wooden table and chair in the kitchen, glowing orange in dusk, and on the table he found a large manila envelope stuffed with documents, manifests and letters. He looked them over long enough to see possible links between Holleque and several groups in Central and South America, and a prominent terrorist operating out of the Middle East.

The business principle of his extortionist was clear. Sell to both sides. He took the heavy envelope and put the briefcase on the table, then left the house and walked leisurely back up the street towards his own home at the edge of campus.

He had gone only two blocks when there were sudden footsteps behind him, and he turned as two red berets grasped his arms in a friendly way on both sides, and walked intimately with him for a brief, frightening moment.

"You have something for Colonel Holleque," said one man: hard, pock-marked features, not a kid, maybe thirty, smelling sour. "We'll deliver it to him."

Lundeman started to protest, but the other man pressed something sharp against his right kidney, and whispered, "I'll gladly gut you right here, if you don't hand it over. We have our orders."

He released the envelope as the man on his left tugged at it, smiling coyly. "Thank you, sir. Now you go straight home, and have a fine evening. The Colonel will be in touch."

They let go of his arms simultaneously, and dropped behind as he walked onwards, eyes straight ahead. When he glanced behind him a moment later, they were gone. In twenty minutes he was home, going up the neat walkway to his spacious porch when he saw a bright flash reflected from the windows of the big house.

An instant later, he heard the explosion.

* * * * * * *

When Lundeman walked away from the house, the thick envelope tucked under one arm, the red berets had followed him, and for a few minutes the street was peaceful. Across the street from the house, three figures emerged from darkness beneath a grove of trees there. Two carried heavy metal shields, a third wore heavy clothing and carried a heavy steel helmet. They crossed the street and entered the house Lundeman had visited. Several minutes later they came out again as a black van pulled up in front of the house. The men got into it and the van drove three blocks down the street. One man got out and looked back towards the house. Something small was in his hand, and he pressed on it with an index finger.

The explosion was terrific, shattering windows a block away and scattering debris to the street. A large, orange fireball ascended fifty meters into the sky.

The man got back into the van, and they drove away.

CHAPTER FIFTEEN

"The maintenance man saw them come through here less than an hour ago," said Tom Mason on the phone. "I'm betting they're in her lab, or somewhere on that floor."

Holleque frowned. "How many people do you have?"

"Four, counting me."

"Weapons?"

"Knives. That's all we need."

"Don't get cocky about it," said Holleque sharply. "Nelson is good. Don't underestimate him, especially when he's with the girl. But get it done. Do it tonight."

"Yes, sir," was the crisp reply, and then silence.

Holleque hung up the phone, picked it up and dialed again, letting it ring a full minute before slamming the receiver down in frustration. All evening long he had tried to call the camp, and there was no answer. He had to get the vial and notebook out there before the group dispersed, along with his buyer's agent who had flown up from Mexico City just to take delivery. Where the hell were they? There was a field phone, but training was over, and everyone would be packing bags in the barracks, cleaning before the next group arrived in only two days. He dialed again. Another long wait. No answer. He put down the phone gently, and sighed. Admit it, man, things are closing in a bit, and they won't leave you alone until you've killed them all.

* * * * * * *

The gunships came in low over the trees, directly out of the morning sun, so that nobody saw them until the chopping sounds of their engines filled the air. Four rockets screamed in to destroy the gate and fence along one entire side of the compound.

Rodríguez was in the barracks, stuffing a pair of pants into his duffle. The concussion slammed him back into the wall. He felt a sharp pain start in his shoulder and dance around the collar bone in a ring of agony that prevented him from lifting his arm. Windows on the southeast side of the barracks exploded inwards in jets of glass splinters, leaving one man leaning against his locker with a bloody face, another writhing on the floor and screaming about his eyes. Men dove for rifles that weren't there, since everything except clothing had been packed in trucks the previous evening. Two red berets pulled knives from boots. A third had found a pistol in his locker, pulling back the slide and releasing it with a snap as the door burst open and two M-16's sprayed a blast of death the length of the room. Bodies tumbled and jerked. Rodríguez screamed when he landed on his shoulder beneath a bunk, and then lay there, groaning. There were footsteps on the board floor, then the bed was pushed aside and a heavy hand turned him roughly over on his back. He saw captain's bars on a camouflaged helmet, and dark-brown eyes glaring at him from a coal-black face.

"You are a disgrace, my man," drawled the captain. "I think we should send you south with the others."

* * * * * * *

They lay drowsily warm in each other's arms, and Jack felt her heart beating against his chest. Their lovemaking on top of the table had been like children playing, wrestling and tugging at each other for an advantage until Jack was on top and in control. They were fully clothed, but Jack couldn't remember ever being quite as hard as he was at that moment when he pinned her arms to the table and felt her pelvis rocking. She giggled, and used her legs to pull him into her, rocking and twisting against him.

Her eyes sparkled in the dim light. "Good way to relieve stress," she murmured.

"It would go a lot better without our clothes on."

"Too cold for that, and dangerous."

"Yeah If I ripped your bra off I could get gassed."

Jack released her hands, and she put her arms around his neck. They moved gently together until she dug a fingernail into his neck, and he yelped.

"This is getting dangerous," he said.

"Life is dangerous. Haven't you noticed?" She ran her hands up and down his arms, and kissed him.

"I'm trying to forget that."

"Then forget it, for just a minute," she murmured, kissing him again, then surprising him with her strength as she used hands and legs to tip him over on his side. They held each other tightly, their breathing slowing and deepening as hands continued to explore lazily.

"I love you," said Jack. "I don't know what I'd do if I lost you."

Karen nuzzled his neck. "My protector. Well, I need to protect you, too. We're both scared right now; I know that. You say silly things to make me feel better, and that's nice, but I'm not helpless, Jack."

"I know. Right now I just want to hold you."

"Mmmm," she murmured, and kissed him lightly.

They were near dozing again when there was a faint sound, barely audible even to a conscious ear. It came from the main floor of the building, and rose along two stair wells before filtering through closed doors to reach them. It was the sound glass makes when broken by a gloved hand.

Air conditioning hummed, sending a freezing vortex around the room. Jack shuddered and stirred, opened his eyes and reached for a blanket that wasn't there. Karen stirred beside him. He sat up, listening. The air conditioner went off with a thud and whir, and as silence returned he heard a rattling sound in the outer office that brought him fully awake. He nudged Karen, and she grumbled. He shook her gently until she reached up and touched his face.

"I think there's someone in the hallway," he whispered, and felt her stiffen.

"God, where's the gun?" she murmured, and slithered off the table. Jack went off the opposite side and started feeling around on the floor. The rattling in the outer office started again, louder this time, and then there were low voices.

"Oh, shit," said Jack. "Whoever it is doesn't sound friendly."

"I found my purse," said Karen, and Jack could hear her rummaging around in it.

"Great, and I found a shoe." The Browning automatic was with his jacket somewhere in the room. Terrific, Jack, and quickly, now, where is that gun? He crawled along a wall, feeling in the corner, finding nothing as there was a crash in the outer office and a voice he had heard before. He wriggled frantically along the back wall, arms reaching out spider-like to snare anything he could find.

No gun. I must have kicked it under the table.

"Stay away from the door, Jack," said Karen, strangely.

He moved towards her voice, at the end of the table, banged his head on a chair, and it hit the table with a thud. There was eerie silence in the outer office as Jack pulled himself up next to Karen, hair rising on the back of his neck, and then the door crashed inwards, half open, motion opposed by the debris stuffed under it. Dark figures moved across the weak light in the hallway. Arms reached out, and there was another crash as the door opened fully.

"Don't move, Jack," whispered Karen.

Light flooded the room, and they blinked painfully.

Four men in fatigues and red berets stood facing them from the other end of the table. Each had a knife in his hand, and a wide grin of lustful excitement reserved for the kill. They were all looking at Karen, who stood calmly at the end of the table, arms at her sides, her blouse unbuttoned,

"We're going to die right now, Jack thought, but when he started to move, Karen grabbed his arm with one hand. Jack knew these men were professionals. No students here, and one of them was Tom Mason, who leered back at him.

"How about that? Hair all mussed up. You guys have been hiding and getting it on at the same time. Get it up again, jock-man, so I can cut it off." Mason and one man moved around to Jack's side of the table, and took a cautious step towards him. His other companions slithered around the other side, looking only at Karen.

"Come and get it, guys," she said menacingly.

"Oooh, I bet you bite and scratch," said one of the men, stalking her.

At that instant, Jack saw the butt of the Browning sticking out from beneath his jacket on the floor at the far corner of the table, behind Mason. There were two men, with knives, between Jack and the gun. He tensed, moving his balance up onto the balls of his feet.

The men saw him move, and lunged in unison.

Karen's arm came up with a vial in her hand, spraying a wide arc of white vapor directly at the men on both sides of the table.

The attackers hesitated, stumbling backwards, awaiting the sting of mace.

Nothing happened. They laughed nervously.

Jack had a sudden, familiar metallic taste in his mouth.

The convulsions began.

Puking and retching, and the smell of evacuating bowels filled the small room as Jack and Karen huddled in a corner. The four men threw themselves into walls and across the table in violent spasms for what seemed an eternity, but was seconds, and then they were still, eyes staring, saliva and vomit trickling from open mouths.

Karen still held the vial, and her hand was shaking. "Oh, how awful, how awful," she said, and repeated it over and over again, tears rolling down her face. Jack retrieved jacket and gun, and complained again about the taste in his mouth.

"Thank God it still worked," said Karen, fastening her blouse again. "I took a terrible chance, Jack. I didn't know how long the dose would last. The gas could have killed us. I didn't know what else to do. Oh, please, CLOSE THE DOOR!"

Jack closed the door to the conference room as the air conditioner went on again, helping him to fight back a wave of nausea. Karen was babbling.

"They're all dead, and I killed them. It's not like the rats; it doesn't happen that way. I can smell it on my hands, Jack, There's vomit on my hands!"

"Easy, easy," said Jack. "there's nothing on your hands. Let's get out of here. I can still smell it, too."

"But where can we go?"

"I'll call Ebensack from here." Jack dialed the office telephone, and waited for a minute before hanging up.

"Not there. Let's go to his place anyway. If there are any more goons around, I don't think they'll expect us to be there."

"But they'll see the car."

"No. We'll walk. It's only three blocks, and we'll take the trail along the hill above town."

They closed the broken door to the office behind them, and felt their way along the hall. Office windows had been randomly broken by the late passage of the Eagle Squad killing team. Broken glass crunched under their shoes until they reached the stairs and went down to a shattered front door to let themselves out. It was cool, and still, and dimly lit on the quad. Jack looked at the glow of his watch. "It's nearly four o'clock. Let's get to Ebensack before someone else comes after us."

They stayed in shadow, skirting buildings until they reached the hill and broke brush for thirty yards. The scenic trail began in town and circled the campus before coming to an end near the president's house. They had walked the trail countless times, in light and dark, to be alone and talk, Now they were fleeing for their lives, but at least in a familiar place. Jack took her hand, and they moved quickly, anticipating every bump and hollow, every root and occasional rock, never stumbling, and soon the lights of the sleeping town were below them and they were using a steep, leaf-filled gully for their descent. Even the birds were silent. They came out on a grassy area that was the edge of a children's park, passing swings and slides, and the bench where they had decided, only weeks before, that they would have two children of their own someday.

There was no traffic, no people to be seen, but fear and imagination created sinister figures in the shadows, bushes and trees, and by the time they reached the county sheriff's home where Ebensack had been staying, their nerves were ragged and torn, their movements mechanical. They rang the doorbell several times, but there was no answer, so they went around in back. The garage was locked, both doors. In the backyard they found a freshly painted gazebo, with vines crawling on two sides. They went inside, out of view from the driveway or the house, sat down on the concrete floor in each other's arms, and waited.

* * * * * * *

Ebensack could not remember a worse night in his entire life. One screw-up after another, beginning with the pickup of Jack and Karen. He should have anticipated something like that; they were lucky to be alive. Now if they would just stay put. He leaned back in the front seat, eyes closed, as the deputy drove him back to an empty house. His aids would be two more hours at the site, looking for bomb parts, but they already had most of what they needed. The fire crew and its Captain were cooperating fully. The ruse had worked, Lundeman would think his tormentor dead, but it wouldn't do for neighbors to know a bomb alone had destroyed the house. Gas was to be the culprit.

Ebensack's mind whirled. I underestimated Lundeman; he can be cool, and deadly. Holleque I understand, a congenital killer, a pro all the way. Wonder if he's heard yet about the camp raid? That'll make him shit green. Watch out, Lundeman, he'll kill you and run like hell. The guy is nuts. All these people are. I have enough on Lundeman, but I need to nail Holleque first. No,

I should arrest Lundeman first, to protect him from Holleque. Shit, I can't think, or feel, right now. Retirement sounds good. Now get me to that bed.

They pulled into the driveway with a bump.

"We're here, Mister Ebensack," said the deputy, shaking his shoulder.

"Thanks, Don. A hell of a night."

"Yes, sir. You want me to go in with you?"

"No. I'm going to stagger in a straight line to bed." He got out of the car, feeling stiff and old all over, and shuffled along the driveway to the back of the house, pulling keys out of a pocket. The garage front flashed with reflected light as the patrol car backed quickly out into the street, and accelerated loudly away. He rounded the corner, thinking only of the soft bed inside the house. "I'm going to sleep for a day," he said out loud, then looked up at two faces beaming at him from the gazebo. "Oh, no," he said, as Jack and Karen bounded towards him.

* * * * * * *

Sleep waited. They made sandwiches and strong coffee laced heavily with sugar, and talked until birds were chirping a welcome to the sun. Their talk was animated, intense. There were things they needed to say, feelings to describe from the nightmares of the previous day and evening. It was direct, and beneath the words Ebensack sensed anger, a covert hostility, directed against himself. He accepted the guilt; after all, he had sent them to a place he deemed safe, and they had nearly been killed there. He had been shorthanded all along, but it was no excuse. He'd not used his people wisely, and for a second time he had made a life-threatening misjudgment. At the moment he felt tired, and oh so vulnerable, and then Jack asked a question long overdue.

"Mister Ebensack, is Colonel Holleque involved with this business?"

"I'm afraid so," said Ebensack.

"In a big way?"

"Looks like he's the head of it. Weapons trafficking, mercenary training, it's a big operation. Lots of money involved."

"The president should be told," said Karen angrily.

"Can't do that. He works with Holleque, and we have good evidence he's the one you've been talking to on the telephone."

Jack and Karen looked at him blankly, as if they had just lost belief in everything. Curiously, he was pleased by that.

"They did the murders?" asked Karen.

"Holleque, or his people, probably. Those chemicals are worth a pile of money on the open market. We have a voice print on Lundeman, even though he used a scrambler, and we have a video of him using it. We can't take any of it into court. Not admissible."

"Is that why you don't arrest them right now?" asked Jack.

Ebensack rubbed his eyes, and sipped coffee. "One of the reasons. We have hard evidence which will stand up against Holleque, and Lundeman will certainly be implicated, but the court case could go on for years, and the taxpayers deserve better than that. These are bad people. With a little encouragement, they will destroy each other, and there won't even be a trial. That's what I'm pursuing at the moment."

He realized his voice sounded cold and hard, but he didn't care. It's a rough world, kids. Open your eyes.

"What do we do now?" asked Karen.

"Sleep. All of us. You take the bedroom, and I'll flop on the couch. We should have an hour or so before the sheriff gets back, and then I have a full day ahead of me."

"All of those guys," said Jack quietly, "they weren't even students. Mercenaries. Professionals. The guys who came after us were professionals. Brother, how much I wanted Eagle Squad, and to think—"

"They were interested in recruiting you, Jack. You and several other students. I guess they figured you'd do it for flag and country. You know, kick the Commies and other bad guys out of Central America, et cetera. Maybe your politics are right for that?"

Jack looked away towards the window. Karen smiled.

"Anyway, Karen's relation with the neuter and nerve gas projects really complicated things for them. By the way, Karen, I want that nerve gas canister you used. I thought we had everything."

"It's empty," she said.

"Give it to me anyway, then let's get some sleep."

She handed the vial to him, yawned, and headed towards the bedroom. Jack stood up, looked at him sorrowfully and said, "They misjudged us, Mister Ebensack. They really did." He turned to follow Karen. They closed the door, and it was quiet again.

Ebensack bagged the deadly glass canister and put it on a coffee table, then stretched out on the couch. He didn't go to sleep right away, but thought about a beautiful young woman who could love a man and a little white rat, and then use a can of nerve gas to kill four thugs armed with knives, knowing they would die horrible. Yes, Jack, they misjudged you. And Karen.

So did I, and it's a good thing, because I really screwed up.

It was light outside when he drifted off to sleep.

CHAPTER SIXTEEN

Sleep can come hard when you've murdered someone, but Curtis Lundeman slept extremely well the night after an explosion ripped apart a ramshackle house at the edge of town. After all, he was only indirectly involved, a delivery boy who awoke refreshed at six, showered and shaved, and settled himself down for an English muffin and coffee breakfast to begin his new work week. Irene lingered in her warm secure bed, not even stirring when the telephone jangled and was instantly answered by her husband.

"Doctor Lundeman, please." A man's voice.

"Speaking."

"Harold Ashworth, sir. I'm with the Minneapolis office of the Federal Bureau of Investigation, and I'm calling to warn you we will shortly be arresting one of your faculty members, Colonel William Holleque. Please avoid contact with this man before the arrest, sir. He is considered to be dangerous, and we don't want hostages involved."

Lundeman's heart froze. "Whatever for?" he stammered. "I mean, what has he done?"

"I can't give you details, sir, but it involves murder, theft of government property, and illegal transport of aliens. We also have a diplomatic immunity situation with Nicaragua, and Holleque is involved with that as well. He will kill you, sir, if you stand in his way to escape. Please don't go near him for the next twenty four hours, regardless of circumstances.'

"I understand," said Lundeman, close to hyperventilating.

"I'm shocked to hear this, but I'll certainly stay out of the way. Thank you so much for the warning."

"I'll call you again when the operation is complete. Goodbye, sir."

The connection was broken, along with the tranquility of his morning. It was finished. All of it. He had to run, and fast. Irene would have to follow later. He couldn't even tell her why right now. Anyway, it would be easy to get back into the country with all the identity papers and passports Holleque had provided him with.

"What am I thinking?" he said out loud. To run was to admit guilt, and Holleque was the only one who could implicate him. Without Holleque there was no proof of his wrongdoing. Honestly, officers, I'm not responsible for the clandestine activities of my faculty members. I didn't know anything about it. Sorry to hear about Holleque. He created a fine Military Science program for us.

Even as he thought it, Curtis knew it was all wishful thinking. Holleque could disappear, but the president of a university could not. Holleque had all the money; all foreign payments had been sent to accounts in several Caribbean banks for a dummy consulting firm he had started. If he disappeared, the money went with him, and Curtis would be left with nothing. Holleque could still implicate him from a distance by letter or obvert transfer of funds to his local account.

Curtis's face heated with a sudden realization. Holleque was a professional killer, If he intended to disappear, he would leave no evidence behind, and that included Curtis Lundeman. He'll kill me, and take all the money for himself, unless I kill him first. He won't be expecting that; he thinks I'm soft.

Lundeman dialed the telephone again, and after several rings Holleque answered.

"Better pack fast. The FBI just called me. They're going to arrest you, and they warned me to stay away."

"So I heard a few minutes ago," said Holleque calmly.

"What?"

"I have my sources, Curt. So why are you really calling?"

"We have to meet. I'm getting out."

"Sounds like a good idea to me. I've been making some travel plans of my own. I suppose you want your split?"

"Of course, and I want it in cash."

"I only have a hundred thousand in cash. That's only a tenth of your share."

"I'll take it, and trust you for the rest later. I don't want any checks or bank transfers, not now."

"Wow, you'll trust me for the rest. I'm really flattered, Curt. It makes me feel like an honest man." Holleque's voice was soft, with a lilt suggesting he was amused by the conversation.

"I want the money right now. Where can we meet?"

There was a pause before Holleque answered. "I'll make it easy for you, Mister President. Drive to the end of George Lake road, and park by the bridge. I'll meet you there with the money, but don't expect me to take you anywhere. Our partnership is finished."

"I'll leave right now. Don't forget the money, or leave me in the lurch. I'll never let go if you do that. Let's make it clean."

"Sounds right to me," said Holleque, and he broke the connection.

Lundeman hung up the phone. His breathing was shallow and rapid. He will try something; I just know he will try something. In the nightstand next to his sleeping wife, there was a Walther automatic Lundeman had bought for her protection. He padded upstairs and retrieved the weapon, then stood looking down at Irene for a moment. I promised you more, he thought. He wanted to wake her and hear her voice. He wanted to pack some clothes, even a small bag. Better not to do that. Try to wait it out a month or two and see how it goes. If necessary, they could take a little vacation, drive to International Falls and cross the border with a false passport. He could arrange a private helicopter to Winnipeg, and then a flight south. In a day they could be lost in South America with enough money to bury them out of sight forever, but only if Holleque actually came through with the rest of his share. He wouldn't of course. Escape was a pipe dream, and Holleque was the one barrier to their freedom.

Curtis pocketed Irene's pistol, left the house quietly, and started the car as it rolled down the driveway. Instead of making his customary right turn towards campus, he turned left and drove through town towards the Lake George road.

* * * * * *

Between the pills and the weed, William Holleque had been on a rollercoaster all night. For the moment he was mellow, so that nothing could disturb his peace of mind or clarity of thought. He took another drag and inhaled deeply, letting the drug seep into every crevice of his being. It was all over, anyway, a long military career with nothing to distinguish it but a good tough image that scared the kids. Rodríguez was a better soldier. Wonder what would happen to him? No pension for us, buddy, but I don't care. There's enough in that briefcase to last forty years where I'm going, and that's with servants. Maybe I'll show it to Lundeman before I kill him. Fucking wimp, always running scared, and then his whore wife. Loose ends. I've got some loose ends, and then I'm gone.

He had been on the phone three times before the frantic call from Lundeman, twice with a security guard who informed him an hysterical secretary had just found four of his cadets dead in a chemistry department conference room, and could he please make himself available in the county coroner's office later that day? Most happy to, he had said with concern, but that had been the trigger. He packed the money, and called Raul at the airport. Mechanic, hell, that guy could fly with the best of them, if you gave him ten thousand dollars. They'd fly low level over the trees into Canada, then a big bird to Toronto, London, Frankfurt, back across to Sao Paulo and on to Bogota. Catch me if you can.

But first, there were loose ends to take care of.

Holleque took a plastic bottle from a pants' pocket and shook two capsules into his hand. The first two amphetamines of his busy day went down dry, but the rush was starting before he got to the street. He cut up a grocery bag, and wrapped the neuter vial and Karen's notebook in a box for mailing. Going through the drop in Texas would lose a week of time, but it was the only option left to him. They were crushing him from all sides, leaving no room, and they would never leave him alone until he killed them all. He could hear his heart pounding, and he was sweating even while sitting still. He exploded into motion, strapped on his service automatic, then added a combat knife to his boot. There were only two things he needed in the dingy rooms: a package, and a briefcase filled with money. The cashier's checks he would obtain in Toronto. Everything else he left, behind an unlocked door.

His entire body was shaking when he reached the car. He drove crazily down side streets until he was a block from the university president's house. He stood in a backyard to watch Lundeman hurry from the house, get in his car and drive away in the direction of town. He walked across the street and into the grove of aspen bordering the house outside a six foot fence which he cleared in a single, graceful vault. His knees were shaking now, and his fingertips burned like fire. He walked boldly across the back lawn to sliding glass doors leading to the kitchen, and pulled. They opened silently.

Loose end number one.

The leather of his boots squeaked easily, so he stayed on the flats of his feet, padding out of the kitchen into the spacious dining area with the crystal chandelier, and the big front room with plush furniture and fireplace. Tables were covered with pictures of dignitaries, the famous and the rich, posing with Curtis and Irene Lundeman. He listened for a moment, then went up the winding staircase and straight to the bedroom, knowing the way, pausing in the doorway to watch the sleeping figure. Perhaps a subconscious part of her sensed his presence, remembering another time, for she moaned softly in sleep and turned over on her back in a kind of invitation. He walked up to her and sat down on the edge of the bed, so that it bounced. His entire body was throbbing with anticipation as his hand slid down towards a boot, grasping the hilt of his knife.

She awoke, startled, and looked into his crazy eyes.

"Hi, lover," he said quietly. "Want to get spread-eagled again?" His hand moved upwards, something flashing in the light.

He thought she would scream, but she didn't do that. It took away some of his pleasure. Instead, she rolled to her right and grabbed at the nightstand drawer, showing a look of pure horror when she found it empty and it was her last complete expression, for at that instant he hit her solidly with a backhand slash that drove her over on her back. He was on her like a lion on a lamb, bearing down on her mouth with his left hand until he felt bone creak. His right hand swept up and down, stabbing her repeatedly and in random places until her body ceased quivering.

He leaned back to admire his handiwork: the open eyes, rolled upwards, the slack jaw, the blood pumping. There was a sort of relief, but something was missing, a monument of some kind for this dead woman beneath him. He needed something to remember her by, a last vision. His chaotic brain, a barely controlled electrical storm just short of seizure, sorted ideas and selected the least bizarre, but designed to implicate Lundeman in the murder of his own wife. Holding the knife carefully with both hands, he carved the word MINE deeply into her forehead, then widened the letters a second time.

He left the way he had entered, over the fence and through the woods to his car, hurrying along because he was late for his appointment with Curtis Lundeman, and loose end number two.

Back in the bedroom he'd just left, on blood-splattered sheets, Irene Lundeman suddenly closed her eyes, moaned softly, and touched her bloody forehead with a finger.

* * * * * *

Lundeman fidgeted nervously in the front seat of the Lincoln, his suspicion of being abandoned growing with each second. He thought again of a possible escape plan, and wondered if he really wanted to include Irene. She had cheated on him so much during their marriage: two men he knew of, both driven from town, and probably others. Did he really need her? He needed no help in spending the money. Ah, yes, the money. He pulled the automatic from his coat pocket, chambered a round, then stuck it in his waistband on his right side, within easy reach beneath his coat. Holleque was crazy, but he had the money. If I play it by ear, maybe I won't have to kill him, he thought.

There was a roaring, clanking sound as the old Chevy pulled up alongside him in the gravel parking area by the bridge. Holleque jumped out and slid into the front seat of the president's car, breathing hard and sweating profusely. The interior of the car suddenly smelled sour as Holleque's grinning skull turned towards him, dilated pupils a window into what was left of his soul. Driven by the drug-induced metabolism of a humming bird, he quivered from head to toe. All these things Lundeman noted, and more.

The blood.

Holleque's hands and forearms were covered with blood, and it was spattered on the front of his khaki shirt, still glistening, still fresh.

"Are you hurt?" asked Lundeman, but Holleque laughed, a cackling sound, demented. Lundeman's hand moved closer to the automatic.

"Oh not me, Curt. Not me, never me, never. I get the sons-of-bitches before they have a chance, before they even think to do it. I read their minds, you know, they can't hide it from me. Oh, no. Loose ends, Curt. I have these loose ends to take care of before I split, and this is what's left of one of them." Holleque wiped a bloody hand across his shirt front, and licked his lips.

"Okay, okay, where's my money, and then we can get out of here."

"In the car," said Holleque, grinning, "but it's not yours,

because you don't need it. I need it, and I'm going to keep every dollar for myself." The black eyes widened, darting around gleefully, teasing. Lundeman's hand gripped the automatic.

"We don't have time for jokes. Get the money."

"I told you, it isn't yours."

"I heard, but it isn't going to happen that way." Lundeman jerked the gun from his waistband and brought it up quickly, but the cold, black eyes had seen every motion with the interpretation of a man who killed for money and survived to spend it. A bloody hand gripped the automatic, a thumb pushing the slide back just far enough to take the weapon out of battery as Lundeman jerked impotently on the trigger. Long fingers grasped his wrist, bending it back even though he pushed on it hard with his free hand. Trapped behind the steering wheel, pushed into a corner, he could not use his feet for leverage, and then Holleque was leaning on him, breathing foully into his face, eyes wild.

"She didn't struggle, even when I stuck her. I used to tie her down, and she'd struggle, and then I'd fuck her brains out and she's cry for more. Fancy lady, your fancy lady, a fucking whore no more. Hee, hee, hee!"

Lundeman screamed.

He opened his mouth wide and screamed, and Holleque twisted his wrist one last time, shoving the gun into his mouth, muzzle upwards, releasing the slide as Lundeman pulled the trigger spasmodically. The gun went off twice, blowing gray matter in a billowing cloud across the ceiling of the car.

Silence.

Holleque released what was left of Curtis Lundeman and got out of the car, quite pleased with the scenario. An obvious suicide, poor man despondent over the murder of his wife. Murdered her himself; you just never know about people, no sir. He got into the Chevy and backed out of the parking lot, then retrieved a downed tree branch and wiped out his tire tracks back to the gravel road. He looked at the big town car sitting by the pretty bridge over the rushing stream. A nice place to die, but no time to admire it. Life is such a rush, and still another chore before getting to the helicopter. He accelerated rapidly down the road, tires spitting gravel.

Time for loose ends number three, and four.

CHAPTER SEVENTEEN

"I have things to do," said Karen.

Jack frowned. "Ebensack said to stay put until everyone is rounded up. They're running for their lives, and they'll kill anyone in the way. I know Colonel Holleque is capable of that, and Lundeman is with him."

"Is that why we have a county sheriff parked in the driveway right now?"

"Karen, this is his house! The guy is giving us a little privacy."

Karen lowered her eyes and watched her spoon stirring dregs of cold coffee in a cup. It was nearly two in the afternoon and they had been up for only an hour, eating a brunch of bacon, eggs, white toast with peanut butter, and strong coffee.

Jack shook his head. "Just last night there were four people trying to kill us. Your memory seems to be short."

"I'm never going to forget last night, and neither are you." She stirred cold coffee reflectively, then said, without looking up, "The evening started out nice, though."

Jack smiled. "It certainly did."

"Orthopedic," she said, and they both laughed.

"Ebensack should call soon and then maybe we can go out to pick up things, but he made it clear we should sleep here," said Jack. "I hope it's quick, because all my books are at the dorm."

"I've got that, and a hungry rat to feed before he destroys my underwear drawer," said Karen. "He's probably started in by now. It would only take a few minutes to go by there, Jack."

"The sheriff won't let us out."

"He's in front. We'll go out the back, and come in the same way. He'll never miss us." Her eyes were bright; she was winning, and knew it.

"We could pick up your car, and leave it in the alley," he said.

"It's on the way," said Karen, getting up from the table. "Let's go now, before it's too late."

There was a reason Ebensack wanted them in the house, but for how long? They would be right back. Surely Lundeman and Holleque were long gone by now. "Okay," he said, "let's go."

They went out the back door, crossed the yard past the gazebo and used the gate to a wide alley, beyond which rose the tree and brush-choked hillside. They followed the alley past high board fences for a block, then cut over to the main street and walked quickly to the visitors lot on campus where they found Karen's car with two parking tickets under a windshield wiper. Karen tossed them into the back seat without comment and started the car with difficulty, the engine sputtering and dying twice before grumbling reluctantly to life. With Jack hunched down in the seat, she drove unobtrusively out of the lot and down the street past the sheriff's house, giggling when they saw the patrol car in the driveway, and its occupant dozing while the radio blared classic rock.

"I feel like a kid playing hooky," she said, and Jack snorted in mock disgust. She could be so childish, and yet other times, like last night, so much a woman, and deadly. Complicated.

They drove to his dormitory, Karen remaining in the car, engine running while Jack rushed upstairs to retrieve two books and a paper tablet from his room. Too impatient to wait for the elevator, he used the stairs coming down, not even turning back when the telephone on his floor started ringing. He didn't stop to answer it, No more trouble this week, thank you. He hurried to the car, which was moving before he got the door closed, and they raced onwards to Karen's apartment.

Something new was wrong.

The car. More specifically, the radiator temperature. It was climbing steadily as they drove, moving up into the red, and there was suddenly a hissing sound beneath the hood of the car. Jack leaned over and tapped the temperature gauge with a finger.

"What's that?" said Karen, suddenly worried.

"Heating up, starting back at the dorm. When's the last time you added anti-freeze to this heap?"

"Oh, God, I don't know," she said, driving merrily along. Her apartment was ahead, less than a block. They passed a Seven-Eleven store. The hissing was louder now.

"Better cool it down, or buy a new engine."

"Gotta feed Morris," she said.

"Okay, I'll take care of the car, and you take care of the rat."

"Fair enough." She parked in front of her apartment and bounded up the walk while Jack lifted the hood, grumbling when a cloud of rancid vapor engulfed him.

"Be back in a minute," she shouted, but Jack didn't answer. His body was lost in a cloud of steam. She went inside, unlocked her mailbox, retrieved two advertisements and a telephone bill. The security door opened with a click, but the light was out and she held onto the hand railing while ascending the carpeted stairs to her apartment. The lock was barely visible in the gloom, and she poked at it with her key until it went in. The whole lock was loose again, she noticed, and then the door was open. Cheap doors. Couldn't keep anyone out. When she slammed the door, it rattled.

The room smelled musty, and there was another odor, like cleaning fluid. She dropped her purse on the couch and walked the short hallway to her bedroom, where Morris lived. The odor was stronger, now, and she thought about opening a window as she entered the bedroom, but at that instant she was grabbed from behind and lifted off her feet, a foul-smelling hand clamped tightly over her mouth, and her arms were pinned against her sides. A big finger crawled under her chin and pulled up until she was staring upside down into the dilated pupils of Colonel William Holleque, the pressure on her face increasing until there were bright flashes of light before her eyes.

"Hi, honey," he growled. "Now, let's get your boyfriend up here, and really have some fun."

The hand clamped tighter, and she felt one arm being pulled up behind her back as darkness swallowed her.

* * * * * * *

There was no coolant in the radiator.

Jack sighed. You'd think the scientist would take care of these things. He left the hood up and walked quickly to the nearby store. He was in and out in a minute, buying a gallon of anti-freeze, a six-pack of pop and two candy bars. No sweat. Back to the car, where he filled the radiator and started the engine, satisfied when the temperature gauge showed a normal reading.

He honked the horn.

He honked it again.

Come on, we want to get back before Ebensack finds out we've left!

A long, steady blast on the horn.

No answer of any kind. No angry shout from a window. No wave from a window.

Nothing.

He got out of the car, went to the door and buzzed her apartment. At the answering buzz he jerked open the security door and stepped inside, so surprised by darkness that his hand moved instinctually behind him to feel the butt of the Browning automatic he had recently slept with. He stumbled once going up the stairs and found the door to Karen's apartment unlocked, the doorknob almost coming loose in his hand as he pushed it open.

"Come on, let's go!"

No answer. He stepped into the front room, looking around, then turned his head sharply at the sound of a drawer closing in one of the rooms ahead. He went down the short hallway in four strides, turning into the bedroom.

"Look, Ebensack is going to give us hell if we don't get—"

Karen was on the bed, lying on her stomach. Her wrists were crossed and pulled up between her shoulder blades, secured there with duct tape. Tape had been tightly would around her upper arms, thighs and ankles. Her mouth had been stuffed with cloth held in place by a bandana wound so tightly that her eyes bulged and her face was bright red. She moaned when she saw him, then tried to yell something and kicked her feet hard against the bed.

Anger overwhelmed caution, and Jack rushed to free her, but he had taken only three steps when something hard hit him on the back of his head. He fell face first, but managed to break his fall enough to avoid breaking his nose. There was a sudden impact in his side, then another, and he felt a sharp pain there. He curled up into a ball, and felt new pain in his arm and shoulder.

"Come on, kid, you can do better than that. I taught you better than that. Get up and fight me like a soldier, but without this little pistol you're carrying."

Colonel William Holleque looked down at him with rheumy eyes. His face glistened with sweat, and his shirt was spattered with blood. He pulled the Browning from Jack's waistband and casually tossed it aside onto the floor.

Jack grabbed at Holleque's leg, but an iron hand clamped onto his shirt collar and jerked him to his feet. He yelled when there was a sharp jab of pain in his side.

Holleque slapped his face hard. "Fight me, damn it! Show your little lady over there what a man you can be before I kill the both of you."

Karen was thrashing around on the bed and screaming into her gag. Jack felt the rage come, but fought for breath, the pain in his side increasing, and now Holleque's hand was tightening the collar around his throat. His vision began to blur.

Jack gasped for breath and dropped into a crouch, got a shoulder into Holleque's hard stomach and drove forward as hard as he could. They crashed into a fragile vanity on the other side of the room, destroying it into splinters. Jack ended up on his knees while Holleque thrashed about like an enraged cat to free himself from the pile of sharp debris. Holleque came out of it in a crouch, his arm extended with a combat knife. His teeth were bared, and his eyes blazed.

"Nice move, Jack," he rasped. "Surprised me. You're a good one; you could have done well with the squad, but we know that's over with, now." Holleque crab-walked to his right, knife level, his eyes on Jack's face, closing the distance then lunging, the knife coming out and up in a slash. Jack ducked under it, sliding along the wall, finding himself in a corner, and Holleque was coming again.

"To the finish, Jack! Winner take all! Winner take this little girl here. Her teacher was a good fuck; I bet she is, too."

He lunged.

Jack got one hand on the thrusting wrist, twisting as the knife point gouged furrows in a wall, putting his other hand on Holleque's throat and focusing his entire being on that hand, which closed suddenly like a pneumatic vise. Holleque's eyes bulged as Jack lifted him off his feet and threw him across the room into the sharp pieces of broken vanity. Holleque's knife went flying, skidded across the floor near the bed where Karen still struggled against her bonds.

The strength went out of Jack's legs, and he dropped to his knees again. There was no pain, now, only a numbness below his waist. He looked to his right and saw the Browning on the floor, only a few feet away. If he could get to it—

Holleque howled like a mad dog and spittle ran down his chin. He lifted himself from the pile of splintered rubble, took two deliberate steps forward and kicked Jack hard on the point of the chin.

"Good fight, kid, but not good enough."

Karen screamed into her gag, and tears burst from her eyes when she saw Jack fall over limply onto his side. Blood ran from his mouth, and his eyes were open. He looked dead, and Karen cried in despair.

"You two sure have been a pain in my ass," said Holleque. "Now, where is that stuff I found? It was in a drawer of this thing we just busted up." Holleque leaned over and began rummaging around in the debris of the vanity, but only for a moment.

"Ah, here it is. My clients might be interested in this."

It was the rack of storage tubes Karen had brought home to hide. Holleque looked at it closely, walked over to the bed and showed it to Karen.

"You been holding out on us, girl? I see some gas here, and some of the neuter stuff I already have. But what are these other tubes? Nano-something. Anything I'd be interested in?"

Karen shook her head weakly. Tears rolled down her face.

"No? Well, hell, I'm going to kill you two in a minute anyway. Why don't we test this stuff out? Let's see here—"

Holleque held out two tubes. "Gas, and neuter, it says here. I won't bother with that. Seems that you and superjock managed to get a dose of neuter before my people tested you with the gas. And you caused me great pain when I had to kill two of my favorite students because of what you did to them."

He held up three other tubes, peered at them close up. "nano this, nano that, and I don't have a clue. So let's check it out." He pulled out one tube. The label had been written with green ink. It was an early sample of Karen's assembler, benign to normal proteins. Holleque unscrewed the top, put a finger on the spray lever above the now uncovered port. He held the tube close to Karen's face, and she winced.

Holleque's eyes widened, and he grinned a skeletal grin. "No? Let's see, I just put my finger here, and press down."

Karen closed her eyes as a burst of cold vapor struck her face, and she growled. There was a tingling sensation on her nose and forehead, but in seconds it went away. She opened her eyes. The pressure from the gag was suddenly worse, her hands had gone totally numb and now her shoulders were aching.

Holleque looked disappointed. "Well, that wasn't entertaining. Let's try another one." He looked closely at the rack of tubes in his hand. Karen got on her side and swung her legs towards the edge of the bed, trying to leverage herself into a sitting position. She looked past Holleque when movement attracted her eye, but Jack was still on the floor, His eyes were now closed, Suddenly his eyelids flickered, and a hand moved.

"This looks interesting," said Holleque, and he held up another tube. The label on this one had been written in bright red ink to distinguish it from the others. Karen's reaction was automatic, and uncontrolled. She recoiled on the bed and kicked her legs hard. Her eyes widened, and her muffled cry was like a whimper.

Holleque's eyes lit up with pleasure. "Well, that's more like it. This must be something exciting. Let's try it on that pretty forehead of yours." He pulled the tube from the rack, carelessly uncapped it, totally ignorant of the horrible contents so close to his fingers. Karen moaned again and tried to roll towards the other side of the bed, but Holleque grabbed her and pulled her back again.

Now his eyes were wild. "Come on, now, scream for me. Do it!" His finger moved to the spray lever, and his hand moved towards her face.

Karen screamed into her gag, but with it came another, deafening sound that numbed her senses.

Holleque jerked upright and grabbed at his leg with one hand. His body twisted crazily around, his other hand clenching in reaction to new pain. There was a hiss, and a cloud of brown vapor enveloped his head and drifted down towards the bed. Karen rolled over twice to get away from it as it settled like dust on the sheets.

A second gunshot caught Holleque in the stomach, and he grunted, dropped the tube on the floor and spun around towards Karen. The skin on his face had begun to boil, and one eye was already a bloody mess. He let out an animal cry, and reached for her. Karen got to the edge of bed, got her feet on the floor and made two desperate hops to the wall. Holleque reached across the bed, one hand on the sheets, and then screamed again. The skin on his hand had begun to boil.

Another gunshot rolled Holleque onto his side, and he slid to the floor, leaving smears of blood on the sheets. Karen would never forget that final, horrible scream as the man somehow staggered to his feet for one final charge.

Jack sat on the floor, holding the Browning in both hands resting on his knees, He made no sound, showed no emotion as he aimed carefully.

Holleque managed to stagger halfway across the room before Jack emptied the sixteen-round magazine into him. He fell in a steaming heap onto the floor, and died there.

There was sudden silence, except for a faint hissing sound coming from Holleque's body. The room was filled with the sharp odors of burnt gunpowder and chemically destroyed flesh.

Jack struggled to get up, and dropped his empty weapon onto the floor. Karen used the wall for balance and hopped to the end of the bed before sinking to her knees. Now it seemed her entire body was numb, and she began to cry again.

The sound seemed to give Jack new energy. He got to his knees, held his left side with a hand. "Wow. At best I have a bunch of cracked ribs and a couple of broken teeth here. I have to breathe shallow, but I'll get you loose now. You okay?"

Karen rolled her eyes at him, and twisted her body angrily.

Slowly, but surely, he came straight to her, so she didn't have to scream at him about going near the bed. He had a small pocketknife, and used it to cut the tape on her wrists so she could relax her arms. He untied the bandana, and pulled the wad of cloth out of her mouth.

"Don't go near the bed. There's disassembler on the floor and all over the sheets," she said breathlessly.

"I saw," said Jack, and he cut the rest of the tape off of her. Karen rubbed her arms, and felt the first tingles of life returning to them. Her tears had dried, and she was suddenly focused again.

"We have to get rid of the evidence."

"What?"

"The disassembler. We have to remove all traces of it. I don't want anyone knowing it even exists. In a few minutes it'll be inert. We can clean up the floor and wash the bedding. But we'll have to do something drastic with Holleque. People will wonder what happened to his skin. I can think of only one thing that might mask it. There's a can of gasoline in the garage. Go get it for me."

"Jesus, Karen, what are you thinking?"

"Please, Jack, just do it. With all those gunshots, Ebensack or the police will be here anytime now. We have to hurry."

"As fast as I can," he said, and grunted as he stood up.

Karen grabbed Holleque's feet and dragged him to the bathroom, then mopped up the floor next to the bed and threw the sheets in the washer. Tube rack and the tube with red-inked label went in a freezer bag and into the freezer in her refrigerator. Jack helped her lift Holleque into the tub, and stood back as she poured gasoline on the body. He watched in horror as she calmly lit it with a single match and added new fuel to the face and hands. The fire burned brightly for several minutes, leaving flesh charred black, and Karen had just stepped back to admire her handiwork when they heard the sirens of approaching police cars.

When the police arrived, Ebensack and several of his agents were with them. "This is a federal matter," he told the police, and ordered them to remain outside while he and his men entered the apartment.

Karen opened the door for him. "We're alive, but Holleque wasn't so fortunate," she told him, and did not hide her anger. Ebensack sniffed the air, looked at the unmade bed, the bloody floor, and a smoke-filled bathroom.

"Now please tell me," he said, "what in the hell just happened here?"

CHAPTER EIGHTEEN

Ebensack was waiting for them in the Chemistry Department conference room when they arrived. An open box of glazed doughnuts was on the table, along with a pot of coffee, a two liter bottle of diet cola, and Styrofoam cups. He stood up when they came into the room, and motioned for them to be seated.

"Have a doughnut on the tax payers," he said. "I hope this isn't too soon for you, but I only have a few questions. How are the ribs?"

"Sore," said Jack, "but only cracked. They wrapped me good. I'll need an implant, though. Holleque managed to knock out a tooth for me."

"I know," said Ebensack. "Don't worry about bills. We'll take care of everything. How about you, Karen? Everything okay?"

Karen gave him the steady gaze of an alpha wolf. "I'm fine, thanks to Jack."

Ebensack winced. "Sorry we were a bit late, of course, but you two have been difficult to trace at times with my limited personnel."

"We did seem to have trouble getting in synch," said Karen, "but I think we did a pretty good job at attracting the bad guys for you."

Now Ebensack frowned. "I did not ever consciously use you as bait, if that's what you mean, but I can see why you might think that. Sorry. Did you sleep well last night? No nightmares?"

"I'm fine, like I said. Now maybe we can get back to our everyday lives. I have a thesis to finish."

"And a wedding to plan," added Jack, and he smiled.

"That, too," said Karen, and her gaze softened.

They each took a doughnut, and poured two cups full with cola. "So, is this a debriefing?" asked Jack.

"A quick one, and also to bring you up to date. President Lundeman is dead, and his wife is in serious condition at the hospital. I'm sure Holleque is responsible; it looks like a sloppy attempt to fake a murder-suicide. The lady was stabbed several times, and her face disfigured. Lundeman was shot in his car, but there were signs of a struggle. Holleque was cleaning house before his escape. I think he came after you two out of vengeance for getting in his way. You were his last stop. We found a suitcase full of cash in his car."

"He was on something," said Karen. "Sweat poured off of him, and he'd switch from murderous rage to deathly calm in an instant. He nearly broke my arms, and I thought he'd killed Jack. He said he was going to kill both of us."

"Ah, but you killed him instead. I must say you did a very complete job of it, but did you really have to burn him up like that? I don't know you well, but it surprises me that you'd do that."

Karen's hard gaze was back again. "He killed my advisor; I'm sure of that. He hurt us, and was going to kill us. I'm the one who poured gasoline on him, and lit the match."

Karen took a sip of cola, then said, "He made me angry, and I let it get away from me, and I don't care."

Jack smiled faintly, and wiggled an eyebrow at Ebensack. "It's not safe to make her angry," he said, then grabbed her hand when she tried to punch him in the shoulder, and held it.

"It's no problem, but people will ask the question, and now I have an answer for them. You're off the hook for revenge. A lot of strange things have happened in this case. The domestic part seems to be solved, but now we have some international webs to untangle. My job isn't finished."

Ebensack bit into a doughnut, and pushed the box towards Karen and Jack, but they refused a second helping.

"What happens to Eagle Squad, now?" asked Jack.

"I'm afraid it's finished, at least for now. The entire military science program will be on hold until a new president is hired. Sorry about that, Jack, I guess you were planning on getting a commission."

"I'd been having second thoughts about that, anyway. Our life will be much simpler if we both end up in industry."

Karen gave Jack an endearing look, and squeezed his hand. "I'd like that, too," she said.

"I don't like disappointing my Dad, but I think he'll understand. I feel badly about Colonel Holleque. I really respected him as a role model for professional military. You think you know people, but you don't."

"I'm sure there's a story behind his involvement. He was nearing military retirement, and money was probably a big factor. There might be others like him, but if there are we'll find them. Now we have better ideas on what to look for."

"Like classified research on a university campus?" asked Karen.

"That's one of them. Speaking of that, are there any other documents or samples I should have regarding the research you worked on with Doctor Reimer?"

Karen shook her head. "You have everything. I went through the lab and her locker again to be sure." Jack looked at her, and nodded his head in agreement.

"Holleque had nothing in his car except the money. We're searching his house right now."

"Whatever he had is probably delivered to his masters, whoever they are. The neuter is bad, anyway. It'll be a disaster for anyone who uses it," said Karen. "I wouldn't want to be there to see that. Once was enough for me."

"Agreed. It's time to get on with more pleasant things. You said you were planning a wedding?"

"Pretty soon," said Karen, and squeezed Jack's hand again. "Jack graduates in June, and I'll probably be finished in February, so sometime after that. We're moving in together in

June, and we'll do our job searches in parallel."

"None of this living apart for us," said Jack.

"I'll expect a wedding invitation," said Ebensack, and he stood up. "You are remarkable people, both of you. Now do me a favor and take these doughnuts with you. The pop, too. I shouldn't have any of this stuff around me."

Ebensack shook hands with them. "You have my card, and if I have more questions in the future I will eventually find you. Best wishes to you both, and remember to send me that invitation."

"We will," they said in unison.

Ebensack left the room and closed the door behind him. Jack closed the doughnut box and screwed the cap back onto the pop bottle. Karen put her arms around him from behind, squeezed lightly, and he grunted.

"Easy. Ribs."

"Sorry. Is it really over now?"

"Looks like it."

"Suddenly I'm sleepy again. Let's go back to my apartment."

"We can party on doughnuts and pop."

"Okay," she said.

And the party lasted until dawn.

* * * * * * *

Sunbathers were scattered on the lawns, early summer heat tempered by a cool wind. Finals were two weeks away, and graduation ceremonies anticipated in the stadium after that. Two presidential candidates had already arrived for on-campus interviews, and discussions about their qualifications had begun in the student senate while the faculty's Presidential Selection Committee was hard at work.

Jack and Karen had cleaned the apartment from top to bottom, removing the final stains and odors that recorded the remains of a bad memory. Jack's worldly possessions had been delivered in a small trailer pulled by Karen's car, and stowed away. Now they sat shoulder-to-shoulder on the couch, and sipped cold coffee.

"That wasn't so bad," said Jack. "With all that smoke, I though sure we'd have to scrub down all the walls."

"You missed the fun part," said Karen. "I did the bathroom weeks ago."

Jack put his arm around her, and she snuggled against him. "Our first place together. And now I am a kept man. No answers on my résumés yet."

"There's no hurry," said Karen. "I'll be sending mine out next week, so I'll just have to keep you for a while."

"Make that forever," he said.

"Okay." Karen leaned over and kissed him lightly. "I can do that."

Jack stroked her cheek with a finger. "You amaze me, so smart and strong, usually so sure of yourself. I've only seen you helpless once."

"Oh God, don't remind me about that." Karen rolled her eyes at him.

"When I first saw you that way I thought it was, well, interesting." Jack's eyes twinkled with amusement as he teased her.

"My shoulders ached for two days after that. If you ever get in a kinky mood you'd better be really nice to me."

"I'll try," he said, and kissed her softly until she suddenly pulled back to look at him seriously.

"Jack, there are a couple of things I need to do, and I want to make a little ceremony out of it. Call it closure if you like, but it's important to me. Wait here."

She went to the bureau and rummaged around in the bottom drawer. Morris squeaked at her from his cage on top of the bureau. His alertness continued to steadily improve, and Karen was optimistic about him. Jack had been assigned the task of keeping his water bottle full. Love me, love my rat, Karen had warned him.

Karen stood up with some papers and a small notebook in her hands. She went to the kitchen, came back with a wash basin, lighter fluid and matches. She motioned Jack to follow her to the bathroom.

"It's everything I could find. I found these little scraps a couple of days ago. Doctor Reimer had them scattered around her office, just a scribble on each paper, but enough to give a good chemist a clue."

Karen put papers and notebook into the basin and set it down in the tub. She squirted lighter fluid all over it and lit it with a match. The paper quickly burned to ash.

"Say goodbye to the complete biography of a protein disassembler humanity is not meant to have," said Karen.

"Good riddance," said Jack, and it seemed enough.

Karen stirred the ashes, and flushed them down the toilet. "One more thing," she said. "You need to take me on a romantic boat ride."

"What?"

"I'll drive us there."

Karen took something out of the freezer and put it into a paper bag. It was a fifteen minute drive to Lake George, and they rented a rowboat for an hour. The lake was only half a mile across, but deep, gouged out by an ancient glacier. Jack rowed them out to the middle. A few boats were scattered around the lake, young people swimming and having an afternoon picnic.

They sat knee to knee in the boat. Karen took the rack of tubes out of the paper sack and used the inner plastic bag as a glove to handle then. "The stuff is probably inert by now, but you never know for sure. And this is the last of it."

One by one, she dropped the tubes into the water, and they watched them sink out of sight. They sat there for a moment, knees touching. Karen frowned, and her eyes seemed to darken when she said, "Now it's over. Now it's really over."

Jack rowed them back to shore again, but it was months later when final closure came for them. Ebensack sent a note accepting their wedding invitation, and enclosed a clipping from a back page of The Washington Post. It was a short article about a military encounter between Zelayan rebels and the National

Police of Nicaragua in a small village near the north Zelaya border. Chemical weapons, a kind of nerve gas, had been in used in an apparently suicidal attack by the rebels, for there had been no survivors on either side.

Ebensack had drawn a large question mark on top of the article. Karen read it, and said, "Probably. I don't think anyone will want to try it again."

"You never know where that stuff comes from," said Jack.

ABOUT THE AUTHOR

JAMES C. GLASS is a retired physics and astronomy professor and dean who now spends his time writing, painting, and traveling. He made his first story sale in 1988 and was the Grand Prize Winner of Writers of the Future in 1990. Since then he has sold eight novels and four short story collections, and over sixty short stories to magazines such as *Aboriginal S.F.*, *Analog*, and *Talebones*. Jim writes science fiction, fantasy, dark fantasy, and suspense fiction. He now divides his time between Spokane, Washington and Desert Hot Springs, California with wife Gail, who is a costumer and healing dancer. There are five grown children and eleven grandchildren scattered around the country. Jim also paints mountain, desert, and red rock scenics in oils and pastels, and is often heard playing didgeridoo and Native American flute. For more details, please see his web site at:

www.sff.net/people/jglass/

www.ingramcontent.com/pod-product-compliance
Lightning Source LLC
Chambersburg PA
CBHW020443270626
47155CB00022B/1302